"You looking for me?"

A deep, velvety-smooth voice had her glancing toward the stairwell where she saw a pair of dusty work boots coming across the plywood floor. Now she could barely wait to see who the guy was who dared call himself The Pick-Up Man. Slowly her eyes traveled up the denim-covered legs to muscular thighs that wore the faded fabric as a second skin. Then a narrow waist and flat stomach...a broad chest with a pair of shoulders Annie figured could hold the weight of any construction beams in the house.

Her eyes traveled the length of him, until she caught sight of the man's face. Then she froze. This was no stranger standing before her. Every angle and plane of his face was familiar: the lips she'd kissed, the blue eyes she'd lost herself in, the hair she'd run her hands through.

No, The Pick-Up Man was no arrogant redneck. He was Jesse Conover, the first man she'd ever planned to marry—and the only man who'd ever broken her heart.

Dear Reader,

Annie Jamison wants to be married but she doesn't quite make it down the aisle—not even on her fourth try. As she says, it's a good thing love isn't like baseball. Three strikes and she'd be out. But just when she's coming up with the ten best reasons to chuck it all and head out to sea, fate throws somebody in her path...and keeps throwing him— Jesse Conover, her first and *best* fiancé. You'll be laughing the whole time it takes Annie and Jesse to realize that some people are just meant to be together!

Pamela Bauer makes her American Romance debut with *The Pick-Up Man*. Many of you will know her as a much-loved Superromance author of about a dozen books, including *Merry's Christmas* and *I Do, I Do*. Pamela makes her home in Minnesota with her husband and family.

Enjoy the laughs—and happy reading!

Regards,

Debra Matteucci
Senior Editor and Editorial Coordinator
Harlequin
300 E. 42nd St.
New York, NY 10017

PAMELA BAUER

THE PICK-UP MAN

Harlequin Books

TORONTO • NEW YORK • LONDON
AMSTERDAM • PARIS • SYDNEY • HAMBURG
STOCKHOLM • ATHENS • TOKYO • MILAN
MADRID • WARSAW • BUDAPEST • AUCKLAND

For the pick-up man I've been married
to for 25 years—my husband, Gerr.
You are truly a hero. Happy Anniversary.

ISBN 0-373-16668-0

THE PICK-UP MAN

Copyright © 1997 by Pamela Muelhbauer.

Chapter One

"Joni's out front. If you want to take a break, I'll send Ginny back to cook," Margaret Jamison called out to the young woman behind the grill in Mom's Café.

Annie Jamison looked up from the pancakes she had just flipped. "Sounds good to me." She slid two eggs onto a plate, added three sausage links, an order of toast, then set it on the serving counter.

"Tell Joni that if she needs any extra money, I'll fit her into the schedule," Margaret said as she added an orange wedge and a sprig of parsley to the plate of sausage and eggs. "We can always use help, and with you being gone…"

Annie knew her mother deliberately let the words dangle in hopes of making her feel guilty that she wasn't going to be around to help out at the café. Annie ignored the innuendo. She stacked the pancakes on a plate and set it beside the eggs, saying, "I'll mention it to her, Ma."

As soon as her replacement arrived, Annie handed her the food-splattered chef's apron. "It's all yours, Ginny."

She pushed her way through the swinging doors, a plate of scrambled eggs in one hand, a glass of orange juice in the other. Unlike the waitresses, who all wore brown-and-white uniforms, Annie had on a pair of black twill pants and a white T-shirt. She headed for the corner booth where her roommate, Joni Tremaine, sat reading a *Glamour* magazine.

"I'm glad you're here. I want to show you something," Annie remarked as she slid across the red vinyl bench seat. She reached into the pocket of her trousers and pulled out a piece of scratch paper. "Here. Read this. It's the ad I put in the *Bargain Shopper*."

Joni picked up the scrap of paper and read aloud:

"For sale. Wedding gown, size 7, never worn.
It's a masterpiece. He wasn't.
Call Annie at 555-7255."

Joni chuckled. "I like it. Too bad you can't put Richard's name in it. He definitely was no masterpiece."

The mention of her ex-fiancé rustled the hairs on the back of Annie's neck. She picked up her fork and dug into her scrambled eggs. "An ad wouldn't do him justice. I'd need a billboard along I-94."

"Well, that dress is a masterpiece, as some lucky woman will discover."

Annie sighed. "I still can't believe I'm selling it."

Joni reached for a caramel roll that was sitting next to her coffee cup. "You did the right thing calling off your engagement. Richard doesn't deserve you."

"No, he doesn't, and I'm glad he's gone."

"It's just too bad he stuck you with all the bills for the wedding."

Annie's blue eyes became cloudy. "I guess he figured it was my idea to have a big ceremony so I should be the one to pay. Selling the dress will at least get me out of debt."

"You still don't want to sell it, do you?"

Annie shook her head, then swallowed back a lump of emotion before she said, "It's so beautiful. Do you know how many times I imagined myself walking down the aisle in it?"

Joni nodded consolingly. "Look at it this way. At least you found out before the wedding that Richard is a jerk."

Annie watched in amazement as Joni applied a generous layer of butter to her caramel roll. Thanks to the blessing of genetics, her roommate could eat as much as she wanted and never gain a pound. She was the only person Annie had ever known who wore a size 1.

"What's wrong with me, Joni? Am I like a jerk magnet? I mean, how many times am I going to have to be engaged before I finally do get to wear white lace?"

"There's someone out there for you," Joni said encouragingly. "You just have to keep looking."

Annie's fork poised in midair. "At one time I would have agreed with you, but now I'm not so sure."

"Don't let a few rotten eggs spoil your appetite. There are men in this world who stay faithful," Joni assured her, using her knife as a pointer.

"Yeah, the dead and the comatose."

Joni clicked her tongue. "You never used to be cynical about men."

"Every time I have to sell another wedding dress, the icing slides a little farther off the cake of optimism." Annie took a long sip of juice.

"All right, so you've had three broken engagements. Annie, this isn't baseball. You don't honestly think that fiancés are like strikes and that it's one, two, three strikes you're out, do you?"

"What's this about three strikes and you're out?" Annie's mother appeared at their booth, coffee carafe in hand. At fifty-four years of age, she still had a trim figure and the same shade of blond hair as Annie's without any coloring—a fact she pointed out to everyone who remarked on the similarities between mother and daughter.

"Annie's worried that just because she's had three fiancés she might have struck out in the romance department," Joni answered, lifting her cup for a refill.

Margaret poured the coffee. "She ought to know better. She's already had four strikes."

"Four?" Joni's brow wrinkled.

Annie shot her mother a stony look.

"Oh-oh. I guess she doesn't know about the Marine, does she?" The look Margaret gave her daughter was apologetic.

"Thanks, Mom," Annie drawled sarcastically. Noticing the curiosity in her best friend's eyes, she said, "It was a long time ago and not worth mentioning."

"You must have been awfully young. We've known each other six years, and you've never mentioned any Marine," Joni remarked.

Annie sensed that not only was her roommate surprised, but she was a little hurt. Not that Annie blamed her. They had been the best of friends since their college days when they had worked together at Mom's Café—Joni doing waitress work and Annie working at the grill. To Annie, Joni was the sister she never had.

"I was young," Annie told her.

"Barely nineteen," her mother supplied, which earned her another look of admonishment from her daughter.

Joni's eyes widened. "And you were engaged?"

"It wasn't exactly a real engagement," Annie said, trying to downplay the significance of fiancé number one.

"What do you mean it wasn't real? You had a wedding gown," her mother argued. "Come to think of it, I have a hunch it's still tucked away in the attic."

Memories that had been pushed to the back corners of Annie's mind came rushing forward. She could see the ivory Jessica McGlintock dress as if she had only tried it on yesterday.

Joni sat staring at her, waiting for more details.

"It wasn't a gown," Annie contradicted her mother. "It was an ivory lace dress."

"Rather Victorian looking," Margaret added. "Her Marine bought it for her."

Annie was grateful when another one of the waitresses needed her mother's attention and Margaret scooted away.

"It sounds as if your mother liked him," Joni remarked.

Annie laughed mirthlessly. "Hardly. It was because of her we were going to elope."

"You were going to run off and get married?" Joni's mouth dropped open. "Who was this guy?"

As if seven years hadn't passed, a handsome face danced across Annie's memory. With it came a brief sensation of being nineteen and madly in love. She reached for her orange juice and took a sip, holding the glass with both hands. As quickly as the memory had surfaced, it disappeared.

She dismissed Joni's inquiry with a shrug. "He was just a guy."

"If you were engaged, I'd say he was more than just a guy." Joni licked the caramel from her fingertips. "So why didn't the elopement happen?"

"It just didn't," she said solemnly, not wanting to remember the circumstances surrounding her broken engagement. "Look, it was a long time ago, and I really don't want to discuss it."

Joni eyed her curiously. "All right. We won't talk about it."

"Good, because what I need to do is concentrate on

selling the masterpiece." She quickly changed the subject. "Are you sure the ad sounds okay?"

"It's great. You should get dozens of calls. Are you going to list a price?"

Annie shook her head. "I'd like people to come take a look at the dress first. I think they're more likely to pay what I'm asking if they see how unique it is."

In between bites of her caramel roll, Joni said, "You know, if I weren't so darn short, I'd be tempted to buy it for myself."

This time Annie's eyes widened. "Have you and Keith decided to get married?"

"No, but I'm hoping he'll pop the question soon." Joni smiled slyly.

Annie had the uneasy feeling that her roommate was headed for disappointment. From what she knew of Keith Hanson, she doubted he was in any hurry to marry. She didn't think Joni wanted to have that pointed out to her. "Even if you were six inches taller, you wouldn't be my size. You're tinier than me."

Besides the fact that she was only five feet tall, Joni had a much smaller frame than Annie.

"I'm bigger than you think," she insisted, which brought a smile to Annie's face. Her roommate was forever adding inches to her petite figure.

"You told me that when you do get married, you want a small, simple ceremony," Annie reminded her.

Joni rested her chin on her elbow. "I do, but now that Keith and I are talking marriage, I'm wondering if maybe I shouldn't have a big wedding with lots of bridesmaids and flowers galore."

"Trust me. It's better to have a small wedding and a marriage that lasts a lifetime than an elaborate affair that isn't even paid for before the divorce papers are signed,"

Annie told her in a voice that made her sound as if she were dishing out grandmotherly advice. "Never again will I plan a big celebration."

"I hate to tell you this, roomie, but you've said that before," Joni reminded her gently. "After fiancé number two—er, I guess I should say three." Her grin was sheepish.

"I know, but this time I mean it." Seeing Joni's dubious look, she added, "I do."

Joni held up her hands defensively. "I believe you. So when is the ad going to run?"

"Thursday." Annie took another sip of her juice. "That means by this time next week, the masterpiece should be gone and I can buy my ticket for Miami."

Joni's face fell. "I wish you weren't leaving, Annie."

"I have to. I need a change." She glanced out the plate-glass windows of the coffee shop at the dull gray November sky. "I hate Minnesota this time of year. Everything's so brown and bare. It's too gloomy."

"You're right about that." Joni sipped her coffee pensively. "As much as I hate to say this, I don't blame you for leaving. If it weren't for Keith, I'd be tempted to go with you. Working on a cruise ship is a great opportunity. Where else can you bask in the sun while you work and be surrounded by single men?" A smile tugged at the corners of her mouth.

"This isn't a vacation. It's a job, and I'm not looking for men."

Joni chuckled. "You won't need to look for them. They'll find you."

Again Annie shrugged. "No, they won't. I'm going to spend most of my time in the kitchen learning how to shape cheese and fruit into bird shapes."

When Joni started humming the theme song from "The Love Boat," Annie stood. "I'd better get back to work."

"So how come you didn't sell the first wedding dress?" Joni asked as Annie gathered up their dirty dishes.

"I don't know. Probably because I was young and sentimental," Annie answered. As she headed back to the kitchen, however, she knew that the truth was she had never given up hope that she would someday wear that dress.

But that was then. No longer was she sentimental and full of false hope. She'd sell the masterpiece and forget all about fiancé number four. As for fiancé number one...she pushed the image of a handsome Marine from her mind and returned to work.

"READY TO GO TO LUNCH?"

Jesse Conover looked up from the set of blueprints to see his older brother standing in the doorway of the partially constructed home. Todd Conover looked so much like his brother that workers on the construction site often got them confused. Both stood six feet tall and had chestnut brown hair. Because they had the same physique, it took a close-up view to tell them apart, which was usually done by the clothes they wore. Today Jesse had on a hooded gray sweatshirt, and Todd wore a blue plaid flannel shirt.

"I'll be with you in a minute." Jesse rolled the blueprints into a tight coil, then shoved them in a cabinet. Before he walked out the door, he reached for a baseball cap with a large *M* on its front.

"What are you doing driving Uncle Henry's old beater?" Todd asked as they trudged across the muddy construction site.

"He wants me to sell it for him."

"Sell it?" Todd made a sound of disgust. "He ought to junk it."

"He can't. He needs the money."

Todd laughed outright. "He's got more money than you and I combined. He's a skinflint. You know that."

"Just because he watches his pennies doesn't mean he's a miser," Jesse defended their uncle.

Todd gave another sardonic laugh.

"The reason he's selling the truck is because he wants to take a winter vacation," Jesse explained.

"With Caroline?"

Jesse shrugged. "Don't know."

"Rumor is he follows her around like a puppy dog. You don't figure he's thinking of getting married again, do you?"

Jesse chuckled. "I doubt it."

"I'm not so sure. He hasn't stopped by the Forty Club in weeks. The only other time he quit hanging out with the guys was when he'd fallen for that blonde who managed to get him to say 'I do.'" The Forty Club was a sports bar on the south side of St. Paul where the Conover men often gathered to watch football games and shoot darts. Seldom a Friday night passed without every male member of the family putting in an appearance.

"That doesn't mean he's getting married again," Jesse said, although now that his brother had mentioned the subject, it didn't seem like such a preposterous idea.

"He's been seeing Caroline for quite a while now."

"Sure. That's because she does that country-western line dancing. Hank likes the way she does the tush push," Jesse said with a grin.

They had reached Todd's Explorer. Before getting in, Todd paused to look at his brother and say, "So long as she doesn't push his tush up to the altar."

"I honestly don't think Hank would even consider marriage again. Once in a lifetime is enough for him."

"And it's one too many times for me," Todd stated with conviction.

"Spoken like a true Conover."

As they climbed inside the vehicle, Todd said, "With good reason. The statistics don't exactly favor happily-ever-after. Speaking of which, I think we'd better have a talk with our cousin Fred and remind him of that. Is it true he and Roxy are finally going to tie the knot?"

"So she says. She's making plans for a wedding."

Todd slowly shook his head. "Then he's as good as gone. Once Roxy gets her mind set on something, she doesn't stop until she gets it."

"Fred could do worse."

"That's true," Todd agreed. "At least it will mean a party for us. They are going to have a big celebration, aren't they?" he asked as he backed the Explorer out of the muddy parking spot.

"Have you ever known a Conover not to go all out for a wedding celebration?" Jesse asked with a raised eyebrow. "It's family tradition."

"I remember when Hank got married." Todd whistled through his teeth. "That was one humdinger of a party, wasn't it?" He shook his head in amazement. "Or were you too young to remember?"

"I was twenty, not ten," Jesse said dryly.

"Was that the wedding where you met—"

Before he could finish, Jesse cut him off. "Yes, it was and if you say another word on the subject, you won't need to come into the restaurant for lunch. You'll be eating a knuckle sandwich."

Todd tossed him a sideways glance. "Still touchy on the subject after all these years, are we?"

Jesse didn't comment.

Todd chuckled. "I do believe Hank's wedding lasted almost as long as his marriage. I'm surprised he let her get away. She was quite a looker, if I remember correctly."

Mrs. Hank Conover had been a looker. And so was her daughter. Jesse rubbed a hand across his eyes as if he could erase the memories, but the image of a blond-haired, blue-eyed girl refused to go away. It was the one time in his life he had let his heart lead his head, and it had been a mistake.

"Beauty's only skin-deep," Jesse recited.

"But ugliness goes straight through to the bone," Todd retorted.

As they passed a brick building marked North Publications, Jesse ordered, "Let me off here. I want to run in and place an ad in the *Bargain Shopper*.

"What for?"

"The pick-up. I told Hank I'd take care of it for him."

"Hank's perfectly capable of selling his own truck."

"I know that, but I'm doing him a favor."

Todd pulled up alongside the curb. "He takes advantage of you, little brother."

Jesse knew there was some truth to what he said. What Todd didn't understand, however, was the soft spot their uncle occupied in Jesse's heart. When Jesse had been a rebellious teenager, Hank was there to take the place of the father Jesse had never known. While Todd was away in the military, Hank had been both big brother and father to Jesse, and it was something Jesse would never forget.

"I don't mind helping the old guy out," Jesse told him as he flung open the door.

"You've got a marshmallow for a heart," Todd said affectionately.

"Only when it comes to family. With the rest of the world, I'm as hard as nails."

ON THURSDAY MORNING Annie flung open the closet doors and pulled out the designer wedding gown. As much as she wanted to hate the dress, she couldn't. She held it up to her as she stood in front of the mirror. Pangs of regret echoed through her. It *was* a masterpiece and deserved to be worn by someone entering a happy marriage.

"Today's the day." She spoke to the dress as if it were a human being. "You're going to get a new home. One where your owner is happy with the man in her life. All I ask is that you present yourself properly so I can recover some of the money I spent on you." She lovingly fingered the beaded pearls edging the neckline.

Eighteen hundred dollars was too much to pay for a wedding gown. How many times had her mother told her that? Selling it secondhand, Annie knew she'd be lucky to get half of what the dress was worth, which only proved one thing—she should have listened to her mother.

But all of her life Annie had done her best to ignore her mother's advice when it came to romance. She hadn't wanted to hear any of her mother's "truths" about men, especially not when it came to her own love life.

And there had been quite a few men in Annie's life. The shoebox full of photos, ticket stubs, florist cards and assorted scraps of sentimental value that she kept in her closet contained reminders of her quest for romance. It was a good thing hiking boots came in a large box, for she was quite sentimental when it came to love. As hard as she had tried to dump the contents of that box into the trash, she hadn't been able to do it.

She told herself she kept the box as visible evidence of

mistakes she didn't want to repeat. Maybe someday she and Joni would do like the roommates on "Friends" had done—have a sacrificial burning of leftover keepsakes of loves gone wrong. And she would recapitulate all those "truths" her mother had recited over the years.

"The truth is, Annie, that men don't know how to be faithful. They try, but they just can't do it. It's a gender defect."

Annie hadn't wanted to believe her. She had attributed her mother's cynicism to her own failed marriages. Stepfathers had come and gone in Annie's life, her real dad a ghost of a memory long forgotten. Annie wanted to believe that had her father not died, her mother would still be married to him. However, considering her mother's track record, that possibility was not a likely one.

Ever since Annie could remember, Margaret Jamison had claimed to be unlucky in love. Annie knew differently. Her mother wasn't a victim of bad luck. She had an extraordinary talent for making foolish choices.

Annie had wanted to believe that luck was made and had refused to let her mother's penchant for picking the wrong men sour her on marriage. When Annie married it would be forever, because she truly believed in her heart that real love did exist. She had proof: Joni's parents recently had celebrated thirty-five years of marriage and were as happy as newlyweds.

Annie had promised herself at a very young age that her life would be different from her mother's. If there was one thing she was determined to do, it was to not make the same mistakes her mother had made.

That's why she had broken her engagements. All four of them. She wouldn't make a wrong choice. Now, upon reflection, she was beginning to wonder if her mother wasn't right. After all, she had had four fiancés and had found four gender defects.

Annie pushed aside the memories that still had the power to cut through her heart. She would soon make a new start, working aboard a cruise ship. She had sold her catering business, subleased her share of the apartment to Joni's cousin and was ready to leave the bad memories behind her. All she needed to do was get rid of her wedding dress, and she'd be on her way to a job that promised excitement and adventure.

As the phone rang, some of that excitement bubbled up inside her. It was only eight o'clock in the morning, yet someone was already calling about the wedding dress.

She eagerly picked up the receiver. "Good morning, this is Annie."

"Ah..." There was a long pause as the caller cleared his throat and coughed. "I'm calling about the Ram." The voice sounded as if the man had stayed up half the night drinking coffee and smoking cigarettes.

Annie's brow furrowed. "What ram?"

"The one in the paper. Is it a stick or automatic?"

Annie's excitement died. "You have the wrong number."

A gruff "Sorry" scratched across the line before a click ended the conversation.

With disappointment Annie slowly let the receiver drop back down onto the cradle. She hadn't taken but two steps when the phone rang again. Upon answering it, she discovered it was the same male voice demanding to know if the Ram had a stick or automatic.

"You've got the wrong number," she repeated slowly with more than a hint of impatience.

There was no "Sorry" before the click. Annie slammed

the receiver down only to have the phone ring a third time. When she said hello, there was no answer, just a click.

Annie held the receiver away from her ear and grimaced. "I'd like to ram you," she grumbled to herself, and went to get dressed. While she dug through her drawers for something to wear, she heard Joni return from her daily run.

The two of them often started the day jogging the city streets. Since she worked for a temp service, Joni's hours were often irregular, while most of Annie's catering business centered around the lunch or dinner hours.

This morning Annie had decided to skip their run so she wouldn't miss any phone calls for the wedding dress. As she was about to pull on a pair of leggings, the phone rang again.

"You got an ad in the *Bargain Shopper?*" Another man's voice.

"I sure do," Annie answered, trying to keep the receiver balanced between her shoulder and her ear as she shoved her legs into her pants. "What would you like to know?"

"I'm wondering what kind of shape your body is in?"

"The shape of my body?" Annie repeated in astonishment. "What are you? Some kind of pervert?" Without waiting for him to utter another word, she slammed the receiver down with a thud, then went to find her roommate.

She found Joni sitting at the kitchen table, drinking a bottle of mineral water, a box of doughnuts in front of her. "Hi. Welcome to doughnut heaven." She shoved the box in her roommate's direction.

Annie peeked into the carton and sighed. "Ah. Hips in the larva stage."

"There's a cream-filled one for you," Joni said temptingly.

"I don't dare. Not after I didn't run this morning." Annie pushed the box back in her direction.

Joni licked raspberry filling from her finger. "Was that a call for the dress?"

"No, it was some guy getting fresh. I hope I'm not going to get a lot of crank calls." She sat down on a chair to put on her athletic shoes.

"Where are you going?"

"To get the *Bargain Shopper*. I want to see what my ad looks like." Annie laced up the shoes, then grabbed her key ring from the counter. "Get the phone for me while I'm gone, will you? If anyone calls for the masterpiece, take their number and I'll call them back."

Annie bounced down the three flights of stairs to the main-floor lobby of her apartment building, where several newspaper racks lined the wall. Still bundled on the floor was a stack of the weekly *Bargain Shopper*. She snapped the twine from the pack and took the top paper.

"You just missed a call," Joni informed her when she got back to the apartment.

"Someone is interested?" Annie looked to her hopefully.

"Uh-uh. It was a wrong number. Some guy."

"Another guy?" Annie sat down at the table and spread the newspaper out in front of her. "That's the second wrong number this morning. And both were men. One guy called three times before he figured out he was punching the wrong buttons."

"That's because the only buttons men know how to push with any accuracy are the ones on the TV remote control." Joni took another bite of her raspberry-filled doughnut. As soon as she had washed it down with a sip of water, she said, "This guy wanted to know if there was a bed liner in the box. Isn't a bed liner one of those plastic things you put on a mattress?"

"I guess. Why would a guy ask for that?"

Joni shrugged. "Beats me. I thought he was talking about the dress, so I told him it wasn't in a box, that it was on a hanger."

"And?"

"That's when he got weird and said he didn't want a wedding dress, that he was looking for a truck and would I put someone on the phone who knows something about the 360? I told him there was no one here with a truck and there was no bed liner in a box, only a size-7 wedding dress in a garment bag."

"He didn't ask for a Ram truck, did he?" Annie asked with a lift of one eyebrow.

"A 360 was all he said. Why?"

"Because the first guy was looking for a truck, too." She chewed her lower lip thoughtfully. "Two wrong numbers, both of them looking for a truck seems to be too much of a coincidence."

"Maybe your number's one digit different from one that's advertising for a pick-up."

Annie flipped the pages until she found the section marked Clothing. In a matter of seconds she had found her ad and read it aloud.

"'Call 555-5050'!" she exclaimed in horror. "They have the wrong number on my ad!"

Joni grabbed the paper from her. "Let me see." Her eyes scanned the small print before returning to Annie's distressed face. "If you have someone else's phone number on your ad, you don't suppose they put your phone number on someone else's ad?"

Annie snatched the paper back and flipped to the trucks

section. "Ram, Ram, Ram," she repeated as her finger trailed across the columns of trucks advertised for sale. When she found what she was looking for, she gasped.

"Here it is. Listen.

For sale:
'85 Dodge Ram PU, 360, loaded.
In good condition. Call the pick-up
man at 555-7255."

Annie groaned. "Oh, my gosh! They switched the numbers. No wonder I've been getting calls for a pick-up!"

Joni came around the table to read over Annie's shoulder. "What kind of guy lists himself as a pick-up man?"

"Obviously one who drives a pick-up," Annie said with disgust.

"It sort of calls to mind an image—you know, a gun rack across the back window, beer cans flying out the doors and a bumper sticker that says Shit Happens."

Annie grimaced. "Whoever he is, I have to call him," she said, frantically shoving the paper aside and jumping up to reach for the phone. "He's getting the calls for my dress, and I'm getting the ones for his truck!"

She dialed the number listed in her ad. After five rings an answering machine was activated. The voice on the taped message belonged to a woman. It was sultry, not exactly the type Annie expected would be sympathetic to her plight.

"If you're calling about the Ram you can see it at 14377 Rosebud Trail in St. Michael. It's red and it'll be parked on the street with a For Sale sign in the window until five o'clock today. Just ask for the pick-up man."

Annie dropped the receiver down with a thud and sank

onto her chair. "Just great. There's no one there. It's an answering machine."

"Don't you think you should leave a message?"

"What for? This pick-up man isn't at home. The voice on the answering machine says I can see the truck until five o'clock at some address in St. Michael." Annie threw up her hands in frustration. "If he doesn't get home until five o'clock I'm doomed! By then, I'll have lost the best of the calls for my dress!"

"You'd better call the paper and tell them they made a mistake."

Annie's shoulders sagged. "It won't do any good. The *Bargain Shopper*'s only published once a week. By the time the next issue comes out, it'll be too late. I'm supposed to be in Miami next Wednesday."

Another call came, and again it was a man looking for a pick-up. Annie wanted to cry. As soon as she had finished giving him the correct number to call, she hung up the phone and said, "I'm going to have to go find this pick-up guy and get this straightened out."

"Maybe I should come with you."

"No, it's all right."

"What are you going to tell this guy?"

"That he better go home and change the message on his answering machine. I'll forward the calls for the pick-up to his number and he can give my number to the people interested in my dress," Annie stated logically.

"And if he doesn't want to do it?"

"Why wouldn't he? He must want to sell his stupid truck." Annie folded up the newspaper and tucked it under her arm.

"Are you sure you don't want me to come along?" Joni asked as she followed her roommate to the door. "I mean, this guy could be a real jerk."

"You forget. I've had four fiancés who were jerks." And with a wave of her fingers, she was gone.

Chapter Two

Hank Conover was only five foot seven, but when he talked, everyone listened. That's why he had the attention of the entire work crew when he stormed up to the partially constructed home on Thursday morning shouting, "They screwed up!"

Jesse was used to his uncle's cranky outbursts. Although Hank had retired from the construction business, he still did odd jobs for Jesse at the work sites. When he heard his uncle hollering, Jesse thought there was a problem with the delivery of aluminum siding that had just been left out front.

"Did they send the wrong color?" Jesse asked as he walked over to the pile of long, flat cartons piled next to the house.

"I'm not talking about the siding." Hank wrinkled his forehead. "It's this." He waved a folded copy of the *Bargain Shopper* in Jesse's face. "They put the wrong phone number on the ad."

Jesse took the newspaper from him, his eyes narrowing as he scanned the print. He frowned, then handed it back to his uncle. "Now, how do you suppose that happened? That number's not even close to mine."

"No fooling!" Hank threw up his arms in helpless frustration. "How's anybody going to buy my truck?"

"Don't worry about it, Hank. I'll take care of it."

"How?"

"I'll have Roxy call and get it straightened out."

"Roxy? She won't give 'em hell."

Jesse sighed. "Getting angry at them isn't going to change the fact that a couple of hundred thousand papers have been printed with the wrong phone number."

"And to think we paid good money for that ad." Hank shook his head in regret. "They ought to give it to us for free—just for the inconvenience," he said stubbornly.

Jesse didn't bother reminding him that he, not his uncle, had paid for the ad. "I'm sure they'll run it again next week without charging us." He was about to walk back into the partially constructed home when he felt a hand on his arm. Hank stamped his booted foot as if he were six instead of sixty-two.

"Next week? By then, the weather could turn cold."

"So?"

"So that truck doesn't want to start when it's below freezing."

"Then we'll have to make sure it's running before anyone comes to take a look at it," Jesse answered patiently. "There's nothing for you to worry about. I told you I'll take care of everything, and I will."

"But I need the money. Caroline and I have made plans."

An uneasy feeling settled over Jesse. Was his uncle planning on getting married again? "I'll loan you the money until the truck gets sold," Jesse offered, even though he knew his uncle had a bank account that had enough commas to allow Hank to retire in comfort.

Hank's features softened. "You'd do that?"

"Sure." Again Jesse started for the house only to have Hank stop him.

"You're forgetting one big problem."

"What's that?" Jesse struggled to hide his impatience.

"The insurance expires on Saturday."

"So call your agent and get an extension."

"You can't get good rates if you only take it out for a week. They make you pay an arm and a leg."

Jesse took a deep breath. "We'll add the difference to the truck price."

"You think you can get more than twenty-five hundred for it?" His eyes lit up at the possibility.

Jesse knew Todd had a point. Uncle Hank could be a skinflint, but Jesse couldn't be annoyed with him. "Look, I've got the heating and air-conditioning man waiting inside for me. Will you trust me to take care of this?"

Hank hesitated before answering. "All right, but I'm not happy about this screwup. I think those people at the paper ought to know what this is costing me," he grumbled as he walked away.

"You mean what it's costing me," Jesse retorted, but Hank didn't hear. He was rummaging through the refuse bin for anything he thought he might be able to sell at the flea market.

HAVING TO DRIVE forty miles out of the city was not in Annie's schedule for Thursday. With lots of odds and ends to tie up before she left for Miami, she had little time to waste looking for a man she didn't even know.

Ominous-looking gray clouds hung low in the sky as she headed up I-94. She hoped it wouldn't rain—or worse yet, snow.

After exiting in St. Michael, she looked for a service station. "Unlike most men, I'm not afraid to ask directions," she mumbled to herself as she found one not far from the exit ramp. She turned off the engine and hurried inside.

"I'm looking for Rosebud Trail," she told the clerk.

"Never heard of it," the balding man said flatly.

"It's not on the map."

"Then I bet it's one of those new roads in the construction area. Everything's springing up so fast around here, you can't keep up with it," the clerk told her. "They're putting up some mighty big houses on the other side of the freeway."

Annie nodded. "How do I get there?"

The man pointed a long arm. "You just go down this road about four miles, then take a right on County Road 12. There are signs all over the place. C & C Custom Homes is the name of the builder."

"Thanks." Annie was about to leave when the clerk called out to her.

"It's awfully muddy out there," he warned, glancing down at her suede pumps.

She understood the reason for the man's words when she pulled into the construction area. Although the roads were paved, the lots weren't covered with sod. It had rained the night before, as was evidenced by the pools of water still standing in the streets.

Annie drove slowly until she came to an area where several trucks were parked. As she looked at the new home under construction, she noticed 14377 painted on a wooden stake stuck in a mound of dirt. Any doubt she had that she was in the right place disappeared when she pulled up behind a red pick-up with a For Sale sign in the window.

"That's in good shape?" she mumbled to herself, noticing the rusty, dented fenders as she stepped outside.

Carefully she followed the path of wooden planks that led across the muddy ground. Navigating the narrow boardwalk, she looked for signs of activity. Certainly with all the trucks out front there must be someone around.

Because a roll of tar paper blocked the front entrance, she decided to enter the house through the garage, which was wide open. It meant having to step off the boardwalk onto the ground that was softer than it looked. As she walked, squishy mud enveloped her shoes.

"Oh, yuck," she murmured, trying to tread as lightly as possible and avoid sinking deeper into the soft ground. With a small leap she managed to reach the concrete floor of the garage, where she stamped both feet, hoping to dislodge some of the earth that clung in globs. To her horror, the floor beneath her feet moved. The concrete was not firmly set. She let out a startled yelp.

"Lady, what are you doing?"

She looked up to see a short, bearded man staring at her from the doorway of the house. He wore a tool pouch around his thick waist and a look of impatience on his face. Unsure whether it would be wiser to step back into the mud or to continue across the wet-concrete floor, Annie stood motionless.

"I'm sorry. I didn't mean to... My shoes were full of mud...." she sputtered, feeling ridiculously inept.

Suddenly, from out of nowhere came a wide, muscular arm that wrapped itself around her waist and without any warning lifted her from the concrete. As it did, the mud-covered suede pumps went clopping to the floor.

"My shoes!" she cried out, unable to see the man dragging her from the garage.

"I'll get your shoes. Quit your hollering," the not-so-gentle voice said in her ear.

She cranked her neck to peek at her rescuer and saw a

thick, bushy mustache and what looked to be the start of a beard. A shock of dark hair peppered with gray protruded from a knit stocking cap.

Annie felt a moment of panic. She wished she had taken Joni's offer and brought her along. She tried not to let her fear show. "Where are you taking me?" she demanded haughtily.

"Inside where you can't get into any more trouble."

He dragged her up the steps, over the tar paper, through the front door, and down a hallway until they were in the middle of what appeared to be the dining room. There he plunked her down on a folding chair next to a table covered with blueprints.

He stomped away, only to return moments later carrying her mud-and-concrete-covered shoes. "Here." He dropped them at her feet.

"Thanks. You don't have a paper towel, do you?" she asked, eyeing the shoes warily.

"You're going to need more than a paper towel to get concrete off of them," he retorted.

"Maybe if I had some water and a rag?" she suggested.

"Rags we got, water we don't. Plumbers haven't been in for the finish."

She studied her suede pumps and groaned. "It's probably too late for water anyway."

The shorter man who had hollered at her in the garage walked over to the table and asked, "What were you doing in the garage anyway?"

"I was looking for the pick-up man."

The two workers exchanged knowing looks.

"You want to buy the pick-up?" Her rescuer looked bemused by her question.

"Oh, no, I just need to talk to the man selling it." She sighed, then added, "Look, it's a long story. If you could just tell me where to find the pick-up man, you could get back to your work."

"He's in the basement," the man with the beer belly answered.

"How do I get there?"

"You'd better wait here. The stairs aren't completed."

She nodded and watched as he walked over to an open stairway leading to the lower level. She could hear his footsteps echo on the wood as he disappeared out of sight. The other worker reached for a tape measure in his tool pouch and returned to work.

It was cold inside the house, and Annie automatically pulled the collar of her coat closer to her cheeks. At the sound of tin clanking together, she looked at the man in need of a shave. He was making marks on the wall with a flat pencil.

"The tin men are downstairs," he stated when her eyes met his. Seeing her puzzled look, he added, "The duct men—you know, the ones who put in the heating and air-conditioning."

She nodded and gave him a weak smile. Was that what this pick-up man was? A duct man? As the clanging and banging increased in volume, she pictured a man she had seen in a TV ad for furnaces. He wore striped coveralls over his rounded form, plastic safety goggles, a duck-billed cap, and a pencil behind his ear.

"That's why it's cold in here. Furnace isn't hooked up yet," her rescuer explained, continuing to make conversation. "I have some coffee in my thermos if you'd like some."

"No, thanks," she murmured, thinking it hadn't taken him long to get over his anger regarding her stepping in the concrete.

A drill boring through metal made a screeching sound

that had Annie grimacing. She added hard-of-hearing and a permanent grimace to the imaginary man she had created in her mind. One of her stepfathers had been a construction worker and he had skin hardened by years of working outdoors. The longer it took the pick-up man to climb the stairs, the older and more weathered his image became in Annie's mind. While she waited for him to appear, she bent over to examine her mud-covered shoes.

"You're looking for me?"

A deep, velvety smooth voice had her glancing toward the stairwell, where she saw a pair of dusty brown work boots coming across the plywood flooring toward her. Slowly her eyes traveled up denim-covered legs to muscular thighs that wore the faded fabric as if it were a second skin. A large belt buckle with the initials JC trimmed a narrow waist and flat stomach, and a tucked-in chambray shirt announced to the world that there was no excess flesh on his bones. No paunchy stomach, no bib overalls, just a broad chest with a pair of shoulders that Annie figured could have carried the weight of any of the timber beams in the house.

As her eyes traveled up the length of him, her body gradually straightened until she caught sight of the man's face. Then she froze in place. This was no stranger standing before her. Every angle and plane on his face was as familiar as the glint in his blue eyes. From the wide forehead that still had a lock of hair dangling across it to the strong jaw that had a tiny, nearly invisible scar on its chin. They all belonged to the first man she had ever loved, the first man she had ever planned to marry. Jesse Conover, the Marine who had broken her heart.

Shock had her rooted in place, her voice locked somewhere deep in her throat.

"Annie?"

She felt bombarded by a rush of memories, all of them provocative. How she would hurry into his arms the moment she saw him. The way he would nuzzle her neck with his lips. The contentment she felt simply by being in his presence.

She swallowed with great difficulty and nodded.

"What are you doing here?" A shiver slithered across Annie's flesh. His voice was as familiar as his face, confusing the logical part of her that wanted to remember this was the man who had hurt her deeply. As if seven years hadn't passed since she'd last seen him, she felt the same familiar tug on her heartstrings. The sound of his voice had always made her feel loved and wanted. Echoes of those emotions vibrated through her now, as well as another. Longing.

She struggled to find her voice, to slow the rapid beating of her heart, but was unsuccessful. His eyes traveled to the floor, where she had one shoe on and one shoe off. "You're the woman who stepped on the unfinished concrete?"

Again she nodded. He shook his head as if to make some sense of the fact that his ex-fiancée was sitting in the middle of his work site.

Finally Annie managed to speak. "I didn't know it wasn't hard," she said apologetically. She wondered what thoughts were running through his mind. Was he as surprised to see her as she was to see him? Was he having the same physical reaction as she was?

"Didn't you see the board at an angle across the opening?" he asked in a tone of voice that made her feel as if she were a child.

The criticism had her lifting her chin slightly. "There wasn't one."

He walked over to the door and stuck his head out. Then he looked back at Annie. "Yes, there is."

"I didn't see it." She held his gaze, refusing to be intimidated by his glare.

Again he looked into the garage. When he turned back to face her, he asked, "What did you do? Jump on it?"

She couldn't prevent the color that spread over her cheeks. "I was trying to get the mud off my shoes."

Once more he glanced down at her feet and shook his head.

The whole scene felt unreal to Annie. Here they were—two ex-lovers seeing each other for the first time in seven years, and they were talking about concrete. All sorts of thoughts were running through her head. Was he a construction worker? Was he married? Did he have any kids?

"I didn't expect to find you working here," she told him.

He came closer so he was standing directly beside her. "How *did* you manage to find me?"

He made it sound as if he had done his best to stay hidden from her. "I wasn't looking for you," she snapped defensively. She could see a tiny pulse beat in his temple.

"I know better than to think that," he answered, and she flushed. "So why don't you tell me why you *are* here?"

"Because of this." She pointed to the *Bargain Shopper.*

"You want to buy the truck?"

"No, I came because of the mistake."

"You work for the paper?"

"No." The way his eyes pinned her with a stare had her shifting uneasily on the chair.

"You don't work for the paper and you don't want to buy the truck, yet you say you came because of the ad." He smiled indulgently. He wasn't letting her finish—but then he never had. It was a habit that at one time she had found endearing. Now it annoyed her.

"Maybe if you'd let me finish, I could tell you why I'm here," she snapped, irritated that her body was responding to him at all.

Her voice was sharper than she intended. His grin slid away, and the two electricians discreetly left the room, mumbling something about checking circuits in the basement.

"See, not all men are insensitive," Jesse stated coldly.

The words stung like the bitter November wind that whistled through the cracks in the unfinished house. When they had parted ways seven years ago, she had accused him of being insensitive. He hadn't forgotten those final words.

"They didn't have to leave." Annie folded her arms across her chest.

"Maybe not in your opinion, but me, I prefer not to have the men who work for me hear while I get chewed out by a woman." A lock of hair fell across his forehead, and he brushed it back impatiently.

"They work for you?"

"I own C & C Custom Homes."

"Oh." So he wasn't a tin man after all, but the boss. "Well, I'm not here to chew you out."

"No? It sure sounded that way a minute ago."

She tugged on her upper lip with her teeth as she tried not to let his presence unnerve her. He pulled out the other folding chair and straddled it backward. Annie could feel herself warm under his scrutiny.

For months after she had broken her engagement to Jesse, she had fantasized what it would be like should she ever run into him again. At nineteen she had felt certain that she wouldn't waste any time being nice to him. After all, he was the man who had cheated on her and destroyed all her dreams of happily-ever-after.

Now, sitting beside him in a partially constructed house, she wanted to ask him questions about his personal life. She quickly pushed those thoughts aside.

"I'm a busy man. Why don't you tell me why you're here," he said a bit impatiently.

"I tried to, but you didn't let me finish," she told him.

He rested his arms across the back of the chair, fixing his gaze upon her. "Shouldn't that be my line? You never gave me a chance to finish what we had started seven years ago. You sent me a letter, remember?"

Her face reddened, and she took a deep breath to steady her nerves. He was the one who had broken her heart, yet he was able to make her feel guilty. "That's all in the past, Jesse. The reason I came here today is because there's a mistake in this newspaper." She held up the *Bargain Shopper*.

"Yes, I know. They have the wrong phone number in my ad."

"That's why I'm here."

"Because they put the wrong number on *my* ad?" One corner of his mouth curled up ever so slightly.

"It may be *your* ad, but it's *my* phone number." It gave her a tickle of pleasure to see that she had caught him off guard.

"Yours?"

She nodded smugly. "Someone at the newspaper must have switched our two numbers. You see, your number is on my ad."

"You're selling a car?"

"No, a dress." She didn't tell him what kind of dress it was. She couldn't. If he knew she was selling a wedding dress, he'd make some wisecrack about not getting to the altar. She'd bet money on it. "Unfortunately the only calls I've had this morning are for a Ram pick-up."

"Then I must be getting the calls for your dress."

She nodded. "I discovered the mistake after about the third call for a Ram."

"So you called my number and heard the recording instructing you to come out here to look at the truck," he surmised correctly.

"Yes. I need you to change the message you have on your machine, tell them to call my number. I'll do the same for you, of course."

"You'll forward the calls for the pick-up?" The look he gave her said he wasn't convinced she would.

"Yes."

He shrugged. "That sounds fair enough. I'll change it as soon as I get home."

"When will that be?"

He shrugged. "Six, six-thirty."

"But that's too late," she protested. "Everyone who reads the *Bargain Shopper* knows that the best sales happen on Thursdays. If you don't change your message until the end of today, I could lose my buyer. Can't the person who left the message do it for you?" She didn't want to mention the woman whose voice was on his answering machine, but she really had no choice.

"Roxy's not there to answer the telephone. That's why there's a recorded message," he explained without telling her who Roxy was.

Curiosity reared its head, but Annie refused to give in to the urge to ask him about the unknown Roxy. She knew what mattered most was that the mistake be corrected.

"Can't you drive home on your lunch hour?"

"We're forty miles out of town. Add another fifteen to get me to my office, and you're talking about losing a couple of hours' work time just to go home and change a message on an answering machine." He made it sound as if it were ridiculous to even suggest such a thing.

That made Annie's temper flare. "Maybe to you it's not urgent that you sell that…that heap of junk out in the street, but my dress is a one-of-a-kind designer original and I—"

"That heap of junk is worth more than any dress," he interrupted her.

"I doubt it."

"Oh, yeah? How much are you asking for your *designer* dress?"

"Eighteen hundred dollars."

He laughed. "That pick-up is worth more than that."

She laughed right back and said just as sarcastically, "Ha!"

"It is. And I can guarantee you that someone's going to get a lot more mileage out of that truck than out of some overpriced rag of a dress," he drawled, an unmistakable note of challenge in his voice.

"The dress is not overpriced," she retorted haughtily.

"No, to someone like you, I'm sure it isn't," he shot back. "You never did have any money sense."

"Just because I believe in buying quality goods doesn't mean I'm extravagant." She remembered how he had teased her about champagne taste on a beer budget. Maybe she hadn't been the best money manager when she was only nineteen, but it didn't necessarily mean she was careless.

"Not everyone can afford to buy quality, especially not a twenty-year-old Marine," he said soberly, a dangerous glint in his eyes. "You know, I never did understand how you could worry about recycling plastic bags and aluminum cans, yet turn around and blow half a paycheck on a pair of earrings.''

"There's no point in dredging up the past, Jesse," she said quietly.

"No, I guess there isn't," he agreed.

There was a brief silence before Annie said, "I wish you would reconsider changing the message on your answering machine. I need to sell my dress today."

"What's the big rush?"

She didn't want to tell him about her job on the cruise ship. Nor did she want him to know that she had overspent for a wedding that had never taken place.

"It's important that I get the money as soon as possible," was all she told him.

"I wish I could help you, but I'm already behind on this home because of the weather. I just can't afford to take a couple of hours off."

Annie could see that it would do no good to argue with him. She reached into her purse and pulled out a pen. She circled the ad for the pick-up and shoved the newspaper under his nose. "You have my phone number on your ad. When you do finally get home, I would appreciate you referring the calls for my dress."

He took the paper from her hands without saying another word.

She forced her feet back into her shoes, then stood. "I've got to go. I have an appointment at noon."

"I'll walk you out the front so we don't have any more accidents." Again a corner of his mouth lifted into a wry smile.

If it had been anyone else, she would have apologized again for stepping on the concrete. She didn't. She simply followed him to the door, her feet feeling like a couple of bricks from the weight of the mud and concrete.

It had started to rain when they stepped outside. To her

surprise he slid his hand beneath her elbow, locking his warm fingers around her arm. Heat spread to every part of her body. As soon as he had helped her navigate the treacherous steps, she snatched her hand out of his.

He looked as though he were about to say something, but a delivery truck pulled up in front of the house. The driver hopped out and called out to Jesse. Annie took the opportunity to slip away without any further conversation between the two of them.

As she drove back to the city, there was only one thought going through her mind. Who was Roxy?

IT WAS DARK by the time Jesse arrived home that evening. He had stayed later than usual at the work site. He had told the electricians that he needed to work off excess energy. The truth was, he didn't want to go home and hear the messages on his machine for Annie Jamison's eighteen-hundred-dollar dress.

It had been a shock seeing her that morning. Seven years hadn't diminished her beauty. She had hardly changed at all. Except for the fact that the poufy bangs she had worn over her forehead were gone, her long blond hair still clung to her shoulders in a most seductive manner. Her skin was just as flawless now as it had been back then. And when she smiled—he felt that familiar tightening in his chest, the one she always had the power to produce with a simple glance in his direction.

He remembered the first time they had met. On leave from the Marines, he had attended his uncle's wedding. With his hair shaved short, he knew his uniform was the only thing that saved him from looking like a total nerd. Not that he expected he'd attend his uncle Hank's wedding and fall in love.

Love had been the last thing on his mind that night—

or the weeks following. Not once in his twenty years had
he allowed a girl to steal his heart. He had always played
footloose and fancy-free, taking the advice of his older
cousins not to even think about settling down with a
woman until he had seen the world.

That's why he hadn't been prepared for the emotions
Annie had aroused in him. His brother had tried to tell
him that his feelings for her were fleeting, that it was only
because he was homesick that he had fallen so hard for
her.

Jesse had known differently. Whether the timing was
right or wrong, he had met the woman he wanted to be
with for the rest of his life. Being apart only made his
feelings intensify, not diminish. Although he didn't have
a lot of money, he figured that if they married while he
was in the service, they could get by living in government
housing. And once he was out, he was going to do as his
uncle had suggested years ago—get serious about a job.

For the first time in his life he had actually felt as if he
had direction. Then she had sent him that damn Dear John
letter. He closed his eyes, not wanting to remember that
such a lovely creature could have done such a thing.

He wanted to hate her for it. He didn't want to feel
anything for her but indifference. Only he had discovered
today that he couldn't be detached when it came to Annie.
Not then. Not now.

Eighteen hundred dollars for a dress! Obviously she
hadn't changed at all. It was a good thing he hadn't married her. She would have had him in the poorhouse by
now. And wasn't it just like her to think that his time
wasn't as important as hers? And that his pick-up wasn't
as valuable as her dress?

As he flipped on the lights in his office, he saw the red
message light blinking on the answering machine. Before

playing the tape, he fixed himself a drink. Just as he was about to press Play, his secretary, Roxy Baxter, walked in.

"I thought I'd drop these off on my way to my night class. Did you just get home?" she asked, her arms laden with carpet samples.

"The tin men stayed late, so I thought I might as well, too."

"I see you still have Hank's truck. No luck on the ad?"

Jesse chuckled. "Luck is something that evaded me today." He explained the mix-up in the ads, omitting the part that Annie happened to be his ex-fiancée.

"I'll call the paper first thing in the morning," Roxy assured him.

"We're going to have to change the message on the machine." He pulled the scrap of paper with Annie's number out of his pocket and handed it to his secretary. "Here's the woman you need to contact about the dress."

"We should probably see what we already have," Roxy suggested, punching the Play button. She sat down in Jesse's chair while he stood, sipping a Scotch and water.

"I'm calling about the wedding dress. I'd like to come see it, but you didn't put an address in the paper. Would you call me? My name is Linda, and my number is 555-1974."

Roxy grabbed a pen and started scribbling on a legal-size pad.

"Did she say wedding dress?" Jesse asked, coming closer to the desk.

"Yeah, why? You look surprised."

Shocked would have been a better word, Jesse thought. Annie was selling a wedding dress. Either she wasn't very sentimental or she hadn't gone through with the wedding.

"I didn't see the ad, that's all," he answered, trying not to let his interest show.

"Hey, Annie! How about a date with a real masterpiece? Give me a call if you want some action," a male voice said huskily.

Roxy wrinkled her nose. "Looks like this Annie's going to get a few crank calls, as well."

The thought of Annie getting propositioned over the phone caused a ripple of uneasiness in Jesse's stomach. "You're not going to put that one on the list, are you?" he asked Roxy.

"She doesn't have to call the guy back," his secretary responded, eyeing him curiously.

Interspersed with calls for the dress were inquiries on the pick-up. Jesse felt a twinge of guilt. Annie had forwarded the calls for the truck to his number, yet she hadn't received any of the calls for her dress.

When the tape had finished playing, Roxy reached for the phone. "I'd better call this Annie Jamison and give her the messages."

She punched seven digits, then said, "It's busy." She let the receiver fall back on the cradle, then glanced at her watch. "If I don't get going, I'm going to be late for class." She held up the notepad. "What should I do about these?"

Jesse took it from her and tossed it on the desk. "I suppose it'll have to wait until the morning."

"Why don't you call her?" Roxy suggested.

Jesse shrugged. "I might."

Roxy didn't move, but sat tapping her pen against the desk, staring at him pensively.

"All right. So what's going through that red head of yours?" Jesse asked.

"I'm just sitting here wondering what kind of a wedding dress it is."

"An eighteen-hundred-dollar one," Jesse answered dryly. "A designer original." He couldn't keep the mockery from his tone.

"If it is, that's a pretty good price. I wonder what size it is? I wish I had picked up a copy of the *Bargain Shopper* this morning."

"I have one. Hank left it in the pick-up," Jesse told her.

Again Roxy glanced at her watch. "I'm going to run out and get it." She disappeared, only to return a few moments later. She spread the newspaper out on the desk and began poring over the columns.

"Look. Here it is. Listen. 'For sale. Wedding gown, size 7, never worn. It's a masterpiece. He wasn't. Call Annie at 555-5050.'" Roxy giggled. "I already like this Annie."

A wedding dress never worn. That meant Annie was single and had Jesse wondering if she had jilted the second fiancé the same way she had left him. And if she was selling this "never worn" wedding dress, did that mean she had sold the lace dress he had bought her for their wedding and told everyone he was no "masterpiece," either?

"I wonder if it's a generous 7 or a small 7," Roxy mused aloud. "You know, I've never thought about looking for a wedding dress in the want ads, but this might be an unexpected find."

"You'd pay that much money for a dress?"

"For my wedding, yes. Most women would, but this Annie doesn't list a price. I'm sure she's willing to sell it for less than what she paid. I wish I had time to go look at it this evening, but I don't dare miss my night class."

"Go in the morning."

"What if it's sold by then?"

"How can it be? We have all the messages right here." He tapped the notepad.

"I'll try calling one more time and then I have to go." She picked up the phone and punched the numbers, only to let the receiver drop in disappointment. "Still busy." She looked up at Jesse with appeal in her eyes. "Would you keep trying for me?"

He groaned.

"Come on, please?" She tugged on his sweatshirt sleeve.

"I don't know a thing about wedding dresses." *Except that the one and only I bought was never worn. It had probably been sold at a garage sale.*

"All you have to do is call and tell her your secretary might be interested in buying it. I'd do it myself, but I have this test in sociology tonight and if I don't get to class on time, I won't get to take it." Roxy tried Annie's number one more time. "It's still busy." She looked at him with doelike eyes.

"All right, I'll do it."

"Thanks, boss." She gave him a quick hug, then hurried to the door. "Don't forget to get the address," she called out over her shoulder. "Tell her I'll be over first thing in the morning, okay?"

Jesse picked up the newspaper ad with Annie's phone number on it. Just what he didn't need—more contact with the one woman who had been able to drive him crazy. He tried phoning her, but couldn't get through. Then he pulled out the phone book and turned to the *J*s. He ran his finger down the page until he found the listing for A. Jamison. She still lived on the east side of St. Paul. That was probably why he had never run into her before now. Most of his work was on the outskirts of the twin cities of Minneapolis and St. Paul.

As he showered and shaved, his mind was filled with memories of the past. Of how they had spent the night on his grandfather's farm, making plans for their future together while they waited for the spectacular sunrise over the creek that rippled through the meadow. Of peanut-butter-and-jelly sandwich picnics, sharing dreams for a house in the country where their kids could have lots of room to ride their bikes and not have to worry about all the traffic on the city streets.

They had agreed they would have two dogs, two cats and enough room for Annie to grow her own vegetable garden. A skylight in the bedroom to make love beneath the stars and fragrant flowering hedges outside the kitchen window were essentials in their dream home. But she had crushed the dream with one Dear John letter.

After seven years he could still picture the way she had looked in his sleeveless T-shirts and baseball caps. He remembered the really clean smell of her skin when she stepped out of the shower...the way she could get him to do just about anything.

He splashed on after-shave and grimaced. That was then and now was now. Never again would he give her the power to pull his strings. He would take the tape-recorded messages to her, give her Roxy's information and that would be the end of things. He liked his life the way it was without Annie Jamison just fine.

BY THE TIME ANNIE arrived home that evening, she was cold, tired and hungry. In her hands she carried a sack of fast food—a concession to her mood. She seldom stopped at the drive-through window of the local burger restaurant, but this evening she needed food and she needed it fast.

Conscious of the fat content in deep-fried food, she'd ordered a broiled-chicken sandwich and a garden salad.

After changing into a pair of leggings and a baggy sweatshirt, she opened the paper sack to discover a fish sandwich, French fries and a hot apple pie. "So what else could go wrong today?" she asked herself.

If it wasn't bad enough that the want ad for her wedding dress had the phone number of one of her ex-fiancés on it, her car had had a flat tire, her best shoes were now coated with a combination of concrete and mud and all the stupid phone did was ring for someone else. As optimistic as she was, she was having a hard time believing that she was going to be able to escape her old life and begin her new one.

She sat down at the kitchen table with her fish sandwich and fries, a notepad and a pen. She had discovered a long time ago that whenever she was in danger of slipping into a blue funk, there were two things that helped stave off the melancholy: food and making lists.

On the top of the pad she wrote, "Ten reasons why I'll be happy as a cruise-ship employee." Number one was "There won't be any ex-fiancés." Second came "There will be no tires to change." Number three read "There will be no mud." She was about to write number four when the phone rang.

Annie had a hunch the caller would be a man inquiring about a pick-up. When she heard the deep voice, her irritation increased.

"What's the body like on that Ram?"

She should have told the man he had the wrong number, that he needed to dial Jesse. It would have been the right thing to do. But she was not in the mood for doing the right thing. She hadn't had one single call on the wedding dress all day. She was irritable, and Jesse Conover was the major source of her irritation.

"The body's shot," she told the caller.

"What do you mean shot? The ad says it's in good shape."

"It's a piece of junk," she answered, then hung up the phone. Immediately she felt remorse. She shouldn't have done such a thing. She wouldn't have done such a thing had Jesse's smirking face not haunted her all day long. It annoyed her that he wouldn't go one inch out of his way to help straighten out the mess of the phone numbers.

Knowing she had behaved churlishly, Annie decided to take a precaution to make sure it wouldn't happen again. She took the phone off the hook. This way she could eat in peace.

She sat back down and continued her list. "There will be no phone calls from dumb men." She took a bite of the sandwich.

When the doorbell rang, she had reached reason number eight. Thinking Joni either had her hands full of groceries or had forgotten her key, Annie went to answer it, chomping on a French fry. Only it wasn't her roommate outside her door, but Jesse Conover.

Chapter Three

Annie nearly choked on the skinny potato. "What are you doing here?"

"I have something for you. Can I come in?"

Reluctantly she stepped aside. As she looked down, she realized she had a big gob of tartar sauce on her sweatshirt. She scooped it up with her finger and licked it. When he smirked as he walked past her, she knew he had seen it.

"Sorry if I'm interrupting your dinner," he said flatly.

She wanted to argue the sincerity of his apology, but decided against it. She needed to have her emotions in control. "Why don't you come into the kitchen?"

He did as she suggested, taking the chair she offered at the small round soda-shop-style table. He wore a leather jacket that was the same rich chestnut brown as his hair, and he smelled like the forest after a rain. Annie knew if she was smart, she'd focus on something not so pleasant—the fish sandwich.

"I tried calling, but your line's been busy," she heard him say.

Even though Annie kept her eyes on the fish sandwich, she sensed his were perusing the kitchen. She sneaked a peek at his face just as he spotted the telephone receiver that was off the hook. Before she could lower her eyes, he had fixed her with an inquisitive stare.

"I was trying to eat my supper in peace," she answered the unasked question.

"You're not going to get any calls for the dress if your phone is off the hook."

"That's my point. I'm not *getting* any calls because a certain *pick-up* owner refused to change the message on his answering machine," she retorted. She wanted to be angry with him, to treat him as if he were a stranger who was causing her an inconvenience, but his blue eyes wouldn't let her be indifferent toward him.

He glanced at the half-eaten sandwich in her hand. "What are you doing eating fish? You hate fish."

The fact that he remembered caused a shiver of pleasure to dance across her flesh. "I ordered a broiled-chicken sandwich." She waved the fish sandwich under his nose. "This is what I got. I hate reconstituted haddock or whatever it is they put in these things." She tossed it on the table, where it landed next to the half-eaten order of French fries. Noticing his eyes peering curiously at the notepad, she flipped it over. She didn't need him to see her happy list.

He didn't say anything, but continued to stare at her. She tried not to think of him as a man with whom she had been intimate, but when she shifted beneath his steady gaze, her legs brushed his under the table. A jolt of awareness flashed through her, and as she met his eyes, she knew he had felt it, too. She pushed her chair away from the table, shoving her fast-food dinner aside.

His gaze remained on her, but to her surprise he made no mention of the brief contact they had made. He simply asked, "Aren't you going to eat those fries?"

"They're cold."

"They just need a little catsup." He smiled easily, a grin that had the power to resurrect even more memories of the past.

She hopped up, welcoming the chance to get away from his probing eyes. She pulled the bottle of catsup from the refrigerator and slapped it down on the table in front of him. Then she shoved the fries in his direction.

"Be my guest."

"You wouldn't have something to drink, would you?"

She went back to the refrigerator, saw two cans of soda, one lemon lime, the other root beer. She grabbed the closest one and set it down beside the fries.

He grinned. "Root beer. My favorite. How nice of you to remember."

"I didn't," she told him, although now she remembered it with startling clarity. Memories of all sorts of his favorites rushed to mind. He liked hamburgers with bacon and cheese, steak medium rare and baked potatoes with sour cream, no butter. After seven years she still knew those details, just as he remembered she didn't like fish sandwiches.

His presence in her kitchen was much too unnerving. She was sorry she had given him anything to eat or drink. She needed to have him gone, out of her home, out of her life.

"I'm surprised you like those things," she commented, eyeing the disappearing fries.

"I can eat anything when I'm hungry," Jesse answered.

"Didn't you eat dinner?"

"Uh-uh. I worked late." When the fries were gone, he leaned back in his chair and asked, "So where's this eighteen-hundred-dollar dress?"

"It's in my bedroom."

"Can I see it?"

She eyed him suspiciously. "What for?" There was a glimmer of curiosity in those dazzling blue eyes that gave her an uneasy feeling that he had seen the ad in the *Bargain Shopper* and knew it was a wedding dress.

He took a sip of the root beer, then said, "I know someone who might be interested in buying it."

"I doubt it."

"Maybe you should let me be the judge of that."

"Trust me, it's not what you're looking for," she said discouragingly.

"Is it a generous size 7 or a small size 7?" he asked.

She could feel her whole body warm. "You've seen the ad."

"Yes." His eyes held hers, and her pulse raced. "So tell me. Did this poor fellow who wasn't a masterpiece get a Dear John letter, too?"

Even though he crooked a smile, there was an undertone of hostility in his question. Caught off guard, Annie searched for a clever comeback.

However, he didn't give her any time to respond, but quickly added, "You didn't tell me that it was a wedding dress you were trying to sell."

She raised an eyebrow. "Was there any reason why I should?"

"Not really." He continued to stare at her with a humorous glint in his eye. In fact, it looked as though he was doing his best not to laugh.

His amusement annoyed her. "Is this why you came over here? To laugh at the fact that my wedding plans fell through?"

"No."

"Were you hoping to discover that this time *I* was the one who had been jilted?"

"No man in his right mind would jilt you, Annie," he

said in a seductive voice that sent shivers up and down her spine.

Her heart began to pound in her throat. She couldn't let him get the upper hand in their conversation, especially not if he was going to flirt with her. From the first day she had met him, he had had a way of making the sexiest compliments out of nothing. In her present state of vulnerability, she couldn't let him work his magic on her.

"Why don't you just tell me why you're here?" she said a bit impatiently.

He reached in his pocket and pulled out a legal-size sheet of paper. "I brought you this."

"What is it?" she asked.

"It's the messages from my answering machine. Most of them are for you."

Guilt washed over her as she remembered the way she had handled the last telephone inquiry on the pick-up. "Oh."

As she tried to decipher the words, her guilt slowly faded. The messages were obviously written in a woman's handwriting, causing Annie to wonder just who it was who had taken them down for her. Was Jesse married? Did he have a significant other?

"You really should put your phone back on the hook," Jesse advised her.

"I don't think it's any of your business," she answered shortly.

He shrugged. "Maybe not, but you should know that I had Roxy change the message on my answering machine. Any calls for the dress will be forwarded here," he told her.

"Roxy?" she couldn't resist asking.

"Mm-hmm," was all he said in response. "She's the reason I want to look at the dress."

The idea that he wanted to buy the dress for a woman didn't sit well with Annie. "So you weren't joking when you said you wanted to see it."

"No, but now that I'm here and I see you in those clothes, I'm thinking it probably isn't going to fit her. She'd probably kill me if she heard me say this, but she's a little broader through the hips," he said with a sheepish grin.

Annie felt a stab of pain at the affectionate gleam in his eyes as he spoke about this Roxy. Who was she? What did she look like? Were they planning on getting married soon? Questions raced through her mind.

Needing to get away from his penetrating gaze, she said, "Wait here and I'll get the dress for you." She hurried into her bedroom and scooped up the crinoline skirt of the designer original, thinking how odd it was that she was actually considering selling her wedding dress to a woman who would wear it to marry one of her ex-fiancés.

Carefully lifting the layers of white organza so the hem wouldn't drag on the floor, Annie made her way back to the kitchen. When Jesse saw her coming, he whistled through his teeth.

"So that's what an eighteen-hundred-dollar dress looks like."

"Correction. It *was* an eighteen-hundred-dollar dress. Because I'm selling it secondhand, I can't get what I paid for it."

"You paid eighteen hundred dollars for a dress?"

"Yes. What's wrong with that? I bet you wouldn't hesitate to spend that much money on one of those fly-in fishing trips to Canada." She remembered how that had been a dream of his—to take a fishing trip to the remote regions of Ontario. There had always been one stumbling block, however. Money.

"That's like comparing apples and oranges, Annie," he chided her.

"No, it isn't. A fishing trip's important to you, my wedding day's special to me."

Annie climbed on the chair so that she could hold the dress in a vertical position and Jesse could get a full view. "These are imported antique ivory buttons, and the lace has been hand stitched..." she began, rattling off the exceptional features of the gown, giving him the sales pitch she had rehearsed all week long. When she was done, an awkward silence stretched between them.

"He must have been mighty special if you were willing to pay that much money for a dress for your wedding." For once the amusement in his eyes was gone.

"I thought he was, but I was wrong," she said quietly, then immediately wished she hadn't said anything about her personal life.

"Did he jilt you, Annie?"

She would have ignored the question, but pride forced her to say, "No, I broke up with him."

The sympathy in his voice disappeared. "Now, why doesn't that surprise me?"

"Because you're a man and can't understand why women need to feel that the men they love will never be unfaithful." She nearly gasped in horror. Were those her mother's words coming out of her mouth?

"Ah, that's right. According to the Jamison doctrine, all men are pigs and make lousy husbands," he drawled in heavy sarcasm.

All the pain and hurt from the past threatened to resurface. Annie couldn't let that happen. "My personal life is none of your business," she said curtly, then climbed down from the chair, carefully shifting the wedding dress as if it were precious cargo. "This thing is heavy. Are you interested or not?"

"Oh, I'm interested. Definitely interested."

She met his eyes and felt her insides tremble. If she weren't holding the wedding dress, she would have thought *she* was the one drawing such an intent gaze. She hated to ask the question, but found she couldn't not ask it. "When's the wedding?"

"The date hasn't been set yet. I guess after six or seven years there's no hurry."

Six years or seven years! He had been dating someone that long and still hadn't married her! That didn't sound like the Jesse she had known. They had only dated for three weeks when he had asked her to elope with him. She pushed those thoughts from her mind and concentrated on the issue at hand.

"If you want to bring—" she cleared her throat "—*Roxy* over, she's welcome to try it on," Annie offered.

"I'm not sure she can get over here. Why don't I take the dress home tonight and bring it back tomorrow morning? I mean, it is getting late and chances are no one's going to come out tonight to look at it...not with the mix-up in the phone numbers."

Annie stared at him in disbelief. He wanted her to give him the masterpiece? Already proprietorial over the dress, she was reluctant to consider such a thought. "I'm not so sure that's such a good idea."

"You can trust me with it, Annie. I won't let anything happen to it."

Trust was a word she did not associate with Jesse Conover. She wanted to say no to him. She didn't want to do him any favors. She didn't want to have to see him again. And she certainly didn't want to have *his* fiancée wearing *her* masterpiece. Yet the thought of a sale had her thinking twice before flat out rejecting him.

"Are you sure you want her to have it? I mean, it is an eighteen-hundred-dollar dress," she reminded him.

He shrugged. "Roxy's the one who has to pay for it."

Another spurt of irritation coursed through her. He was so quick to criticize her for spending that much money on a dress, but when it came to his precious Roxy, it was another story.

"Here are your choices, Annie." He picked up the yellow legal-size sheet of paper and held it before her eyes. "You can call all these numbers on this list and hope that one of them is still interested in the dress, or you can send the dress home with me and maybe make a sale without any further hassle," he finished smugly.

Hassle? Didn't he realize that any further association with him would be a hassle greater than a thousand phone calls from strangers who might not buy her dress?

"Oh—and by the way—one of these calls is a proposition. Apparently when you advertise a wedding dress for sale, you send up a red flag that you're single."

She snatched the paper from his fingers, annoyed with the glint of amusement in his eyes.

The sound of a key turning in a lock announced Joni's arrival. Annie cringed. She would have liked to explain the situation and all of the day's events to her roommate before introducing her to Jesse. It wasn't going to happen.

"Hi." Joni bounced into the room in her usual perky fashion. "Oh—you have company. Sorry." She set a bag of groceries on the counter.

"No, it's all right. This is Jesse Conover. He's the man whose phone number is on my ad in the *Bargain Shopper*."

Annie could see Joni's eyes light up in an appraising fashion. She recognized a piece of beefcake when she saw one and wasn't above flirting with him, even if she was practically engaged to Keith.

"You're the pick-up man?" She smiled and moved closer to him. "Hi, I'm Joni."

"He's interested in buying the masterpiece," Annie interjected before Joni's eyes devoured him completely.

"I don't think it's going to fit you," Joni said with a giggle.

"It's all right. I'm not much for antique ivory buttons," he returned with a flirtatious grin.

"He's not buying it for himself," Annie snapped irritably.

"Lighten up, Annie. I know that," Joni chastised her affectionately.

"I was just asking Annie if she'd mind if I took it home so the woman who would like to wear it could try it on," Jesse stated with a beguiling smile.

Before Joni could voice her opinion, Annie said, "I really don't think I want the dress to leave this house."

"She has a point," Joni agreed, coming to her defense, much to Annie's surprise. "It's a very valuable dress, and you are a perfect stranger."

"Oh, I'm no stranger, am I, Annie?"

That had her roommate's eyes widening. "You two know each other? Well, isn't this a small world!" Joni gushed. "Did you go to high school together or something?"

"Or something," Annie mumbled.

Joni looked to Jesse to elaborate, but thankfully he let the remark slide.

"Well, I guess if you know each other, that's a different story," Joni stated cheerfully.

"No, it's not!" Annie protested. "I don't want the dress to leave the apartment. It could get dirty." Thoughts of the rusty old pick-up and the mud that was probably in the interior flashed through her mind.

"I'll be careful," Jesse assured her.

Again there was a humorous glint in his eyes, and it annoyed Annie. "No, I don't want it in that pick-up," she said stubbornly.

"Annie, it's in a plastic garment bag," Joni reminded her.

"And if you want, I could leave a deposit on the dress—a cleaning fee," Jesse offered.

The longer Jesse Conover stood in her apartment, the less sure of herself Annie felt. She needed to get rid of him, and if sending the dress home with him would accomplish that, then she would do it.

"All right. You can take it. But I'd like it back tomorrow morning by nine o'clock."

Satisfaction gleamed in Jesse's eyes. He pulled out his wallet and handed her three hundred-dollar bills. "This ought to cover cleaning charges if it gets dirty in the *pick-up*."

Annie stared at the three hundred dollars in her hand. Obviously Jesse's business was prospering. While she went to the bedroom to get the protective dress bag, she could hear Joni and Jesse talking. When she returned, her roommate's cheeks were flushed, her eyes sparkling. Jesse had that reaction on a woman. Within minutes of meeting, he could have any female eating out of the palm of his had. Annie felt an ache in her chest.

"You'll bring it back tomorrow morning?" she said after she had zipped the dress into the plastic bag and handed it to Jesse.

"I'll stop by—either with the dress or a check. Is seven too early?"

Before Annie could answer, Joni spoke up. "Don't worry. If Annie wants to sleep in, I'll be up by then."

Annie waited until Jesse was gone before chastising her roommate. "What do you mean, you'll be up at seven? I thought you didn't have to work until noon tomorrow?"

"I don't, but I have lots of stuff to do tomorrow morning, so I might as well get up early," she said, suddenly remembering her groceries. She pulled a carton of milk from the brown paper bag and put it in the refrigerator.

Annie clicked her tongue. "You just want to see him again."

"He is awfully cute."

"Yes, well, let me tell you something. He chases skirts the way squirrels chase nuts." Annie finally replaced the phone on the hook while Joni continued to put away the food.

"Oh-oh. Sounds like you learned that the hard way." Joni stacked several frozen dinners in the freezer. "Since you practically snapped the guy's head off when he was here, it makes me think he's more than an old acquaintance."

Annie knew there was no point in keeping the truth from her roommate. When Jesse returned tomorrow, he could easily let it slip that he was her ex-fiancé.

"Remember when we talked about striking out in the romance department and I told you I had already had a fourth strike?"

"Yeah." Joni paused to stare at her roommate. "Are you saying that Jesse is...?"

"My first fiancé," Annie finished for her.

"And you let him get away?" she shrieked.

"No, I didn't *let* him get away. I kicked him out the door. Trust me, he's no prize," Annie stated with angry authority.

Joni was apologetic. "I'm sorry. I just meant that it's hard to imagine not wanting to marry someone who looks like that."

"Looks aren't everything, Joni," she reminded her.

"I know that, but the guy seems really nice. What did he do that was so awful?"

Annie grimaced at the memory, and Joni said, "He hurt you, didn't he?"

"Someone always gets hurt when a relationship ends," she said quietly.

"Look, if you'd rather not talk about it, it's okay."

Annie wasn't sure she should talk about it. Just thinking about what had happened seven years ago brought back emotions she thought she had long ago forgotten. Yet she knew if there was anyone who would understand, it was Joni. She had been there to console and support her when Annie's other engagements had ended.

"Relationships have a way of burning hot and then fizzling. It's all part of being young, I guess," Annie said with a sigh as she sat down at the table.

"How did you meet him?"

"At one of my mother's weddings. She married his uncle Hank," Annie reluctantly admitted. "It was before you came to work at the coffee shop. The marriage only lasted six weeks. But it was long enough for Jesse and I to fall in love—or at least think that we were in love."

"Your mother said he was in the Marines."

"Mm-hmm. He was home on leave when we met, which could account for how fast things moved. I mean, when you only have three weeks to be together, things get rather intense right from the start."

"They must have been if you got engaged," Joni remarked.

A wistful look clouded Annie's eyes. "Not the smartest

move I ever made—especially considering Jesse's reputation.''

"A love-'em-and-leave-'em type?"

"I didn't want to listen to any of the gossip. Besides, I figured I was different than the other girls he had ever dated. So before he went back to the service, we made plans to elope. I was going to fly out to the base at Christmastime.''

"So what went wrong?"

"Shortly before Thanksgiving his grandmother died. He managed to get a special leave to come home for the funeral.''

"And?"

"And everything was so different from the last time I had seen him. I mean, we argued over little stuff, but I thought it was because he was upset over the death of his grandmother. He told me I was immature because I didn't want him spending time with his friends instead of me. And then there was the problem with my mother and his uncle.''

"They weren't getting along?"

"They had separated and were in the process of getting a divorce.''

"And you let that come between you?"

"No, but it certainly didn't make things any easier for us. My mom started including the Conover men in her little quotes about the unreliability of the opposite sex, which wasn't what I needed to hear when I was feeling insecure about Jesse.''

"His uncle probably said the same kind of things about you Jamison women," Joni volunteered.

"Probably, but even if my mom and Hank had been happy, it wouldn't have mattered. Jesse wasn't ready to settle down. I found that out the last night he was home.''

"What happened?"

"He didn't spend the last night of his leave home with me. He took me out to dinner, but after he dropped me off at home, he told me he was going to go say goodbye to some of his buddies who were playing cards at a friend's house."

"And that's why you broke off your engagement?"

"He didn't go to see his buddies, Joni. He went to see another girl."

"Are you sure?"

She nodded. "I followed him."

"Why?"

"Because my mother had me feeling insecure. Whenever Jesse wasn't with me, she'd raise all these doubts. That night she asked me if I thought he was really with the guys. I wasn't sure he was, so I decided to go see for myself."

"And you found him with a girl?"

The memory cut through Annie's heart like a hot knife through butter. "I watched him walk up to this house where a girl answered the door and wrapped her arms around him."

"Then what did you do?"

"I went home, but I couldn't sleep. So at five o'clock in the morning I got up and drove back to that house, and guess what? His car was still there."

Joni shook her head in sympathy. "Men can be such pigs! Looking at Jesse, I would have never suspected that he could do such a thing."

"No, he's pretty smooth when it comes to talking. But luckily I discovered that the Conover men all have one thing in common—they like to chase women. I didn't want to end up like my mother—married and divorced six weeks later."

Joni heaved a long sigh. "And to think I was nice to the guy." She shook her head in remorse.

"I let him take the masterpiece home so his girlfriend could try it on."

They stared at each other and burst out laughing.

"She probably won't look good in it. Very few women can wear that style and not look like her butt's as big as a house," Joni said reassuringly.

"I hope her butt *is* as big as a house," Annie said with a giggle.

"She probably has warts."

"And crooked teeth."

"And ratty hair."

"Squinty eyes."

"A pug nose."

"No neck."

The phone rang, interrupting their litany. Since she was the closest, Annie picked it up. This time it was no man's voice, but a woman's.

"Hi, my name is Roxy," the husky voice said, and Annie's stomach plummeted. "Did Jesse tell you I'm interested in the wedding dress you have for sale?"

"Yes, he did," Annie managed to answer, clearing her throat before she added, "he took it home with him so you could try it on."

"He was there?"

"He just left about fifteen minutes ago."

"Well, isn't he the sweetest man on the face of this earth!" Roxy gushed. "I would have come over myself, but I had this night class I couldn't miss. That was awfully kind of you to let him take the dress home with him."

"Yes, well, he left a three-hundred-dollar deposit," Annie told her.

"He did! Oh, my goodness. Miracles never cease, do they?" She chuckled.

Obviously Roxy knew Jesse well. There was static on the line, and Annie guessed she was calling from a cellular phone.

"I can see I'm going to have to give him a big hug and—" She must have driven through interference, for her next words were indistinguishable.

Annie was grateful. She didn't need to hear what Jesse's fiancée wanted to do to him. Just imagining him with the unknown woman made her grimace.

When the line was clear again, Annie said, "I told him I'd like the dress returned tomorrow unless you decide you want to buy it."

"Jesse doesn't have to take time off from his busy schedule to return it. I'll come over myself. What is the price you're asking?"

"That's negotiable," Annie replied automatically, and then immediately regretted it. For Jesse's fiancée, she should have asked full price.

"Great. I can't wait to see it!" she said enthusiastically. "Thank you, Annie."

Annie hung up the phone with a clunk. "You're never going to guess who that was," she told her roommate.

"Roxy?"

"She didn't sound like she had warts or a big nose." Annie slid onto a chair. "She sounded nice."

"Do you think he's going to tell her that you're his ex-fiancée?"

She shrugged. "I don't know and I don't care."

"Annie, think about this. The woman could be wearing *your* dress to marry *your* ex-fiancé."

Annie didn't want to think about it. She wanted to forget everything that had happened today, especially meeting Jesse Conover.

"Chances are it won't fit. She sounded like a big person." The words were spoken more for Annie's benefit than Joni's.

Again the phone rang. This time Joni answered it. It was her boyfriend. Quietly Annie slipped out of the room.

She went into the living room and switched on the television. One of her favorite comedians was hosting an awards program. Annie listened but didn't laugh. She wasn't hearing the words of the monologue. The only voice she heard was Roxy's husky one saying she would have to give Jesse a big hug and…and?

Annie shook her head. She wasn't sure what would be worse—seeing Jesse again tomorrow or meeting the woman he was going to marry. Both made her want to be gone come seven tomorrow morning.

Before she went to bed, she decided she wouldn't answer the door. She would make Joni do it. She had to because the thought of Jesse with his hands on another woman was enough to make her heart ache.

"YOU GOT MY MESSAGE," Jesse said as he opened the door to Roxy.

"Actually I didn't. I called that Annie person to check and see if you had remembered to tell her I was interested in the dress, and she told me you had taken it home with you." She stepped around him, her eyes perusing the room. "Where is it?"

"Over there." He motioned toward the leather sofa, where the plastic garment bag was draped across the back.

"Thanks." She gave Jesse a quick hug, then hurried over to the sofa. "I heard this cost you three hundred bucks." She didn't wait for him to reply, but crooned appreciatively as she unzipped the bag. "Oh, this is gorgeous! Look at the lace on it!"

"For what it cost, it ought to be something special," Jesse remarked dryly.

Roxy held the dress up to her shapely figure. "Oh, this is just too good to be true. I hope it fits." Without another word to Jesse, she disappeared into the bathroom, leaving Jesse alone with his thoughts about the woman who was selling it.

Annie Jamison hadn't changed much since the first time he had seen her. She still wore her blond hair shoulder length, and her complexion was as creamy now as it had been seven years ago. She looked as if a feather would knock her over, yet he knew better. There was a strength and determination behind that innocent look that could take the wind out of any man's sails.

No, nothing much had changed about Annie. She had the same smile, the same hand gestures when she talked. And he still reacted the same way when she batted those long lashes at him. He wanted to take her in his arms and kiss her senseless. He shook his head as if he could erase those thoughts. His body told him differently. Even though she wasn't even here, the mere thought of her could make his blood pulse to areas he didn't want it to be.

He wanted to be angry with her. She had led him to believe that he was the man she hoped to spend the rest of her life with, only to write him off with a letter. Even though seven years had passed, she was the one woman in his past he had never truly been able to forget.

"Look at this! It's absolutely wonderful, but..."

Jesse looked up to see Roxy standing before him in the wedding dress. "But what?"

She turned around, and he saw that she couldn't get the

back buttoned. "It's too small," she said in an agonized voice.

That didn't surprise Jesse. He had known the minute he saw Annie that she was slimmer than his secretary. "You didn't really want to spend that much money on a dress, did you?"

"She said she would be willing to take less." Roxy fingered the lace sleeves lovingly. "I wonder if I could get it altered."

Jesse wasn't listening. He was imagining what Annie would look like in the dress. A vision of her preening and turning for his inspection brought a smile to his face. Seven years ago they had planned to elope. If he were marrying her today, he would insist on a big church wedding where all of the world could see what a beautiful bride he had.

"Jesse, did you hear anything I said?" Roxy interrupted his musings.

He shook his head to chase away the images. "Yeah, you want to get it altered."

"I asked if you thought this Annie would let me keep it one more day so I could take it to a seamstress and see if it's possible."

"Don't count on it. She seemed rather uptight about me taking it at all."

"Really? I didn't get that impression when I called."

"You don't know Annie Jamison." The words slipped out automatically.

"And you do?" She fixed him with an inquisitive gaze. "*Do* you know this Annie?"

With as little emotion as possible he said, "I dated her when we were kids."

"Kids…what do you mean kids? Thirteen and fourteen?"

"Nineteen and twenty." Reluctantly he gave a brief explanation about Hank marrying Annie's mother.

"Is she the Annie you were dating when you were in the Marines?"

He nodded.

"So why did you break up with her?" Roxy wanted to know.

"What makes you think I broke up with her?"

"Because you always do the breaking up. Jesse, I've worked for you long enough to know that women come and go in your life at your choosing," she reminded him.

He dismissed her inquiry with a shake of his head. "It doesn't matter. We dated, it didn't work out. End of story."

Roxy eyed him suspiciously. "Now you have my curiosity aroused. I'll take the dress back tomorrow and talk to this Annie myself."

Jesse shrugged. "Go ahead. I have no burning desire to see her again." *Liar,* a little voice echoed in his head. "Just make sure you get my three hundred bucks back."

Chapter Four

When seven o'clock came and went without so much as a knock on the front door the following morning, Annie began to feel uneasy. By seven-thirty she was pacing, wondering what was going to be worse—if Jesse didn't bring the dress back or if he showed up with his fiancée.

"You're going to wear a hole in the carpet," Joni warned her.

Annie gestured wildly with her arms. "Where is that man?"

"Maybe he overslept. Why don't you call him?"

"I'm not going to call him!" she said stubbornly. "I won't call him." She continued her ritual—moving from the window to the kitchen to look at the clock and back to the window, watching for some sign of him or the unknown Roxy.

"Maybe he's tied up in traffic," Joni said logically.

"He's probably doing this to get even with me." Annie knew she was being irrational, but she couldn't help it.

"Aren't you overreacting a little bit?" Joni suggested. "He is only thirty minutes late."

"It's an eighteen-hundred-dollar dress!" Annie exclaimed impatiently.

Joni mumbled, "Sorry," and then disappeared to her

room. Annie continued to pace. When Joni reappeared, she carried a laundry basket full of dirty clothes.

"Are you leaving?" Annie asked.

"If you want me to stay, I will, but I have to get my laundry done before I go to work."

"No, go ahead. I can deal with this on my own," Annie assured her, giving her a weak smile of thanks.

When eight o'clock rolled around and the dress still hadn't been returned, she convinced herself that Joni was right. Jesse was probably still in bed. Only she doubted he was sleeping. Had he and the unknown Roxy been unable to resist making mad, passionate love that morning? By eight-fifteen Annie was slamming cupboards and cursing the memories that reminded her of what it was like to wake up in Jesse's arms.

At eight-thirty the doorbell rang. Annie took a deep breath and prepared to meet the woman who not only would wear her wedding dress, but was now the recipient of all those wonderful loving touches Jesse knew how to give.

As Annie pulled the door open, she saw that the deep breath wasn't necessary. Standing in the hall was her mother.

"Oh, it's you." The words were automatic and sounded dull, even to Annie's ears.

"Why, thank you, it's nice to see you, too," Margaret Jamison drawled sarcastically, stepping around her daughter to enter the apartment.

"I'm sorry, Mom. I didn't mean that the way it sounded," Annie apologized. Seeing the hurt expression on her mother's face, she reached over to give her a hug. "What I should have said is 'This is a nice surprise.' How come you're not at the café?"

"I took the morning off." She peeled off her raincoat

and draped it across the back of Annie's sofa. Instead of the brown-and-white uniform the waitresses wore, she had on a navy blue shirtwaist dress. "Do you have any coffee?"

Annie regarded her suspiciously. In the twelve years her mother had owned Mom's Café, not once had she opted to have a cup of coffee at Annie's place rather than go to work.

"What's wrong?" Annie asked, her hands on her hips.

"Nothing. Why does something have to be wrong before I can have a cup of coffee with my daughter?" she asked innocently as she moved to the recliner.

"This is your busiest time of day at the café," Annie reminded her. "I've been trying for years to get you to put someone else in charge, and you never do it."

"Surprise. I did. Cleo's in charge." She pulled the lever that lifted the footrest. "She can handle it." She made herself comfortable, stretching out in the overstuffed recliner. "I love this chair. I can't believe you found it at an estate sale."

Annie knew her mother was behaving rather strangely, but before she could ask her what was going on, the telephone rang. Thinking it might be Jesse, Annie hurried into the kitchen to get it.

Only it wasn't Jesse.

"Annie, this is Roxy. I'm sorry I haven't returned the dress. Jesse told me you wanted it back this morning, but I'd like to take it to a seamstress to see if it can be altered. It's a little snug."

Annie's imagination loved that statement. Roxy was chubby. She smiled to herself.

"Would it be all right if I bring it to you around noon?" Roxy wanted to know.

"It's not a problem," Annie answered, forgetting her earlier frustration.

"Terrific. Hopefully the alterations will work and I can bring you a check instead of the dress," Roxy told her.

"Okay. I'll see you at noon." She wanted to ask if Jesse would be coming with her, but decided against it. What she didn't need for her mother to overhear was Jesse Conover's name.

Annie must have been frowning when she returned to the living room, for her mother asked, "Got a problem?"

Annie shook her head. "No, everything's great. I think I have a buyer for my dress."

"Then you haven't changed your mind about the job on the cruise ship?"

Annie shoved her fists to her hips in a defensive stance. "Why would I?"

"A mother can hope, can't she?"

The job was a topic of conversation she avoided with her mother. When Annie had been notified that she had the job, Margaret's first response was not a congratulatory hug, but a warning that running away from problems never solved them. Annie had given up trying to convince her mother that she wasn't running away from anything. Besides, she didn't want to have to defend her decision to try something new.

Annie leaned her hip against the arm of the sofa and asked, "Why are you really here, Mom? I know it wasn't to have a cup of coffee."

"There is something I need to tell you...." she began.

A feeling of déjà vu crept over Annie. The last time her mother had had such an uncomfortable look on her face was when she had announced she was divorcing her fourth husband. "You and Neil aren't having problems, are you?"

That brought a sarcastic laugh from Margaret. "You ought to know by now that life with Neil is one big problem."

Annie groaned. "Aw, Mom, not again?"

She didn't reply but asked, "Are you going to get me a cup of coffee?"

Annie went back to the kitchen, where she poured her mother a mug of coffee. After adding a heaping teaspoon of sugar, she carried it into the living room.

As soon as Margaret had taken a sip, she leaned her head back and closed her eyes. Annie studied her face and saw wrinkles that she hadn't seen previously.

"Mom, you're not sick, are you?"

Margaret kept her eyes closed and answered flippantly, "Sick of Neil or sick sick?"

"Your marriage is not a joking matter," she admonished her. "Tell me what it is that's bothering you." She knelt down beside the recliner.

Margaret opened her eyes and looked at her daughter. "Neil has found someone else he'd rather grow old with."

Annie reached over to place her hand on her mother's forearm. "He wasn't good enough for you, Mom."

"You're right." Margaret patted her hand. "I should have never married him. I shouldn't have married any of them." She shook her head in regret. "Men." She made a sound of disgust. "They're all alike, you know."

Annie didn't want to agree with her mother, but after four fiancés and no marriages, who was she to refute her mother's declaration? Every single one of her stepfathers had hurt her mother. And the truth was, Annie didn't think her mother *should* have married any of them.

"I should have known better. Lucky in cards, unlucky in love," Margaret recited with authority. "That honeymoon in Vegas was like the kiss of death. We won twenty-four hundred dollars, you know.''

"I know, Mom," she said consolingly.

Margaret rubbed her forehead. "Do you have any aspirin?"

"I'll get you some." Annie went into the kitchen and opened a cupboard. She pulled out the bottle of aspirin and carried it into the living room. "Do you know what you're going to do?" She shook two tablets into her mother's hands.

"I'm going to file for divorce." Her mother tossed the aspirin onto her tongue, then washed them down with a sip of coffee. "That's why I'm not at the café. I have an appointment with my lawyer at ten-thirty."

"It's already gone that far?"

Her mother nodded. "He packed his things and left last week."

Annie's chest tightened. "Why didn't you tell me?"

Margaret shrugged. "No point in rehashing it when you know what the outcome's going to be. You know what I always say. It's okay to make a mistake as long as you recognize it as a mistake and move forward. I'm moving forward."

Annie understood very well about mistakes and was in total empathy with her mother. Besides, she had never liked Neil. Privately she had called him Steel Neil. He had about as much sensitivity as a steel beam.

"It's a good thing we had a prenuptial agreement. It'll make things easier," Margaret remarked before taking another sip of coffee. There was a slight tremor in her voice, and Annie wondered if her mother was as unaffected by Neil's defection as she wanted her daughter to believe she was.

"Mom, are you sure you're okay? Maybe I should come with you to see the lawyer," she suggested.

"Why? I'm not upset, Annie. I'm relieved to be getting out of a bad situation," she stated adamantly.

Annie wasn't convinced. "I wish you would have told me you and Neil were having problems. I could have come over and helped you through this."

"I don't need a baby-sitter, Annie," her mother said with a hint of irritation. "I'm getting divorced, not having an operation."

"I guess it's not like you haven't been through this before, is it?" Annie stated in a matter-of-fact tone.

Some mothers would have been offended by her comment, but not Margaret. "That's right, and we both know I'll be fine."

Annie knew she spoke the truth. She had seen four stepfathers come and go in her life. Number five would be no different. "Well, if there's anything I can do to help, just let me know."

"There is something." Margaret pushed herself forward. "I know yesterday was your official last day at the coffee shop, but I could really use another pair of hands for the lunch hour today." She looked at Annie hopefully. "You wouldn't have to cook—just help out the waitresses."

Annie's shoulders sagged. As she'd expected, her mother hadn't come to have a heart-to-heart, but to seek her help. Just once she wished her mother would need her for something other than cooking in the kitchen at Mom's Café.

When Annie didn't respond right away, she added, "It's only for a couple of hours. Just until I get back from the attorney's office."

Annie glanced at the clock. "I really want to help you

out, Mom. But I can't leave. You see, I sent my wedding dress home with someone last night so she could try it on, and she's returning it to me this morning at noon.''

Margaret pushed herself out of the chair. "It's all right. I'm sure Cleo will do just fine on her own. You stay here and wait for your dress." She reached for her raincoat.

Guilt washed over Annie. As much as she wanted to think Cleo could handle the lunchtime rush, she knew there was a good reason why her mother never left the older woman in charge. Having worked at the café, Annie knew that reason. Cleo was easily flustered.

"Mom, wait. I'll call and change my appointment. That way I can be there for the lunch rush."

Margaret reached for her hand and gave it a squeeze. "Thank you, dear."

Unable to reach anyone at Jesse's number, Annie left a message for Roxy on the voice mail instructing her not to bring the wedding dress back until after three, as she would be at work. Then she found the brown-and-white uniform she had packed away with her winter clothes, gave it a quick press with her iron and put it on.

"This is the last time," she told her reflection in the mirror, then headed for her mother's restaurant.

"HI, JESSE." Roxy waved to her boss as he crossed a vacant lot where a bulldozer was busy pushing around mounds of dirt. "I just came from the seamstress and I'm going back to the office," she told him as he approached her car.

"So what was the verdict? Is it going to be the dress you wear when you march down the aisle with Fred?" Jesse asked, glancing in the window to where the wedding dress lay across the back seat of her car.

Roxy sighed. "No. Not even the world's greatest diet

will get me into it, and there isn't enough fabric to let out the seams."

"So you're going to return it?"

"Well, it's like this. I was supposed to meet your Annie at noon, but she called and—"

"Wait a minute," Jesse interrupted her. "She's not *my* Annie."

Roxy's eyebrows rose. "All right. I was supposed to meet the Annie whose wedding dress I have in my car, but she left a message saying she won't be home until three. The problem is I have a dentist appointment at two-thirty in downtown St. Paul."

"So call her and tell her you'll be late."

"I tried calling, but she's not at home. She's working."

Automatically the image of Annie in the brown-and-white waitress uniform she used to wear when she worked at her mother's café flashed across Jesse's mind. He would sit on a stool at the counter for hours, content to simply watch her scurry about with people's food. He wondered if she still worked there.

"Don't you have to drive over to city hall this afternoon to get those building permits?" Roxy asked, interrupting his musings.

A suspicion arose in his mind. "Roxy, you're not thinking that I should return the dress, are you?"

"If you're going to city hall, you'll be driving right through her neighborhood. Could you do it for me?"

He could. And what made him all the more annoyed was that he wanted to do it. The thought of seeing Annie again sent blood pumping through his veins in double time.

He took off his baseball cap, ran a hand across his head, then replaced the hat. "I think you should just call her and leave a message that you'll return it this evening."

"Jesse, I've already kept it longer than I should have. What if she has other buyers lined up to look at it?" Her voice softened as she said, "It wouldn't be that big of an inconvenience, would it?"

It wasn't the inconvenience that worried him. It was seeing Annie again. He had spent far too much time thinking about her the way it was. If he wasn't careful, she'd work her magic on him all over again. He'd be caught like a spider in a web, doing whatever he could to please her.

"You're going to go right by her place," Roxy reminded him for the second time.

"All right. I'll do it," he said against his better judgment.

"Great. What should I do with it?" she asked, opening her car door.

"Put it in Hank's truck," he told her.

"Oh—that reminds me. There've been several calls for the pick-up, including a guy who wanted to stop by and test-drive it, but he couldn't do it until this evening. I took his number down." She reached into her purse and pulled out a slip of paper, which she gave to Jesse.

He ran a hand along the back of his neck as he glanced at the number. Todd was probably right. He should have left the sale of the truck to his uncle. "I think I'll let Hank handle this."

Roxy lifted the garment bag from the back seat of her car and carried it over to the red pick-up. When Jesse unlocked the back of the topper, she hollered at him, "You can't put a designer wedding gown in the back of a pick-up."

"It's in plastic."

The look that she gave him had him opening the passenger door and gesturing eloquently for her to set it inside. "You will be careful with it, won't you?" she asked as she laid it across the seat.

"It's my three hundred bucks she has on deposit," he reminded her.

That seemed to put Roxy's mind at ease. "I'll stop by the office on my way home from the dentist and make sure everything's okay."

What's not to be okay? Jesse wondered, but didn't raise the question.

As soon as Roxy had driven away, he pulled out his cellular phone. With his hip propped against a rusty fender, he dialed his uncle's pager.

Within a few minutes his cellular phone rang.

"It's Hank."

"I might have a buyer for the pick-up," Jesse told him. "Stop by the office on your way home tonight, and I'll give you the information."

"I'm probably not going to be done much before four."

"That's all right. Just come over whenever you're finished. I'm going to have some lunch and then go get those building permits we need for the Sanderson project."

"Will do, boss," Hank said before hanging up.

Just as the conversation ended, Todd pulled up in his Explorer. "Hey, little brother. It's Friday. The broomball team is meeting for lunch at Champps. Want to come along?"

Jesse shrugged. "Sure. Why not? Just let me talk to Larry before we go." He walked over to the man operating the bulldozer, made sure he understood the work that needed to be done, then waved and headed back toward Todd's Explorer.

"Your truck or mine?" Todd asked as Jesse approached.

"Yours," Jesse answered. "Hank's got something in the front seat."

"ANYBODY HERE?" Hank called out as he stepped into Jesse's office. Hearing no response, he closed the door behind him and walked over to the desk. He put the invoices he had found at the work site next to the memo pad and started to write a note when he noticed the yellow legal pad with the phone messages concerning the pickup.

His eyes lit up as he read the list of names. He whistled through his teeth. "It's a good thing I left the job early," he said aloud to himself as he sat down at the desk. "I need to get on this right away." He reached for the phone, punching in the first phone number on the list.

Someone answered on the first ring. Hank's eyes widened. "You want to see the '85 Ram? Where are you at?" He paused, then said, "Sure. I'll meet you there. Give me forty-five minutes. I have to go pick up the truck."

He dug deep into his pockets for the spare set of keys and headed back out the door.

ALL DURING LUNCH Jesse had had a hard time concentrating on the subject being discussed—broomball. While Todd and several of the team members talked strategy and practice dates, Jesse couldn't stop thinking about Annie. Where was she working and what would she say when he showed up at her door again?

Every time the waitress in the bar returned to their table, she flirted outrageously with Jesse. But he didn't notice. There was only one shapely blonde on his mind, and that was his ex-fiancée.

That's why he decided he would return the dress first

and visit city hall second. That way he would have no reason to stay at Annie's. He'd drop off the wedding gown and split. He didn't need to find out what she had been doing with her life. He didn't need to know why she had refused to see him when he had come home from the service. He didn't need to get involved with her again.

On the way back to the construction site, Todd asked his brother, "Didn't you say you had to stop at city hall?"

"Yeah, why?"

"I have to pick up a pair of work boots I had resoled at a shoe repair over on Seventh Street. Why don't I drive over there now, and you can get the permits on the way back? It's right in the same area."

Jesse shrugged. "It's fine with me."

As it turned out, the shoe repair was located smack-dab in the center of a city block. Todd parked at a meter out front of a two-story brick building that also housed a barbershop and a tailor. But it was the building on the corner that caught Jesse's eye. It was a café with a red-and-white-striped awning. The marquee over the awning said Mom's Café. Seven years ago Annie's mother had owned the place.

While Todd went into the shoe-repair store, Jesse sat debating whether he should go find out. Unable to resist, he climbed out of the truck and walked down to the corner. One glance through the plate-glass windows told him the café was just as he remembered it. A row of stools lined the counter, and leather-padded bench seats filled the booths. The aroma of fried foods drifted out as the door opened and closed.

Jesse was about to walk back to the truck when he noticed Annie, a pen and pad in hand, waiting on a customer at the counter. She wore her hair tied back in a ponytail, the brown-and-white uniform hugging her body in a way it hadn't done seven years ago. The older gentleman she was serving looked delighted to have her for his waitress. Who wouldn't be? Jesse thought.

As if she sensed someone staring at her, she glanced toward the window. Caught in the act, Jesse had no choice but to go inside. He took one of the empty stools at the counter. Annie ignored him and turned her attention back to her customer.

Another waitress with the name Cleo stitched over her pocket came to take his order.

Jesse grinned at her and said, "I'd like to see Annie."

Cleo smiled back and called out, "Annie, this fellow wants you."

Oh, how true, how true, Jesse thought as he watched Annie's face flush ever so slightly. Whether it was from the heat of the kitchen or his presence, he wasn't sure.

She finished scribbling out the other man's order, slipped it on the revolving metal carousel on the counter separating the kitchen from the restaurant, then approached Jesse.

"Did you come to eat?" she asked.

"This place hasn't changed much, has it?" he observed, noting that instead of blue-and-pink packets filled with sugar substitute, there was a canister dispensing the real stuff. "A new coat of paint and different curtains, but still the same old café."

"Prices have gone up," she answered, shifting impatiently.

"How come you're not cooking? Isn't that the reason you went to cooking school—so you could cook?" He deliberately brought up the subject to let her know that he knew her enrollment in a culinary course in Chicago was partially due to the fact that she had wanted to be away from home when he was discharged from the service.

She ignored his question. "Why are you here, Jesse?"

"I was in the neighborhood and just thought I'd drop in—for old times' sake," he answered.

Again she shifted impatiently. "I'm afraid you're going to have to take your trip down memory lane by yourself. I have work to do." As if to prove her point, a burly man in a plaid flannel shirt called out, "I could use another cup of coffee, Annie."

"I'll be right there, Will." She gave Jesse an I-told-you-so look.

"Go ahead and get him a cup."

When she had finished serving the gentleman, Jesse signaled for her.

Reluctantly she returned. "Have you decided what you want to order?"

"I'll have a soda." He watched as she reached for a glass, the fabric of her skirt rising as she stretched. She filled the glass, grabbed a straw and set it before him. "You look the same as you did seven years ago. Same smile, same ponytail, same great legs."

He could see he had flustered her with his comment. She shoved her order pad back into her pocket and reached for a rag to wipe off the counter space next to his. The brown cotton fabric stretched across her bust, and Jesse felt his body react.

"If you're not going to order something else, why don't you leave?" she said tightly, her eyes on the counter, not him.

"I came to pass along a message from Roxy."

That had her attention. "What is it?"

"You'll have your wedding dress back later this afternoon."

"How much later?"

"Is three-thirty okay?"

"Do I have a choice?"

He grinned. "Not really."

She tossed the rag back into a dishpan of soapy water. "You could have left that message on my answering machine."

"As I said, I was in the neighborhood."

She didn't look convinced. Without another word she picked up the coffee carafe and worked the length of the counter. As she refilled each of the cups, she smiled at the customers. Jesse wished she would smile at him the way she smiled at the other men.

When she had finished, she returned to Jesse. "You know, this whole dress thing is really one big inconvenience for me."

"You told Roxy she could take it to the seamstress," he reminded her.

She heaved a long sigh. "Look, I really don't have time to stand here and argue with you. Just make sure she gets the dress back by three-thirty."

"It'll be there. She's not bringing it back. I am."

"And that's supposed to reassure me?" she asked sarcastically.

"My word's as good as gold. It always has been."

Annie stared at him in disbelief. Of all the nerve! Did he actually expect that she'd buy that line? "I wasn't born yesterday, Jesse."

"And what's that supposed to mean?"

"At one time you gave me your word I was the only woman you would ever love," she threw back at him, then moved to the far end of the counter. She could feel his eyes on her as she busied herself with straightening the counter.

Just when she thought his gaze would burn the clothes off her back, he got up to leave. She hurried over to give him the check. "You can pay the cashier," she said coolly.

When she would have set the ticket on the counter, he grabbed her hand and said in a dangerously soft voice, "I think you're a little confused as to just whose word it was that was broken."

Annie looked down at her hand enclosed in his and felt a tremor echo through her. With the slightest of tugs, he released it, but not before she had seen the flash of anger in those blue eyes.

She was not about to let Jesse Conover make her feel guilty over ending their engagement. "Save your breath for someone who cares, Jesse," she snapped back. "All I want from you is my dress."

"You'll get it. Just make sure you hold up your end of the bargain."

"Which is?"

"I want my three hundred bucks back."

BY THE TIME JESSE returned to Todd's truck, his brother was tapping his fingers on the steering wheel.

"Where have you been?"

"I needed some fresh air so I took a little walk," was all Jesse said.

"Obviously it didn't improve your mood."

Jesse didn't answer. They rode in silence until they reached the construction site. As Todd pulled up in front of the area where the bulldozer was still at work, Jesse sat forward. "What the heck...?" he murmured.

"What's wrong?"

"Where's Hank's truck?"

"He must have taken it. You said you were going to let him handle the sale from now on."

"I was, but he wasn't supposed to come get it until after four." Jesse climbed out of the Explorer, slammed the door shut and stood with his hands on his hips, staring at the street where, instead of the old red Ram, there sat a shiny black pick-up. "I told him to meet me at the office."

"Maybe he had a hot buyer and didn't want to wait," Todd suggested.

"Damn." Jesse headed for his pick-up.

"Where are you going?"

"To find Hank."

Chapter Five

Annie thought about Jesse all the way home from work. His presence in her mother's café had been a distraction she didn't need. It had reminded her of all the times he had come and sat on that very stool and sipped Cokes while he waited for her to finish working. She didn't need the reminder. Nor did she want his compliments. She could still hear the huskiness in his voice when he had said, "Same smile, same great legs." The way his blue eyes had roved up and down her figure had caused her heart to skip a couple of beats.

She mentally shrugged. So what if Jesse Conover had the power to make a woman's heart miss a beat. She would not allow him to charm her a second time. Once had been enough. She was no longer nineteen, but twenty-six—an adult woman who didn't respond to flirtatious remarks as if they were manna from heaven.

She needed to put him out of her thoughts, to focus on the matter at hand—preparing for her job on the cruise ship. Jesse was just another source of irritation—like the flat tire on her car had been. She'd had a small run of bad luck, but unlike her mother, she believed she could change that.

And she would. As soon as Jesse returned her wedding

dress, she would never have to see him again. She would put him out of her mind for good.

With that resolution firmly entrenched in her thoughts, she unlocked her door and entered her apartment, slinging her jacket across the sofa as she kicked off her work shoes. In her hands she carried a stack of mail. She was about to flip through it when the phone rang. She hurried to answer it.

"Hi. I'm calling about the wedding dress. Is it still for sale?" a feminine voice said in her ear.

Optimism bloomed in Annie's cheeks. "Yes, as a matter of fact it is." She went on to explain in great detail what the dress looked like, giving a sales pitch she was convinced no one could refuse. To her delight it worked. The woman asked when she could come see the designer gown.

Annie glanced at the clock on the kitchen wall. "How about seven?"

"Seven would be great," came the eager response.

After giving her directions, Annie replaced the receiver with a smile on her face. Then she hurried into the bedroom to change out of her waitress uniform. The last thing she needed was for Jesse to see more of her legs. She pulled on a baggy sweatshirt and a pair of sweatpants. Her hair she left in the ponytail.

"So there, Mr. Conover." She preened in front of the mirror. "Your efforts to foil my attempts to sell the masterpiece aren't going to work."

Before leaving her bedroom, she reached for a small atomizer and doused herself in its mist. "That's not for you, Jesse. I just don't like the aroma of Mom's Café."

JESSE HAD ONE EYE on the bulldozer pushing dirt across the vacant lot and one eye on the paved road. He glanced at his watch. Three o'clock, and there was still no sign of Hank. Why had he come and taken the pick-up? More important where had he gone? Although, it wasn't the truck that was foremost in Jesse's mind, but the dress—Annie's eighteen-hundred-dollar wedding dress.

That damn dress. How many times in the past two days had he cursed it? Hank could be anywhere—outside the Forty Club, in St. Michael at the work site, at Caroline's. He groaned. Certainly his uncle had seen the dress lying across the seat when he slid behind the wheel?

When three-thirty came and went with still no sign of his uncle, Jesse knew he had to make a decision. Either he went looking for Hank or he drove over to city hall for the building permits. As much as he wanted to go look for his uncle and the missing wedding dress, if he didn't get to city hall before four-thirty, he wouldn't get the permits, and that would mean work wouldn't get started on the Hawk's Ridge addition. He kicked the mud from his work shoes and climbed into his pick-up. As he turned the truck around in the cul-de-sac, he reached for the cellular phone and punched in seven numbers.

"Hi, this is Annie."

The sound of her voice made his skin grow warm. "Hi, it's Jesse."

"Where's my dress?" The coolness in her tone chased away the heat on his flesh.

He maneuvered the pick-up out into traffic. "I'm going to be a little later than I thought. I've run into a problem."

"With my dress?"

He sensed the note of panic in her voice. "No, I'm just tied up with some business at my office, that's all," he answered. "Would it be all right if I stopped by around six?"

"Six?" she shrieked.

"Aren't you going to be home then?"

"Yes, but I have a potential buyer coming to look at the dress at seven. That's cutting it awfully close."

He could hear the irritation in her voice. "That leaves you an entire hour. It's not like you need to shine it up or anything, is it?" When he heard her swift intake of breath, he knew her blue eyes were flashing.

"The point is, you said you'd return the dress by three-thirty," she reminded him.

"I know and I'm sorry, but this can't be helped. Look, I'll try to get over there as soon as possible, but I promise I'll be there by six at the latest."

"Jesse, your promises aren't worth much."

"That's not fair, Annie."

"Isn't it? Yesterday you told me the dress would be here this morning." She didn't try to hide her anger.

"And it would have been if you hadn't agreed to let Roxy take it to a seamstress," he retorted.

"So what are you saying? That you think it's my fault that she's not a size 7?" Before he could respond, she quickly added, "Gee, while you're at it, why don't you also blame me for having to go to work instead of waiting at home all day for your Roxy to decide when it's convenient for her to return the dress."

"Roxy felt bad that the dress didn't work out," he said in defense of his secretary.

"I'm sure she did."

Her sarcasm annoyed him. "I don't have time to argue with you. The dress will be returned to you today, all right?"

"It better be," she warned.

He hung up the phone, then dialed his office. Instead of Roxy, he got the answering machine. As soon as the recorded message had played and the beep had sounded, he said, "This is Jesse. See if you can track down Hank for me. Tell him to get his butt over to the office and wait for me."

ANNIE WAS NOT HAPPY. Once again she was forced to wait for Jesse. Why was it so difficult to get him out of her life? While she waited, she folded her winter clothes and packed them into boxes to be stored at her mother's while she was gone.

That's how Joni found her—running packaging tape across the cardboard to seal the boxes.

"Is the dress still for sale?" Joni asked as Annie shoved a box against the wall.

With a grunt she heaved the second box on top of the first. "Yes. It didn't work for Miss Roxy."

"Oh-oh. Do I detect a hint of irritation with the unknown Roxy?"

"It's because of her I don't have the masterpiece." Annie explained what had happened, starting with Roxy's phone call that morning and ending with Jesse's that afternoon. She left out the part about Jesse stopping in to see her at the diner.

"Why is Jesse returning it for her anyway?"

Annie shrugged. "I guess he's one of those macho types who wants to do everything for the little lady in his life," she drawled irritably.

"Then he has the dress?"

"Mm-hmm."

"Well, if that's the case and he's too busy to bring it over here, why don't you go over there and get it?" Joni suggested. "You said he was tied up at his office." She walked over to the closet and pulled out the telephone book.

"What are you doing?"

"Looking up his address." Joni flipped through the pages until she found what she was looking for. "Here it is. C & C Custom Homes. It's on Pilot Knob Road. That should be easy enough to find."

Annie hesitated. "I don't think I want to go over there."

"Do you want your wedding dress back on your terms or on his?"

Annie was quiet as she mulled over her roommate's suggestion.

"What if he doesn't show up at six? Then what are you going to do?" Joni asked.

Annie thought it over briefly, then said, "You're right. It's my dress. I'm going to go get it."

"Good. I'll go with you."

Fifteen minutes later when Annie turned her car onto Pilot Knob Road, the gray clouds that had been threatening rain all day opened, releasing a downpour that pelted the windshield. She could feel butterflies winging around in her stomach. "Maybe he won't be there. What if he was called to some construction site?"

"It's Friday afternoon and it's raining. My bet is that he's here," Joni stated confidently. "You'll get the dress and then we'll leave. Easy-peasy."

Annie wished someone would telegraph that easy-peasy stuff to the butterflies in her stomach. When Joni called out, "There it is on the right," Annie's heart joined the butterflies in their escapade.

"Whoa! The home-building business must be prosperous. Look at the size of this place!" Joni gushed. "Why do you suppose he drives such a beat-up pick-up when he owns all of this?"

As Annie pulled into the long, curving driveway, she had similar thoughts. Jesse may have been a poor Marine seven years ago, but now he was definitely living on the right side of the tracks. The driveway forked, with a sign indicating C & C Custom Homes was on the left.

"Maybe he's a cheapskate like Hank," she told Joni. "Mom thinks all the Conovers are."

"Well, he certainly didn't spare any money when it came to building his own home," Joni remarked as Annie followed the paved driveway to the left. They soon discovered that the office was actually a detached garage that had been converted into business space. Where garage doors had once been, now were French doors and plate-glass windows.

Annie pulled into a space marked Visitors' Parking and turned off the engine. Seeing no other cars, she said, "It doesn't look like anyone's here."

"He probably parks at the house and walks over," Joni told her. "Come on. Let's go inside."

"Maybe we should wait until the rain lets up. Otherwise we're going to get soaked."

"We'll make a dash for the door."

Reluctantly Annie got out of the car. She followed Joni up to the French doors and rang the bell. No one answered. Because the blinds were drawn, they couldn't see if anyone was inside. Joni tried the door handle, but it was locked.

"He's not here and we're getting soaked," Annie stated irritably.

Joni looked toward the multilevel home on the hill. "Maybe we should try the house."

"No, I'm already wet enough." Annie dashed back to the car and climbed inside. As soon as Joni was seated across from her, she started the engine.

"Are you sure you want to leave without the dress?" Joni asked.

"I'm freezing." She set the heater fan on high and was about to back out of the parking space when headlights from another car appeared in her rearview mirror.

"Someone's coming," Joni called out.

"I know. I see the car." She waited and watched as a red Miata pulled into a parking space about twenty feet away on Joni's side of the car.

"It looks like a woman. Maybe it's Roxy," Joni remarked.

The butterflies returned to Annie's stomach with a vengeance. "It could be a customer."

"Maybe. At least she was smart enough to carry an umbrella."

"She has to walk past us to get to the door. We'll be able to see if she has a key and goes inside."

"I'll just ask her." Joni rolled down her window and called out to the woman. "Do you work here?" Annie couldn't hear the reply. Joni rolled the window back up and said, "I think she said her name is Roxy. Turn your windshield wipers on high so we can get a better look."

Annie did as Joni instructed. As the woman went scurrying by, she glanced at the two of them sitting in the car. She gave them a smile and a friendly wave, indicating they could come inside.

But Annie wasn't going to go anywhere. She couldn't. For the minute she saw the woman's face, a chill swept over her body, causing her to shiver. This Roxy looked amazingly like the woman who had come between her and Jesse seven years ago.

"Come on. She's waving for us to go in," Joni said.

"I can't."

"What do you mean you can't?" Joni didn't miss the way Annie's white knuckles clutched the steering wheel.

"Joni, I think that might be the woman I saw with Jesse the night I caught him cheating on me."

"She's the reason you broke off your engagement?"

"Yes," came the painful admission. Annie's teeth had started to chatter. Whether it was the wet clothes or the shock at seeing the redhead again, she didn't know.

"Are you sure?"

"Yes...no...it looks like her," she stammered, then quickly shoved the car in reverse and backed out of the parking space.

"Wait. Don't just drive off. Let me go inside and get the dress," Joni offered.

But Annie was beyond thinking rationally. All the pain of seven years ago came rushing back. "No. It doesn't matter."

"Of course it matters," Joni insisted. "Annie, listen to me. You don't even have to see the woman. I can run in and get the dress, and that'll be the end of it."

But Annie wasn't listening. She was getting away from C & C Custom Homes as fast as she could. "I can't believe I was stupid enough to let him talk me into taking the dress in the first place." She chuckled in a self-deprecating manner. "I mean, think of it, Joni. I almost sold *my* wedding dress to that...that...!" Her voice rose on a note of hysteria.

"Almost, but it didn't happen," Joni said reassuringly. "And obviously he's no prize if here it is seven years later and they're still not married!"

"What can he possibly see in her?" she asked in a voice choked with emotion.

"I don't know. She looked like she had hippie hair. Maybe it was wet from the rain, but it looked like she had a center part and it hung straight down."

"That's the way she wore it back then, too, except she had a big pouf of bangs on top. I'm sure she dyes it. No one has hair that shade of red."

"So now what?" Joni asked.

"I think I should keep the three hundred dollars he left as a deposit. I mean, he didn't fulfill his end of the bargain, right?" She looked to Joni for approval.

"Why do you want to keep it? Because he didn't bring the dress back on time or because he's still dating Roxy?"

Annie didn't answer.

"HAVE YOU HEARD FROM HANK?" Jesse asked Roxy the minute he got back to the office.

"No. What's wrong?"

Jesse removed his rain-drenched jacket and hung it on the coat tree near the door. "He came and swapped trucks this afternoon when I was out to lunch."

"Maybe he found someone who wanted to buy it," Roxy suggested.

"Could be, but if that's the case, I wish he would have left the wedding dress in my truck."

Roxy dropped the pen she was holding and grimaced. "Oh, no. Tell me you're not saying the dress hasn't been returned."

He shook his head grimly. "Hank took the pick-up before I had a chance to take it over to Annie."

"Good grief. That poor woman is probably ready to string us up. Have you told her what's happened?"

"I called and said I was tied up with business but I'd have the dress there by six." He glanced at his watch. "If Hank doesn't show up soon, I'm going to have to call her again."

"It's almost five now. He should have been here by now. I've never known Hank to miss picking up his check on payday," Roxy said with a wry grin. "He won't be able to stop at the Forty Club if he doesn't."

Jesse's laugh was without humor. "Todd says he hasn't

been stopping at the Forty Club lately. He thinks Hank's in love again.''

"With that Caroline?'' Jesse nodded, and she added, "Maybe you should try calling her place. Hank might have stopped there.''

"I suppose it's worth a try,'' Jesse said, picking up the phone. After dialing and getting no one, he turned his attention to the mail Roxy had left on his desk. "Anything happen this afternoon that I should know about?''

"Nothing, except a couple of inquiries about the new development.'' Roxy pulled open a file cabinet and inserted several manila folders. "Oh, and there were two women here, but they didn't come in. It was kind of weird. One of them asked if I worked here. When I said yes, they left.''

"What kind of car was it?''

"An old white Honda.''

Jesse put the mail aside. "Did you get a good look at them?''

She shook her head. "It was raining too hard. All I know is they were both blond.''

Jesse immediately thought of Annie and her roommate. She had driven a white Honda to the construction site.

"It was probably someone looking for directions, but the rain was coming down so hard, they left.'' She finished putting the folders away, then said, "That does it for me. I'm going to go home.'' She held up a brown envelope. "What about Hank's check?''

Jesse put his hand out, palm upward. "I'll see that he gets it.''

Roxy deposited it in his hand. "Do you have plans for the weekend?'' she asked, pulling on a navy blue trench coat.

"Todd and I are playing broomball on Sunday. What about you?"

"Fred's taking me to dinner in Stillwater tonight. It's the sixth anniversary of our first date." She retrieved her umbrella from the corner of the room. "Are you sure you don't mind me leaving? I feel responsible for the wedding dress."

"I already told Annie you had given it to me," Jesse reassured her.

"Yes, but maybe I should stick around until Hank brings it back. That way I could take it over to Annie myself and apologize in person."

"Don't worry about it." He put his hands on her shoulders and gently pointed her in the direction of the door. "Go have a nice dinner with my cousin. I'll take care of the dress."

Little did Jesse know how false those words would be. At five-thirty the phone rang. He picked it up, hoping it would be Hank. It was.

"Where the hell are you?" Jesse couldn't keep the anger from his voice. "I thought we had agreed that you would come back to the office and get the pick-up. I don't remember telling you to take it from the job site."

"I had a party interested in buying it. Why are you yelling at me for taking my own truck?" Hank demanded.

"Because you have something inside that I'm responsible for."

"What's that?"

Jesse had to struggle to remain calm. "What do you mean, what's that? I'm talking about the wedding dress."

"Oh—is that what that was in the plastic bag?"

An uneasy feeling crept over Jesse. "Yes. It *is* still in the truck, right?"

"It might be, but I can't say for sure."

The uneasiness became a sick feeling in the pit of his stomach. "What do you mean you can't say for sure?" he asked in a dangerously soft voice.

There was a long pause, then Hank said, "Because someone stole the damn truck right out from under my nose."

"What?" Jesse screamed into the receiver.

"My pick-up—it's been stolen!" Hank exclaimed excitedly.

"With the dress inside?" Jesse barked.

"Yes, with the dress inside," Hank barked right back.

Jesse took a deep breath to calm himself, then said, "How did it happen?"

"I stopped at that little convenience store over on Grand Avenue and when I came out, it was gone. Stolen right from under my nose!"

Jesse leaned back in his chair and closed his eyes, rubbing the bridge of his nose with his fingertips. "Who would want to steal that old pick-up?"

"Beats me. I can't believe it happened, either. What is the city coming to when a man can't even leave his pick-up running for two minutes and—"

Jesse's eyes flew open and he sat forward. "Wait a minute. Did you say you left the truck running?"

"Yeah. I couldn't turn the thing off. I was worried that it wouldn't start again, and I was on my way over to meet a fellow who wanted to test-drive it."

Jesse sighed. "Did you notify the police?"

"Yup. They're here with me now. Taking down all the particulars. It's a good thing I took out that extra insurance, isn't it?"

"Yeah," Jesse said absently, wondering how he was going to tell Annie her dress was stolen.

"I'm going to need a ride home. Can you come get me?"

"Can't you call Caroline?"

"She's out of town for the weekend."

Jesse grimaced. "All right, I'll be right there."

Before he hung up, Hank asked, "Whose wedding dress was it anyway?"

"It's a long story. I'll tell you when I see you."

BY THE TIME JESSE DROPPED Hank off at home, it was after six. Instead of calling Annie and telling her what had happened, he decided to go see her in person. He told himself it was because he owed her that much, but deep down inside he knew he wanted to see her again.

For seven years he had carried around a dull ache—a result of the Dear John letter she had sent him. He had always thought that the first time he saw her again he'd have to use every ounce of self-control not to strangle her. But that hadn't happened. From the moment he had set eyes on her, he had wanted not to hurt her, but to kiss her.

He knew she would be upset over the wedding dress. He had thought he would be able to enjoy her anxiety, but despite everything that had happened, he couldn't take pleasure in her misery—no matter how badly she had hurt him.

As he drove the short distance to her apartment, he tried to think of an easy way to break the news that the dress had been stolen. None came to mind. He had thought that after talking to the police, he would have a better idea of what to tell her. He didn't. Any way he looked at it, the outcome was still the same. The dress had been stolen.

As he waited for a traffic light to turn green, he noticed a young man standing on the street corner selling cut flowers. Jesse pulled over to the side of the road and got out of his truck. He selected a small bunch of deep red roses. He knew it wouldn't make up for what had happened, but at least it was something to give her.

He parked in front of her apartment building. With the falling temperatures, the rain had gradually turned to snow. White flakes dusted the shoulders of his leather jacket as he hurried up the steps into the lobby. He paused in front of the nameplate that said A. Jamison/J. Tremaine. With a deep breath he pushed the button.

"You're late." Her voice was sharp over the intercom.

"Sorry. It couldn't be helped."

When he heard the buzz, he opened the lobby door and took the steps two at a time. She was waiting for him in the entrance of her apartment, her arms folded across her chest.

Annie expected to see Jesse carrying her wedding dress, not a bouquet of flowers. The sight of him standing on her doorstep with red roses in his hand, his blue gaze assessing her, made her body grow warm. During their short courtship he had only brought her red roses on one occasion, and that was the day after he had proposed. He had said they were a symbol of his love and devotion to her. The memory sent a chill across her flesh that chased away the warmth.

"What are those for and where is my dress?"

He ignored the second part of the question and said, "You used to tell me that whenever I could think of nothing to get you, flowers would always brighten your day." He offered them to her. "I figured you could use a little brightening."

Cautiously she accepted them. "Thank you." She couldn't resist sniffing the fragrant blooms. Her eyes met his over the tops of the flowers, and she wondered if he was remembering that other occasion when he had brought her roses.

She couldn't afford to be nostalgic. The reason he was here had nothing to do with proposals or love or devotion. "You haven't answered my question. Where is my dress?"

He shifted uncomfortably from one foot to the other. "Do you remember that time we went to the sculpture garden and we sat on that bench admiring that piece that was a bronze man? The one you thought didn't have a head?"

She blushed, and Jesse knew that she remembered very well that they had spent more time kissing on that bench than they had viewing the art in the garden. "What does that have to do with my dress?" she asked impatiently.

"When we moved on to the next exhibit, you left your mittens on the bench."

"Yeah, and someone stole them. So what is your point?"

He didn't answer, and she released a tiny gasp. "What are you trying to tell me?"

Gently he urged her inside and closed the door behind the two of them.

"Jesse, did you or did you not bring me back my dress?" she asked, her eyes widening in horror.

"Didn't," he said soberly, moving closer to her. He fixed her with a penetrating gaze and reached for her free hand. A jolt of awareness shot through Annie as his fingers wrapped around hers. She tried to pull away, not wanting to be affected by his magic touch. But as his thumb gently rubbed the back of her hand, her heart raced and her mouth became dry.

She could see tiny white snowflakes glistening in his dark hair. A faint shadow darkened his chin, calling up a sensory flashback of what it had felt like to have that rough jaw brush against her smooth skin. Her eyes focused on his mouth, and without any effort on his part she could taste the way it had felt when he had kissed her all those years ago. She closed her eyes briefly, wanting to dispel such memories.

"There's no easy way to tell you this," he said quietly.

"Tell me what?" she asked cautiously.

"The pick-up I had for sale was stolen."

When he paused, she asked, "What does that have to do with you not returning my dress?" As much as she wanted to pretend she didn't understand, the chill that ran down her spine told her what she already knew. "Are you saying…?" She trailed off uneasily.

He nodded. "Your dress was inside. It's gone with the truck."

Chapter Six

Annie stared at Jesse in disbelief. "Tell me you're joking."

"I'm sorry, Annie. I know that's not what you wanted to hear, but the good news is the police think that the truck was probably stolen by a couple of kids who'll take it for a joyride and then abandon it. With a little luck they'll be able to recover the truck and its contents."

She rolled her eyes. "That's supposed to be good news?"

"Hopefully within the next twenty-four hours you'll get your dress back and everything will be fine."

She didn't respond, but simply stood with her mouth agape, staring at him.

After a few seconds he said, "Annie, say something."

She slowly shook her head. "I can't believe this is happening. As if yesterday wasn't bad enough...now this. Do you realize what this means?"

"I know it's creating a little inconvenience, but—"

"A *little* inconvenience?" she interrupted him. "It's one big, fat inconvenience and it's all your fault." She groaned and pressed a hand to her forehead. "If you hadn't taken the stupid dress home with you, none of this would have happened."

"But it did happen, and now we have to deal with it," he stated with an annoying calmness.

"That's easy for you to say. I'm the one who's expecting someone in fifteen minutes to look at a dress I don't have. What am I supposed to say to her? 'Call back tomorrow. Maybe by then the police will have tracked it down and if we're lucky, it'll still look like a wedding dress and not someone's oil rag.'"

"You don't have to say anything. I'll handle it for you." He took off his jacket and laid it across the back of her couch. He was wearing a denim shirt that clung to his broad shoulders and emphasized his lean physique.

Annie couldn't help but notice he was much bigger than any of the other men she had almost married. She realized that as intimate as they had been, she had never found out his shirt size. Not that it mattered—it probably wasn't the same now as it had been then.

He stood too close to her, looking as if he belonged in her apartment, seemingly relaxed despite the fact that *he* was the one who had lost *her* dress. Unlike the other men she had dated, he emanated a magnetism that warned Annie he was all male and dangerous to her emotional health.

"I'll talk to this prospective buyer," Jesse offered, dragging her attention back to the subject at hand.

"I don't think so."

"You don't want me to explain to her what happened?"

What Annie wanted was to be rid of him before her body betrayed her into doing something she would regret. "I don't want you here. Period." She threw the bouquet of flowers at him, then picked up his jacket and tossed that at him, too. "You've given me the bad news. You can leave."

"Come on, Annie." He set the jacket and the flowers aside. "Let me help you with this," he urged.

"You want to help me? Then give me the other fifteen hundred dollars." She folded her hands across her chest and faced him in a challenging stance. "Then we'll call it even."

"Annie, be reasonable."

"I am."

He chuckled mirthlessly. "You already have a three-hundred-dollar deposit."

"Yes, and it's a good thing I took it when I did." She clamped her mouth shut and glared at him.

"There's a chance you'll get the dress back, and even if you don't, your insurance will cover its loss." Again there was that irritating calmness to his voice.

"*My* insurance? It was stolen from *your* truck," she reminded him. "Oh, no! Don't tell me you don't have insurance on that old thing?" Panic widened her eyes.

"It's not my truck. It's my uncle Hank's. I was just selling it for him."

At the mention of her former stepfather, Annie's anger escalated. Until now she had conveniently separated her mother's man troubles from hers. Now they seemed to blur together.

A look of horror crossed her face. "My dress is in Hank's truck? Well, that explains why there's no insurance. He's too cheap to buy any," she snapped angrily.

"He may be careful with his money, but he's not stupid enough to break the law," Jesse shot back. She tossed him a dubious look. "He has the truck insured, but even if he didn't, it wouldn't affect you. It's not his insurance company who is responsible for your dress."

Perplexed, Annie asked, "What's that supposed to mean?"

"Any personal property inside the vehicle is covered under your homeowner's policy. In your case your renter's insurance should cover it. If you give me the name of your insurance agent, I'll call him and explain what happened."

She threw up her hands in frustration. "Oh, this is just great! *You* lose *my* dress, and *I* have to file a claim with *my* insurance company?"

"That's the way it works," he said apologetically.

Annie felt as though she might explode with anger. "I don't believe this is happening!"

"It's not that big of a deal."

She stared at him in disbelief. He had no idea what this meant to her. Without the money for her dress, she was going nowhere. No trip to Miami. No job on the cruise ship. Nothing.

"If you think about it, this could turn out to actually work in your favor," Jesse continued.

She held up her hands in protest. "Don't even try to explain how this could be a lucky break for me, please."

He ignored her plea. "If the dress isn't recovered, you'll get reimbursed for the cost. Isn't that better than not having a buyer?"

"That doesn't solve the problem of the buyer who's coming at seven!" she exclaimed. Again she groaned. "All of this could have been avoided if you would have just gone home at noon yesterday and changed that stupid message on your answering machine."

"There's no guarantee you would have sold it yesterday," he argued.

"You don't think I can sell it at all, do you?" she accused.

"Come on, Annie, be practical. First of all, there aren't many women out there who are built like you, and secondly there aren't many who are willing to spend that kind of money.''

Both statements annoyed her. What did he mean *built like her?* She wasn't exactly a perfect size 7, but she wasn't out of proportion, either. And what did he care how much money she spent on a dress?

"Oh—and you know all about the women out there, don't you, Jesse?" she drawled.

He ignored her sarcasm. "At least if you file an insurance claim, you know you're going to get back the money you spent for the dress. That might not happen if you get the dress back and no one buys it.''

"Someone will buy it. It's a masterpiece," she stated emotionally.

"Yeah, I know, but *he* wasn't," He spouted the words in her advertisement. "Just what was wrong with this one, Annie?''

"You mean besides the fact that he cheated on me?"

That produced a startled look on Jesse's face and had him at a loss for words.

"It doesn't take an Einstein to figure out that if a man can't be faithful to a girlfriend, he's going to have problems being faithful to a wife," she told him, trying to keep the hurt out of her voice.

"I agree," he said soberly.

"You do?"

"Yes, why would you think I didn't?''

Annie was about to blurt out, *Because you cheated on me,* but the sound of the buzzing intercom stopped her. "That's probably my buyer." Annie shot him a nasty look. "She came all the way from Wisconsin to look at the dress.''

"Then you'd better have her come up. It's much better to explain something like this in person instead of over the intercom,'' he told her, gently urging her toward the door.

Annie buzzed the woman up. "I can handle this," she told Jesse when he followed her to the door. Still he clung to her side as she opened the door.

The woman standing outside was a petite brunette wearing a trench coat and a rain hat. Although she looked to be the same height as Annie, she was definitely heavier. Before Annie could explain to her what had happened to the dress, Jesse took over the conversation. With the same charm that had caused Annie to fall madly in love the first time she had seen him, he mixed apology with flattery.

"I'm afraid it was just one of those things beyond our control. Annie didn't realize the truck had been stolen when you called," he explained to the brunette, fixing her with a gaze that could have raised the heartbeats of most warm-blooded females.

It worked on this particular female. "I'm so disappointed," she told Jesse, sighing helplessly. "I've been looking for a gown by that designer for months, and this one sounded perfect." Glancing at Annie's trim figure, she lifted one eyebrow skeptically and asked, "Do you think it would have fit?"

Annie would have told her no. Jesse, however, let his eyes travel over the woman's ample figure and said, "I don't see why not, since you and Annie are nearly the same size."

The brunette glowed at the comparison.

Jesse went on to ask her about her wedding plans, listening intently as she relayed the boring details. Any antipathy the woman might have had when she had first arrived disappeared as she and Jesse discussed everything from limousines to Limoges china. By the time she was ready to leave, she was giggling and smiling at Jesse as if he were a long-lost friend.

"Since it was my truck that was stolen and I'm responsible for this mix-up, I'd like to reimburse you for your inconvenience." He pulled out his wallet, but she waved her hands vigorously.

"Oh, no. That's not necessary," the blushing bride-to-be told him. She slipped a business card in his hand, instructing him to call her if the dress was recovered. Then, with a wink at Jesse and an expression of sympathy for Annie, she was gone.

"See, that wasn't so bad," Jesse told her as they watched the girl's retreating figure disappear down the hallway.

"She was not the same size as me," Annie declared irritably.

"Same height," he countered with a devilish grin. "Admit it—she felt much better about making the long drive here knowing that the reason she couldn't purchase had to do with the dress and not her figure."

"Maybe," Annie grudgingly conceded. "But offering to *pay* her for her inconvenience?" Her eyes flashed indignantly. "What about my *inconvenience?*"

"If it's that important to you, I'll pay you for the dress," he offered.

Annie stared at him in disbelief. "*All* of the money?"

"It's what you want, isn't it? Money?" He was looking at her the same way he had looked at her seven years ago when they had argued over money.

She considered his offer carefully. Her first instinct was to say yes, to accept his offer and be done with it. She'd never have to see him again—except to reimburse him when the insurance money came through. Or to give the money back if the dress was found.

What if the dress was found and she couldn't sell it? She'd be indebted to Jesse Conover. She'd have to make arrangements to pay the money back....

"You can keep your money, Jesse." She marched over to the sofa and scooped up his leather jacket, then shoved it in his direction. "Here. You've done everything you came to do. You can go."

"I don't understand you, Annie. You tell me you won't be happy until I pay you for the dress, and now that I want to give you the money, you tell me to keep it." He fixed her with a bemused stare. "What is it you want from me, Annie?"

She wished she knew the answer herself. The more she saw of Jesse, the more confused she became. Some of those mixed emotions must have shown in her face, for he reached for her, pulling her into his arms.

"Jesse, what are you doing?" He had her trapped in his arms, the leather jacket between them.

"Something I should have done yesterday." The huskiness of his voice had Annie's heartbeat racing.

"I don't want—" she began, only to break off when his eyes darkened as they stared into hers. Watching them change, she knew what was coming. He was going to kiss her. As he leaned even closer, she felt her breasts tingle and her stomach ache with a sweet desire. She tried to tell herself this was not what she wanted, but she did nothing to break loose of his arms.

It felt so natural to be there. Annie melted against him, her lips parting, her breath coming out on shallow puffs. She released her grip on his leather jacket and moved her hands up his chest, across the denim covering his warm flesh.

She pressed herself closer to him and boldly rubbed herself against him. He stiffened momentarily, then as if he could no longer hold back, he settled his mouth against hers, not with the passion that Annie knew he possessed, but with a caution she could only guess came from restraint.

But they both soon realized that there was no such thing as restraint or caution when it came to their responses. What started as a tender kiss quickly turned into a blaze of passion that had their mouths hungrily devouring each other and taking them into a world where nothing mattered but basic instincts.

With a groan Annie welcomed the invasion of his tongue, arching gently as she allowed him access to the sweetness of her mouth. She trembled as a delicious heat spread through her, making her aware that this was an experience she had been craving for a long, long time. Every instinct she possessed told her to let her guard down and give in to the swirl of emotions that was turning her world into a whirlpool of passion.

They were like spontaneous combustion, and their desire burned away any protests their brains might have made.

Jesse whispered her name, then pressed kisses over her eyelids and cheeks. Annie tipped her head back so he could trail kisses down the column of her throat. Shivers of pleasure tickled her spine. Then she lifted his chin so that her mouth could once again meet his. When his hand moved to the hem of her sweatshirt, a restless sensation stirred deep inside her.

She heard him groan, then realized the reason he had pulled away from her was because the phone was ringing. It took several seconds before she was aware of just what had happened. She recognized that look in his eyes—it had been there every time they had made love.

On wobbly legs she went to the kitchen to answer the

phone, every part of her body tingling. It was another call for the dress. Distracted by the man's presence in her living room, she told the caller in broken sentences that the dress hadn't been sold but wasn't available for showing. By the time she got off the phone, she had regained some of the balance Jesse's kiss had taken away. She didn't return to the living room right away, but stayed in the kitchen, thinking about what had just happened between her and Jesse.

Why had he kissed her like that? Worse yet, why had she responded the way she had? Her whole body warmed, then she shivered at the memory of his touch. It had felt so good. So right. She brought herself up short. It was not right. He was engaged to another woman. He had no business kissing her.

Stiffening her shoulders and pulling down on her sweatshirt, she returned to the living room. Jesse was sitting on the sofa, a grim expression on his face.

"I think you should go," Annie said quietly.

"Don't you think we should talk about what just happened?"

Annie rubbed her temple where a dull ache had started to make its presence known. "All that happened is that we proved nothing has changed between us physically. Ever since you asked me to dance at my mother's wedding, our bodies have always been like a couple of highly explosive sticks of dynamite waiting for the right circumstances to ignite."

"And that's what you think happened between us?"

She wished he'd quit staring at her as if she were a lab specimen waiting to be dissected.

"Yes. What else would it be?" she asked, examining her cuticles as if they were more important than her conversation with him.

A glance in his direction told her he didn't like her answer. He picked up his jacket and without another word left.

Annie dropped down onto the couch and closed her eyes. If only it were that simple, she thought to herself.

Within a few minutes the intercom buzzed, indicating there was someone at her door. Her breath caught in her throat. Had he come back? She hurried over to the button on the wall and poked a finger at it.

"This is Annie," she said shakily.

"It's your mother."

Just the fact that she referred to herself as her "mother" and not her "ma" alerted Annie to the fact that Margaret Jamison was not happy about something. Annie buzzed her up and waited with her door open for the storm to arrive.

"Why was Jesse Conover at the coffee shop today?" her mother demanded as she swept past Annie into the apartment.

"It's a free country. He can go wherever he wants," Annie answered dully.

Her mother shed her overcoat and faced Annie with hands on her hips. "You don't look surprised. That must mean he came to see you. Oh, Annie. You're not letting that man back into your life, are you?"

"It's not what you think." She gestured for her mother to follow her. "Come into the kitchen, and I'll explain."

She followed Annie, her eyes not missing the cups that sat on the small table. "You had company?"

"It's a long story. Sit down, and I'll make some coffee." She pulled out a chair for her mother, then while she filled the coffee maker, she recounted the events of the past two days involving Jesse Conover. She deliber-

ately omitted two things—the kissing and the fact that the
stolen pick-up belonged to Hank.

"So it's just one big mess. It's like there's a curse on
that dress or something," Annie lamented as she sat down
across from her mother.

"Thank goodness you never wore it. Who knows what
would have happened?" Margaret took the cup of coffee
Annie had poured and stirred in a generous spoonful of
sugar. "Jesse must have insurance?"

"I don't want to collect on the insurance, Ma." She
explained the details of the claim and how it would take
a month before she received any payment. "I need the
money this week, not a month from now."

"Then Jesse should pay for the dress," Margaret stated
unequivocally. "Let him be the one who waits to be reimbursed from the insurance company."

Annie pushed her blond hair back from her face. "It's
not that simple, Ma."

"Of course it is. You have to demand that he pays you.
After all, he lost it and he owes it to you."

"He offered to pay, but I turned him down," Annie
said wearily.

"You did what?"

"I can't take any money from him."

"Of course you can. He can afford it. He's a Conover.
They're all skinflints. When I think of how Hank made
me account for every single penny I spent..." She trailed
off, her blue eyes flashing indignantly.

"Don't think about it, Mom," Annie urged her. "Your
trouble with Hank is separate from this."

"I still regret the day I let that man into my life. Look
at the heartache it caused us. I should have known better.
Those Conover men are nothing but trouble."

Annie could see her mother was getting worked up. "It's not your fault my wedding dress is missing."

"You're my daughter," Margaret stated emphatically. "I think I ought to be the one who straightens this mess out. Besides, it would give me great pleasure to make a Conover pay for the injustice done here."

"No!" What Annie didn't need was for her mother to get involved. She couldn't let her tangle with any of the Conovers, not after her disastrous marriage to Hank. "Please don't. I want to handle this on my own. I'll figure something out."

"Unless they recover the stolen truck, it doesn't sound like there's anything to figure out. You either wait for the insurance money or you get it from Jesse," Margaret stated matter-of-factly.

Annie knew what her mother said was true. There was no way she could leave for Florida without the money from her dress. Her credit cards were maxed out, she still owed a bunch of money on her car and her savings account had been drained by expenses for a wedding that never happened.

She probably had been a fool to think Richard would ever pay for any of their prenuptial plans, but she had put her trust in him. How was she to know that he would betray that trust six weeks before the wedding, when all of the arrangements had been made, a great deal of money had been spent. Instead of a happy marriage, all she had to show for her efforts was a stack of bills. Never before had she felt as if she were destined to follow in her mother's footsteps. The thought was enough to send a shiver across her slender frame.

Margaret drained her cup and took it over to the sink to rinse it out. "This just goes to show you how lucky you are you never hooked up with Jesse. Life with him would have been nothing but a series of bad-luck stories.''

Annie didn't comment.

"Here's my advice on the subject, and I'm only going to say it once and then I won't mention it again," her mother promised. She leaned up against the counter and used her right hand as a pointer. "Just think about this. There's not a Conover alive who doesn't have a fat bank account. Jesse is no exception. He's responsible and he should pay." Then she reached for her purse and headed for the living room to pick up her coat. "Promise me you'll think about it, okay?"

"Yes, Ma, I'll think about it," Annie echoed.

"Good. And I wouldn't wait too long to act, either," she added, slipping her arms inside her coat.

Margaret pulled on a pair of driving gloves, then gave her daughter a hug. "Thanks for helping out at the diner today."

"It's all right, Mom. How did things go at the lawyer's?" she asked, feeling a momentary spurt of guilt at having totally forgotten her mother's plight.

"He's not contesting the divorce, so it's all pretty cut-and-dried."

Annie knew that as much as her mother wanted her to believe that it was just another interruption in her schedule, the truth was there were bags under her mother's eyes. She looked tired and sad.

"How about if I take your place at the diner tomorrow and you sleep in?" Annie suggested, forgetting that earlier that day she had vowed she had put on the brown-and-white waitress uniform for the last time.

"Cleo could use a day off more than I could," Margaret answered.

"I'm not giving Cleo a day off. It's either you stay home or else I don't come in," Annie told her.

"All right. I'll sleep in, but I'm coming in for the lunch hour."

"Good. Consider it my going-away present," Annie told her.

Her mother sighed. "I'm the one who's supposed to be giving you something. I'm sorry I don't have any money to loan you, but you know we had to replace the grill at the café and then the freezer was on the blink."

Annie dismissed her mother's comments with a toss of her head. "Mom, I got myself into this financial mess, and now I have to get myself out."

"Make Jesse pay, Annie. After what he did to you, he owes you big-time."

"Who owes you what?" Joni had come home and walked in on the middle of their conversation.

"Just the gal I wanted to see," Margaret said, wrapping her arm around Joni's shoulder. "Talk some sense into my daughter, will you?"

As soon as Margaret had left, Joni asked, "What was that all about?"

"You're not going to believe what's happened." And for the second time that evening, Annie found herself explaining about the stolen truck and the wedding dress.

When she was finished, Joni said, "Your mother's right. You should take the money Jesse offered. Where is this Forty Club anyway?"

"It's a bar on the outskirts of the city—no place for a woman to go alone."

"If you want me to come with you, I will," she offered.

Annie glanced down at her sweats. "I'd have to shower and change," she said wearily.

"It's only a bar."

"That's easy for you to say. Look what you're wearing." Her eyes roved up and down Joni's petite figure, which was dressed in black slacks and a tweed wool blazer.

"Do you want the money or not?"

Annie reached for her car keys.

AN HOUR LATER the two of them were sitting in Annie's car outside the Forty Club. It was a combination bar and restaurant that was a blue-collar hangout on the southern edge of the city. Friday nights were usually crowded as workers came to unwind after a tough week at work.

The snow had increased in intensity, limiting visibility. Annie parked in the back row of the crowded lot, but they could still see the neon Open sign over the club's door blinking out a welcome to the cold and weary.

"I'm not sure this is such a good idea," Annie said to her roommate as the door to the bar opened and the faint sound of country-western music could be heard.

"What's bothering you?"

Annie didn't want to tell her roommate that it was the kisses that she and Jesse had shared earlier that evening. Nor did she want to admit how difficult it was going to be to see him if he was with another woman.

"I say let's do it," Joni suggested. "It's getting cold sitting out here."

"At least you have your winter jacket." Annie turned the collar up on her fleece anorak and sank deeper into its folds. She had packed away all of her winter clothes, thinking she'd be gone before the snow fell in Minnesota.

"There certainly are a lot of people going in. What's this place like anyway?" Joni asked, watching a couple of women scurry to the door.

Annie shrugged. "When Jesse and I were here, we were

on the restaurant side. I guess the bar is like any other bar." The memory of dinner for two came rushing back. They had sat in a booth in the back, a red candle burning in an amber glass in the center of the table. Jesse had been unable to resist kissing her in public. It was there he had told her he wanted to marry her. The memory sent a knifelike pain through her chest.

"This isn't a good idea." Annie started up the car.

Joni reached across and stopped her from putting it into gear. "Wait. We came all the way out here in a near-blizzard. You don't want to turn around and go home without at least making the effort to collect your money."

Annie thought about it for a moment, then pulled the keys from the ignition. "All right. Let's do it before I chicken out."

They put their heads down against the blowing snow and headed for the door, dodging the puddles of slush. As they neared the building, the music grew louder. When the heavy wooden door swung open, a blast of warm air greeted them.

"Which way?" Joni asked as she dusted the snow off her hair.

"The bar's to the right, but I need to use the ladies' room first," Annie answered, gesturing to a sign that indicated the rest rooms were straight ahead.

Unlike the rest of the establishment, the women's rest room was vacant. Annie grimaced as she caught her reflection in the mirror. She reached in her purse for a tube of lipstick and a comb.

"Look what the snow did to my hair," she wailed as she tried to put some life in the damp tendrils. As soon as she had reddened her lips and combed her hair, she applied a fresh coat of mascara.

"Annie, this is your *ex-fiancé*," Joni reminded her.

"Yeah, I know, but there might be some other cute, eligible guys out there," she answered. *And the man who kissed me senseless only hours ago,* she added silently to herself. "Oh, my hair is awful." She moved over to the hand dryers and punched the button activating the flow of hot air. She bent over so that her hair was under it.

After a brief spell under the dryer, she straightened and asked Joni, "There. How's that?"

"If nothing else, your cheeks are now flushed. Come. Let's go." She gently steered her toward the door.

When they reached the bar, Annie stopped. Joni urged her forward, nudging her in the small of her back as they ventured into the dimly lit room. Most of the tables were full, the horseshoe-shaped bar surrounded by men and women, some standing, others sitting on the padded stools. Several televisions suspended from the ceiling sat at various angles for customers to watch sporting events.

"I smell popcorn," Joni said in a loud voice, then quickly added, "Oooh...food," as a waitress carrying a tray of hamburger baskets walked by.

"We didn't come here to eat," Annie reminded her, perusing the room for Jesse.

"Do you see him?" Joni asked, close to her ear.

"No. He might be around the other side of the bar."

"Then let's move," Joni suggested, again nudging her roommate in the back to get her going.

As they walked past the jukebox, they were approached by two men looking for fun. "You ladies look like you need a couple of guys like us to find you a place to sit," the taller of the two said to Joni in an obvious come-on.

"That's mighty sweet of you to offer," Joni flirted harmlessly, "but we're meeting someone." The guy shrugged and stepped aside.

"That's why I hate coming to places like this." Annie

spoke quietly beside Joni's ear. "I'm not good at this bar thing."

"I don't see why not. You have no trouble talking to men when they come into the diner."

"That's different. They're not drinking beer and looking for a good time."

"Oooh...check out the good-looking guy in the corner," Joni said as they reached the other side of the lounge. "The one in the dark green shirt. He is c...u...te," she drawled.

"He's also Jesse's brother," Annie announced, her fingers clenching as she searched for her ex-fiancé.

"Is he married?"

"Why do you care?"

"Just wondering, that's all," Joni answered. "Look. He sees you."

Annie saw Todd Conover get up and start toward them. Still there was no sign of Jesse. Maybe he and Roxy had a date this evening.

"Annie? Is that you?" Todd asked, his grin widening in recognition as he approached. He eyed Joni with interest, then said, "It's been a long time."

She nodded. "Seven years." That was one of the advantages of living in a metropolitan area the size of Minneapolis and St. Paul. The cities were big enough that you didn't need to worry about bumping into ex-boyfriends.

"I'm surprised to see you on this side of town," Todd remarked.

Annie took a deep breath and said, "I'm looking for Jesse. Is he here?"

"Not yet, but I'm expecting him any minute. Come sit down and have a drink." He ushered her toward the corner table where three other construction workers sat sipping on beers. Todd pulled two more chairs up to the table and signaled for the waitress.

"What brings you here?" he asked after all the introductions had been made.

"Jesse didn't mention that he'd seen me?"

"No, but then he always did want to keep you to himself." He grinned, and Annie's skin warmed.

"We have some unfinished business," she said a bit more sharply than she intended. "It's a long story," she added on a softer note.

"Well, let me buy you two ladies a drink while you wait," he said amiably as the waitress came to take their order. Annie refused the offer, simply asking for a glass of water. When Joni would have declined the offer, too, Todd turned on the Conover charm. She ordered a margarita. Annie shot her a warning glance, but all Joni did was raise her eyebrows and shrug.

"You know, you look really familiar to me," Todd said to Joni, leaning closer to her. "Have we met before?"

Annie rolled her eyes while her roommate answered, "I don't think I would have forgotten you." Joni flirted shamelessly, causing Annie to cast her another admonishing look that she chose to ignore. "You don't work out at the health club on Lexington, do you?"

He laughed. "Good heavens, no. I get all the exercise I need lifting two-by-fours into place," he boasted. Annie saw Joni's eyes fly to the muscles bulging beneath the sleeves of his henley, then down across the flat abs of his stomach.

"It's a great place to have fun," Joni answered back cheekily, her eyes widening the longer she talked with Todd Conover. "On Tuesday evenings we have volleyball tournaments for singles."

Annie could hardly believe it. Joni was batting her eyelashes at the man as if she were interested in him.

"Now, you hardly look big enough to play volleyball with the guys," he teased, eyeing her petite figure with interest.

Annie waited for her roommate to put him in his place. If there was one thing Joni hated, it was for men to remark on her size. To Annie's surprise, however, Joni simply flirted coyly, saying, "Sometimes the smallest player packs the biggest punch." To emphasize her statement, she wiggled her fist in the air.

So engrossed was Annie with the flirting going on between Todd and her roommate, she didn't notice Jesse's arrival. It wasn't until something brushed across her shoulder that she realized someone was standing behind her. She knew without looking that it was him.

Her heart began to beat in double time, her palms became sweaty and her mouth went dry. What would she see in his eyes when she turned around? Surprise? Desire? Satisfaction?

Slowly she turned and looked up at the man she had kissed less than two hours ago.

He bent over and whispered in her ear, "What the hell are you doing here?"

Chapter Seven

"I need to talk to you, Jesse."

Annie looked like a frightened kitten, her blond hair sticking out in all directions, her eyes wide and luminous. Her vulnerability evoked all sorts of protective feelings in Jesse, feelings he didn't want to have.

"Why don't we go to the bar," he suggested, not wanting to have five sets of ears listening to their conversation.

She looked as if she would protest, but decided against it. Reluctantly she scraped her chair back and stood. Taking hold of her elbow, Jesse steered her away from the curious stares of the others. He didn't stop until they were on the opposite side of the room.

She stood before him, her arms folded across her chest, her feet planted firmly on the tile. With her untamed blond hair, she reminded Jesse of Annie the teenager. She looked as if there weren't a mean bone in her body, that she couldn't hurt anyone if she tried. He knew differently.

Even though she had jilted him, he still wanted her. Nothing had changed in the time they had been apart. What had happened at her apartment had proved that. His body still craved the sweet smell of her, the softness of her skin, the sound of her voice.

It annoyed him, this power she seemed to have over

him. As she stood before him, he tried to concentrate on the fact that this was the woman who had sent him a Dear John letter in the service, the woman who had tossed back his offer to pay for her missing wedding gown in his face, the woman who had denied that the kisses they had shared meant anything except physical release.

Consequently his voice was a bit gruff when he said, "I think you've said all that needs to be said at your place."

She licked her lips nervously. "Jesse, you're not making this any easier for me."

"What is it you want to say to me?"

"I need the money for my dress." She looked up at him in supplication.

"And you want me to be the one who gives it to you." He kept his voice even, despite the turmoil that was swirling inside him simply by being in her presence.

"You can have the insurance money when it comes," she offered. "I'll sign the claim over to you."

Only a few hours earlier Jesse would have freely given her the money. But that was before she had teased him with kisses that left him longing for something she could never give him. If it had been any other woman asking, he would have agreed. But this was Annie, the girl who had promised to always love him. The girl who couldn't even bring herself to tell him to his face that she didn't want to go through with their marriage. The woman who had told him their kisses meant nothing.

When he didn't respond immediately, she added, "You said you'd give me the money."

"Maybe the offer's no longer good," He avoided looking at her smoothly painted red lips, focusing instead on his fingers—just as she had done earlier that evening.

Annie felt as if the wind had been sucked out of her

sails. Having to come here to ask him for money was the last thing she wanted to do. This was the man who had played a cheating game with her seven years ago. Now he was playing another kind of game with her, and she didn't like it one bit. Anger seeped through her, but she refused to let him see it.

"This is really important to me, Jesse." She placed her hand on his forearm, and he immediately jerked it away.

"You don't need to tell me that, Annie. Money has always been important to you," he said sharply.

"That's not fair!"

"Isn't it? What's so important that you can't wait thirty days for a check?"

She bit down on her lower lip, debating whether or not to answer. Finally she said, "I'm supposed to start a new job next week. I'm going to Florida to work on a cruise ship."

He chuckled sarcastically. "Oh, well, that changes everything. I didn't realize you wanted the money to go on a cruise. Gee, maybe I should throw in a couple of hundred extra."

The sarcasm caused her smile to fade. "It's a job, not a vacation."

"That may be, but I'm not a bank," he stated firmly.

This time she didn't try to hide her anger. "I should have known you'd be like this."

"Like what?" he asked innocently.

"Petty. Just because I didn't accept your offer earlier this evening, you won't even consider giving me the money. You haven't grown up at all, Jesse. You're still playing games just like you were seven years ago." Her chest heaved in anger. "All right, fine. Don't give me the money, but I want you to know I'm keeping the three hundred dollars.'' And without another word, she turned and stomped off.

Jesse didn't go after her, but stood watching her from across the room. After she had gathered her things, she motioned for her roommate to follow her to the door. Jesse waited, knowing she had to walk past him to leave. She tried to avoid him, but he stood smack-dab in the center of the entry, waiting.

As she tried to step past him, he grabbed her, pulling her into his arms. He slid his hand up the back of her neck and lowered his mouth toward hers. ''You weren't going to leave without giving me a goodbye kiss, were you?''

Not waiting for a reply, his lips captured hers. He only meant it to be a brief brushing of his mouth on hers, but once he tasted the sweetness of her he couldn't control the passion that flared between them.

It was only when Joni's voice called out Annie's name that they pulled apart.

Jesse lifted his hand to her face and gently brushed his thumb against her cheek. ''Enjoy your cruise,'' he said in a husky voice.

ANNIE RACED OUT to the parking lot as if a pack of wild dogs were after her. When she reached her car, she was panting. As soon as she and her roommate were inside, she turned to Joni and cried out, ''Are you nuts?''

''Me?'' Joni looked completely taken aback. ''I'm not the one who stormed out of there as if someone had just shouted 'Fire.' What were you doing kissing Jesse?''

''What were you doing flirting with Todd Conover? Did you forget you have a fiancé?''

''Keith and I are not engaged. Besides, I was only being friendly.''

Annie grunted in disbelief. "Being friends with a Conover man is not possible for any woman." She turned on the windshield wipers, but the rubber blades didn't move. While they were in the bar, a thin layer of ice had accumulated on the windows. "Damn. I don't have a scraper."

Joni rummaged around in her purse and pulled out two credit cards. "Here." She passed one to Annie. "Try this." They both climbed out of the car and began chipping away at the ice on the windshield, squinting against the blowing snow.

"You know, just because your romance didn't work with Jesse doesn't mean all the Conover men are bad news," Joni insisted as she scraped at the ice.

"Are you forgetting about my mother?" Annie shot back. "Joni, they're skirt chasers...every one of them."

"Todd seemed rather sweet to me."

"Sweet?" she shrieked in disbelief. "He's thirty years old and has never been married...and for a good reason."

"Maybe he's never met the right woman."

Annie jabbed at the ice zealously. "I don't believe this! All the guy had to do was bat those baby blues at you, and you're a marshmallow."

"You're just irritable because you didn't get the money from Jesse," Joni retorted.

"How do you know I didn't get it?"

"Because you wouldn't be this ticked off if you had." Joni straightened. "That's it. I can't chop anymore. It's too thick, and my fingers are frozen."

"And you wonder why I want to take that job on the cruise ship," Annie commented sarcastically as they slid back into the car. She pushed the blower fan to high and held her fingertips up to the dash to warm them. "Thanks to Jesse, I might be stuck here in the cold."

"He and his brother look so much alike they could almost be mistaken for twins," Joni remarked.

"That's what I've been trying to tell you. They are alike, and that includes their behavior. Joni, there's a good reason why neither one has married. They can't stay faithful to one woman."

"You still haven't told me why you were kissing him," Joni reminded her.

That brought an ache to Annie's chest. "I wasn't. He was kissing me. I don't make a habit out of kissing men who have fiancées."

"He doesn't have a fiancée."

That brought Annie's head up with a jerk. "What?"

"Roxy's his secretary. Todd told me. You would have heard it, too, had you not rushed out of there like a gazelle."

The news came as a surprising shock to Annie. Jesse wasn't engaged to be married. Of course, that didn't mean she felt any less charitable toward this Roxy person. After all, she was convinced that even if the woman wasn't having a relationship with Jesse currently, she had at one time been his lover.

"Are you sure you don't want to go back in?" Joni asked.

"No, why would I?"

Joni shrugged. "It's just that there are lots of single women in there...." She let the words dangle on purpose.

"Even if that kiss had meant something—and it didn't—Jesse wouldn't want me in there. This is boys' night out. Every Friday night is," Annie sneered, remembering how much she had hated to give up the few Friday nights she and Jesse had had together. Even though his military leave was short, he'd always managed to spend Fridays with the guys.

"I guess it's no different than when we get together every Tuesday, is it?"

"Of course it's different," Annie declared indignantly. "We don't go looking to pick up men in a bar when we have our night out."

"Speak for yourself," Joni quipped.

"We don't!"

"All right, all right. Hold your horses. I was only teasing," Joni said placatingly.

As soon as the defroster had cleared away the remaining ice from the window, Annie put the car in gear and backed out of the parking lot. "Just take my advice, Joni. Stay away from the Conover men."

Annie only wished that her heart didn't beg her to ignore her own advice.

GETTING UP and going to work at 5:00 a.m. was not what Annie had planned to be doing the weekend before she was scheduled to leave for Miami. The more she thought about her job on the cruise ship, the faster her optimism faded that it was ever going to be a reality.

After a restless night she nearly slept through her alarm, which meant when she did finally get out of bed she barely had time to shower and dress. Pulling her hair away from her face and securing it with a large barrette, she skipped her makeup. The only cosmetic she used was a light layer of lipstick to keep her lips from getting chapped by the blustery, cold air.

When she arrived at the café, she had no time to think about her appearance, as one of the waitresses had called in sick, leaving Annie and Cleo to work the entire restaurant. On a normal morning it wasn't easy to work short a waitress, but on a Saturday it was next to impossible. It meant no breaks until the lunch-hour help arrived.

By the time the breakfast rush was over, every bone in Annie's body ached. Hungry and tired, she was grateful for the appearance of Inez, a longtime employee and friend of her mother's who only worked the noon hour. Annie poured herself a cup of the homemade vegetable soup, grabbed a glass of soda and headed for an empty booth in the rear of the restaurant.

She sat with her back to the door, sipping the warm broth. If it wasn't for the fact that she was in her mother's eating establishment, she might have been tempted to put her feet up and rest. She forced herself to sit erect and hoped the soup would restore her depleted energy. As she ate, she blocked out the sounds of the diner and thought of ways to get the money for her move.

"Annie Jamison?" a husky feminine voice interrupted her musings.

Annie glanced up to see a stunning redhead standing beside her. Even before the woman introduced herself, Annie knew who she was. The mysterious Roxy.

Annie wondered what else could go wrong with her life. If the past two days hadn't been bad enough, she now was confronted with the woman who had come between her and Jesse, smiling and wanting to make cozy conversation.

Despite what every instinct in her body was telling her to do, Annie gestured for the redhead to sit down.

"I called your place this morning, and your roommate told me I could find you here," Roxy said, shrugging out of her fur coat. Apparently she was going to stay for a while. Annie couldn't help but notice the woman wore rings on nearly every finger, including a gigantic white rock on her engagement finger.

"Did you want something to eat?" Annie asked automatically.

"Maybe just some coffee."

As tired as she was, Annie didn't hesitate to get up to fetch it. She needed a few minutes' breathing space to get over the shock of sitting across from the woman who had been responsible for her broken engagement. She took several deep breaths, then brought the cup of coffee over to Roxy.

"Thanks." She gave Annie another warm smile. "When Jesse told me what happened to the wedding dress, I thought I should apologize in person. I'm really sorry for everything that's happened," she said sincerely.

Annie counted to ten, reminding herself that it would do no good to take out her frustration on this woman. Yet she couldn't keep the edge from her voice. "Unfortunately apologies aren't going to get my dress back."

The woman looked taken aback by her tone, and Annie felt an immediate remorse. She suddenly was self-conscious about the way she looked. Here she was sitting across from an immaculately dressed, beautifully made-up woman, and she knew her face was shiny and her hair was straggly where it had come loose from the barrette. "You'll have to excuse my bad mood. I've been working since six this morning, and it hasn't been the best week of my life."

The other woman's eyes softened in understanding. "It's a beautiful dress. If I were as thin as you, this would have never happened. I would have bought it."

Annie knew it was a compliment, but she still shifted uncomfortably. "Look, it was nice of you to come, but there's really not much anyone can do, is there? I'm sure the insurance will eventually pay for the dress."

Roxy pushed her arms back into the sleeves of her coat, obviously getting the hint that Annie wanted the conversation to end. "I should go. I'm sure you need to get back to work."

Annie forced a smile. "Yes, I do."

"I hope the police find your dress," Roxy said sincerely.

"Me, too." Annie grabbed her half-empty cup of soup, the glass of soda and the coffee cup and headed for the kitchen, not once looking back.

When Margaret Jamison saw Annie's face she asked, "What was that all about?"

"Nothing."

"It sure looks like something by the frown on your face. Who was that woman?"

Annie faced her mother. "Her name is Roxy Baxter. She's the reason Jesse had my dress."

Margaret gasped. "He's engaged?"

"No, she is, though. She's his secretary."

"Why would she come here?"

"She wanted to tell me how sorry she was about my dress."

Her mother made a sound of disgust. "Sorry isn't going to pay your bills. Did you tell her you expected Jesse to pay for the dress?"

Annie shook her head. "I couldn't."

"Well, why not? Annie, it's just as much her fault as yours that you don't have your dress. You should have told her you wanted the two of them to pay. She didn't look like she was hurting for money. Did you see that fur coat she was wearing?"

"Yes, I saw the fur coat. Mom, please. I don't want to discuss this." She walked away, but her mother followed.

"Did she say something to upset you?"

"No!"

"Then why are you slamming dishes?"

Annie turned around. "Because I'm pretty certain that she was the girl I saw kissing Jesse that night seven years ago. You know, when he was supposed to be playing cards with the guys but he was really with another girl." She had to bite down on her lip to choke back her tears. Still her eyes misted over.

"Oh, dear," was all her mother managed to say in a near-whisper. "No wonder your feelings are hurt."

"I'm not hurt. I'm angry," she insisted.

"You have every right to be." Her mother comforted her, placing an arm around Annie's shoulder.

"Nothing's gone right since that stupid mix-up in the want ads," Annie lamented. She sank down onto the bar stool at the end of the counter. "I'm never going to get to Florida at this rate."

"Things are looking a little bleak," her mother agreed, "but I've never known you to be a pessimist, Annie."

"You'll have to forgive me if I'm fresh out of optimism at this point," she retorted wryly.

Her mother stared pensively out the plate-glass windows. When the door opened, admitting several customers, she said, "Oh-oh. Looks like the lunch crowd's starting to arrive, and I haven't gone to pick up Dorothy."

"I didn't see her name on the schedule," Annie remarked.

"She's a late addition," her mother said, untying her apron. Seeing Annie's questioning look, she added, "She refuses to drive when the roads are slippery, so I told her I'd pick her up."

"Why didn't you get her on your way in?" Annie asked.

"She wasn't ready. I don't suppose you could stay until I get back?" She looked at her daughter in supplication.

Annie slowly boosted herself to her feet. "All right, but I'm warning you. I'm leaving as soon as you get back."

Margaret smiled. "Deal."

ONE OF THE ODD JOBS Hank was hired to do was to see that snow was removed from all of C & C Custom Homes' premises. Although Jesse contracted for someone to plow the driveways, Hank always made sure that the walkways were clear and the icy spots were covered with salt pellets.

That's why when Margaret pulled into the parking lot of the contractor's headquarters, Hank was the first person she saw. He stood with a snow shovel in his hands, watching her maneuver her big old Buick LeSabre into a parking spot.

"I've come to see Jesse. Where is he?" she demanded to know as she stepped out of the car.

Hank ignored her question. "You gonna leave that car like that?" he asked, eyeing the Buick with distaste.

"What's wrong with it?"

"You're hogging two spaces."

"Tough." She walked past him toward the office doors.

He didn't move, but watched her waddle away as if she were stepping on eggshells. When she reached the door and tried the handle, she looked back at him. "It's locked."

"Of course it's locked. It's Saturday."

She carefully plodded on back over to him and said, "I need to see Jesse."

"Well, you're out of luck. He doesn't work on Saturdays," he said smugly.

"So where can I find him?" She glanced toward the house. "Does he live there?"

"Yes, but I wouldn't go over there if I were you," Hank advised her.

She paid no attention to his warning. With a determined set to her shoulders, she set off on the recently shoveled path toward the house. She hadn't taken but a few steps when her foot slipped on a patch of ice and she fell to the ground.

Hank dropped the shovel and hurried over to help her. "I told you not to go over there. I haven't put the salt pellets down yet."

"Oh, my ankle," she moaned as she lay sprawled on the ground. Her skirt had risen when she had fallen, exposing a long length of leg that didn't escape Hank's eyes. She quickly tugged it down, giving him a nasty look.

"You still got a great-looking pair of legs, Margie," he said with an appreciative grin.

"I'll be lucky if I'll be able to use them again." She grimaced as she attempted to stand.

"Here. Let me help you." He placed an arm around her waist and shoved a shoulder beneath her arm. "Okay, lean on me," he instructed, then helped her up.

"Ouch!" she exclaimed as she hobbled into an upright position, putting all of her weight on her left foot.

"Let's get you inside. Then we can see what damage has been done," he told her.

When it was apparent she wouldn't be able to walk, he swiftly lifted her into his arms.

"Put me down right this minute, Hank Conover," she ordered, but he paid no attention. He carried her back toward the office.

"Reach inside my pants pocket," he ordered.

"I will not!" she said indignantly.

"For the keys."

She blushed, then slid her hand into the small opening

in his corduroys. Her fingers found a large ring of keys, which she pulled out and held in front of his face. "Which one?"

"The one with the red tape on it," he answered. "Put it in the lock."

For once she did as she was told, unlocking the glass door on the office. Hank pushed the door open with his knee, then carried her inside, huffing and puffing. He set her down on a leather wing-backed chair.

As soon as he had closed the door, he knelt down beside her. "Take off your boot."

She ignored his command. "Are you crazy carrying me around like that? You could have given yourself a heart attack," she scolded.

"I'm sixty-two, not ninety-two," he snapped back. "Now, are you going to let me take a look at that ankle or not?"

Reluctantly she removed the boot.

Margaret winced as he gently fingered her ankle. "It's swelling up. You must have sprained it."

"Now what do I do? I can't even put any weight on it! How am I going to drive my car?"

"Don't worry. I'll take care of you."

ANNIE DIDN'T REALIZE how long her mother had been gone until Cleo said, "I think the lunch-hour rush is over."

Annie glanced at the clock and frowned. "What do you suppose happened to my mother?"

"Streets are slippery, so the driving's slow going, but she should have been back by now," Cleo answered, wiping down the eating counter. "Maybe you ought to phone Dorothy."

Before she had a chance, Inez called out to her from

behind the counter near the cash register. She held up the telephone receiver. "Annie, it's your mom."

Annie hurried over to get it. "Mom, where are you?" she asked anxiously.

"I've had a minor accident. I slipped on the ice and sprained my ankle."

"How did that happen?"

"It doesn't matter, dear. It happened, that's all. I'm not going to be able to come back to work. I hate to ask you this, but can you cover for me until Leila gets there? She's promised me she'll be there by four."

"Of course, Mom. Are you sure you're all right? You sound sort of...I don't know, distracted."

"It's probably the painkiller the doctor gave me."

Worried, Annie said, "I'll stop by on my way home from work, okay?"

"No—that's not necessary. I'm fine. Really. I know how tired you must be from working all day. You go home and put your feet up, and I'll call you later."

"All right. Take care," Annie said, giving the receiver a puzzled look before handing it back to Inez.

"Is everything okay?" the older woman asked.

Annie informed her and the other employees of her mother's injury. Each time she told the story, her face became a bit more grim.

"Cheer up, Annie. Things aren't that bad," Cleo remarked a short time later while Annie leaned against the kitchen wall lamenting the events of the past three days.

"Yes, they are. Look." She turned around so that the other woman could see the back side of her uniform. Streaks of dark brown liquid covered her back.

"What happened?"

"I bent down to pick up a fork, and a kid at table seven spilled a glass of chocolate milk on me."

"Oh, Annie," Cleo commiserated. "You know what? I think you're in luck. There are extra uniforms in the storage room."

"I don't know if I have the energy to change," Annie said dispiritedly.

"You do." Cleo gave her a gentle shove in the direction of the storage room. "Do it now while things are quiet. You can use the washroom."

Annie nodded and trudged back to the storage room, where she found several uniforms hanging on a metal rack. With the exception of a few wrinkles, they looked fine. Instead of going into the washroom to change, she decided she would switch clothes right there and save time.

After removing her apron, she slipped out of the soiled brown-and-white uniform, leaving it in a heap on the floor. She was about to put the clean dress on when she noticed the tags were still attached. Except for cans and jars of foods, the only other items in the storage room were paper goods and cleaning supplies.

There must be a knife, Annie thought, searching the shelves for anything sharp that could cut through the plastic wire that kept the tags firmly in place. Thinking there might be old utensils in a box on one of the top shelves, Annie set the dress aside and reached for the step stool. She was on the top riser when the door opened. Startled, she screamed when she saw Jesse standing in the entrance.

"Annie?" He walked toward her. "What are you doing?"

She froze, suddenly aware that all she had on was a bra, underpants, panty hose and a pair of cushioned work shoes. The way Jesse's eyes were raking over her, she might as well have been naked. Heat spread through every inch of her body.

"I'm looking for a knife," she finally managed to answer, scrambling down from the step stool. "I need to cut the tags off my uniform."

He grinned as she snatched the dress from the shelf and held it up in front of her. "I've seen you in your underwear before, Annie," he said huskily.

She didn't need him to remind her of that. Or the fact that he had delicately removed every piece of her clothing until she lay naked in his arms. She wondered if he was remembering the same things and shivered when his eyes darkened appreciatively.

"What are you doing here?" she asked him, clinging to the uniform as if it were a lifeline.

"I wanted to see you. One of the other waitresses said you were back here."

"I'm not talking about in here specifically." She backed up until she felt the wooden shelf at her back. "I meant what are you doing at the café?"

"I wanted to talk to you."

From the look in his eyes, he wanted to do more than talk. "You shouldn't be in here. It's only for employees."

He gave her a devilish grin. "I always did like to take risks where you were involved." He reached in his pocket and pulled out a little gadget that looked like a miniature wrench. With a twist of his wrist, a sharp edge appeared. He moved closer to her until he was within inches of her face.

Annie knew he was a dangerous man—and not simply because he had a knife in his hands. With a sparkle in his eyes, he reached for the dangling tags and severed the plastic wire. "Better?" he asked in a seductive voice.

She couldn't find her voice, but managed to nod. She took a step backward, needing to put distance between them. Then she slipped the uniform over her head, pulling it into place. When she would have reached for the zipper, he stopped her.

"I'll get it for you. Turn around."

"I'll get it myself," she said tightly, then ignored the humor in his eyes as she struggled to reach the zipper. Normally she didn't have trouble zipping up the back of the uniforms, but for some reason, this one stuck. She winced as his cold fingers took over for hers. With his breath warm on her neck, the zipper closed and she was completely clothed again. Once again she found it necessary to step away from him.

"You look tired," he remarked as she tied her apron around her waist.

"I've been here since six this morning," she told him, wishing she didn't see sympathy in his face. It was much easier to deal with her emotions when he was being difficult.

"I thought maybe you didn't sleep well last night. I know I didn't."

He was waiting for her to ask him why. She knew she shouldn't give him the satisfaction, but she couldn't help herself. "Why? Were you worried about the valuable pick-up that's missing?" Her feeble attempt at sarcasm sounded just like that—feeble.

"No, I was thinking about you. How good you felt in my arms yesterday. Wondering if you still wore those dainty little flowered bikini briefs." Again there was that devilish grin. "I see you do."

Annie could feel her emotions succumbing to his charm. She fought to remember that this was not a man she could trust with her heart. She turned her back to him, but he simply stepped around her so that he was once more facing her.

"I'm wondering why I keep thinking about the way

things used to be between us," he said huskily. "Why I can't forget how good I always felt when I was with you."

Her breathing was becoming more shallow as he leaned closer to her. The scent of his after-shave teased her nostrils, and she found herself staring at his mouth. It would be so easy to give in to the temptation to reach up and touch those lips....

But then the door opened and Cleo stuck her head inside. "Sorry to disturb you, Annie, but there's another phone call for you."

"I'll be right there," she answered. Cleo nodded, then quietly shut the door. Annie felt as if the magic spell had been broken. "I have to go," she told Jesse, then started for the exit.

"Annie, wait a second. Have dinner with me."

"That's not a good idea."

"I'll give you the money for your dress," he said temptingly.

She eyed him suspiciously. "Why do we have to have dinner for you to give me the money?"

"We don't, but we both have to eat, so I thought I'd buy you dinner to try to make up for all the inconvenience I've caused you."

Annie was too tired to examine the pros and cons of such an idea. "All right. I'll meet you for dinner. Where?"

"How about if I pick you up at seven?"

"Make it seven-thirty," she echoed. "I want to stop by my mom's on the way home from work."

He nodded and accompanied her out into the restaurant, where the watchful eyes of Cleo followed their every move. Annie wasn't surprised. The older woman had worked at the café for the past ten years and knew all about her engagement to Jesse Conover. Annie half expected a maternal warning from Cleo when Jesse left with a "See you at seven-thirty."

Annie didn't need any warnings. She was already wary of Jesse. She'd have dinner, get her money and say goodbye. That was all.

Chapter Eight

Annie didn't know why she had agreed to having dinner with Jesse. In her present state of fatigue, she needed a hot bath and her bed, not a dinner date. She mentally corrected herself. It wasn't a date—or was it?

She sighed as she thought how complicated her life had become all because of someone else's clerical error. If the paper hadn't printed her phone number on Jesse's ad, she'd be· packing for Florida instead of worrying about how she was going to sit across from him and eat dinner when every time she saw him he tied her stomach up in knots.

After finishing her shift at the diner, she dragged her tired and aching body out to her car. She debated whether she should go straight home or stop to check on her mother. If she went home, she would have enough time to take a short nap before Jesse picked her up. Concern for her mother, however, had her driving in the opposite direction. When she pulled up in front of her mother's house, she saw a shiny new blue pick-up parked in the driveway.

Curiosity quickened her steps as she made her way up the shoveled walkway. When she pushed open the back door, she heard the faint echo of a man's voice. Had Neil returned? Annie wondered as she kicked off her boots. Then she heard laughter—male and female—and noticed the two empty beer bottles on the kitchen table. Her stepfather didn't drink beer.

Without taking off her coat, Annie padded across the cold linoleum floor toward the living room. "Mother, whose truck is that in the...?" As she stepped onto the plush carpeting, she stopped short. Her mother was stretched out on the sofa, a pillow behind her back, a plaid lap robe across her legs, a glass of beer in her hand. Her cheeks were full of color, her eyes sparkling. But it was the man sitting on the chair across from her that caused Annie's jaw to drop open. It was Hank Conover.

Annie's face twisted in a combination of surprise and horror. "Mother?"

Startled, Margaret turned her torso toward the doorway. "Annie! What are you doing here?"

"I came to check on you. I...I was worried," Annie stammered, taking tiny steps into the room.

"You didn't have to come. I'm fine."

Annie thought she looked better than fine. She was glowing. "What's he doing here?" she asked, pointing a finger in Hank's direction.

"Annie, your manners," Margaret scolded her gently.

"Hi, Annie. Long time no see." Hank got to his feet.

"That's your truck outside?" she repeated inanely.

"My new one. Just picked it up this morning." He smiled and made small talk as if nothing out of the ordinary had happened in the past three days. "How have you been?"

"I've been better," Annie murmured, still not comprehending the picture before her. What was Hank Conover doing drinking a beer in her mother's living room?

Margaret Jamison said smoothly, "Hank was kind

enough to give me a ride home." She gestured toward her foot. "I can't drive with my ankle like this."

"A ride home from where? The hospital?" Annie questioned.

Neither Hank nor her mother answered her question. "Don't you worry about your car. I'll have someone return it to you first thing in the morning." Hank's eyes were on Margaret as he spoke.

"Annie could probably ride with you to get it," Margaret suggested, looking at her daughter in supplication.

"Go where?" Annie asked.

When Margaret didn't answer, Hank spoke up, gesturing with his thumb. "It's over at the office."

"You mean the doctor's office, right?" Annie asked, although she had a sneaky feeling she wasn't going to hear the answer she wanted.

"No, Jesse's," Hank answered.

For the second time Annie's jaw dropped open. "You fell on the ice in front of C & C Custom Homes?"

Again Hank was the one who replied. "Yup, but you don't need to worry about a thing. We're insured against accidents. All of your mother's medical bills will be paid."

"You're darn right they will be," Annie said irritably, annoyed that her mother had gone looking for Jesse to get the money for the missing wedding dress. She gave her mother a look that expressed that displeasure.

"I was only thinking of you, dear," Margaret said piously.

That brought contrition from Hank, as well. "I'm really sorry about your wedding dress, Annie. Your mother's been telling me how important it is that you get it back."

Annie cringed. What she didn't need was for her mother

to be discussing her problems with Jesse's uncle. Actually she didn't want her mother to be talking to Hank at all.

It was obvious that Hank didn't share that sentiment, for he said, "I wish there was something I could do to help."

Annie didn't believe for one minute that Jesse's uncle would be any more sympathetic toward her plight than Jesse was.

"Do you really mean that?" Margaret asked, her eyes sparkling with an emotion Annie didn't want to see there.

"You don't have to worry about a thing," Hank boasted. "I'm going to straighten this whole mess out the minute I see Jesse."

Unable to refrain, Annie made a sound of disbelief. That earned her a warning look from her mother.

"I'm sure we can come to a resolution that will work for all of us," Margaret stated smoothly, looking at Hank as if he were an unsatisfied customer at the café who needed to be placated.

"*We* don't have to do anything. This is a matter between Jesse and me," Annie spoke up, disliking the way her mother's eyes twinkled every time she spoke to Hank Conover.

Hank glanced at his watch, then cleared his throat. "I should probably get going." He set the empty glass down on the end table next to Margaret's head. "Thanks for the beer, Margie. Now, remember, if there's anything at all you need, you have my number."

Annie watched her mother's face flush as he fussed over her bandaged ankle. As soon as he was gone, Annie wasted no time in confronting her mother about his visit.

"Margie?" She wrinkled her nose in distaste. "I thought you hated it when he called you that name?"

She fluffed the pillow behind her back. "He didn't mean any harm by it."

"I can't believe you let him bring you home." She hovered over her mother as if she were the parent and Margaret the child. "What happened to this I-will-never-let-that-man-within-six-feet-of-me-again stuff?"

"Annie, I fell on the ice. I needed help. He was there. Why are you making such a big deal out of this?"

"Because it is a big deal. What were you doing at Jesse's office in the first place?" she demanded, hands on her hips. "You told me you were going to pick up Dorothy."

She chortled. "I never had any intention of getting Dorothy. I just told you that so you wouldn't get upset with me." She held up her hands and examined her recently painted fingernails. "I knew you weren't going to get the money, so I thought I'd go see him myself. And it's a good thing I did."

"Oh, yeah. It looks like it turned out just great. Now you're out of work with a sprained ankle," Annie drawled sarcastically.

Again Margaret gestured to her foot. "This could have happened out front of the diner. There are slippery patches everywhere."

"I still don't understand why you were being so friendly to Hank Conover. He *is* one of your ex-husbands," Annie reminded her.

"For Pete's sake. All he did was take me to the doctor," she snapped a bit impatiently. "I treated him like I would have treated anyone who had done me a favor."

Annie groaned. "Come on, Mom. You were drinking beer with the guy."

"He's the one who bought it. He stopped on the way

home from the clinic because he thought it would help me relax."

She chuckled sardonically. "Yeah, right."

"It's true. He was concerned about me being in pain."

She made another sound of disbelief. "I'd say he's more concerned that you might sue him."

Margaret gasped. "He knows I would do no such thing. It's just a little sprain." She shifted on the sofa, wincing as she moved her right leg.

Annie dropped down onto the chair where Hank had sat. "It never would have happened if you hadn't lied to me."

"Like daughter like mother," her mother said smugly.

Annie's brow wrinkled. "What's that supposed to mean?"

"You didn't exactly tell me the truth. You deliberately let me believe that your dress was in Jesse's pick-up."

"What does it matter whether it was Hank's pick-up or Jesse's? The dress is still gone!"

Margaret straightened the lap robe. "Yes, but I would have done things differently if I had known Hank was involved."

"That's my whole point. I don't want you involved, Mother."

"I would think you'd be happy with what I've accomplished. Hank's going to talk to Jesse on your behalf."

"That's not necessary."

"It can't hurt. Jesse always did listen to his uncle." She gave a sigh of satisfaction. "I learned some rather interesting things this evening."

Annie eyed her suspiciously. "About what?"

"Jesse."

Annie didn't say a word. She knew her mother was waiting for her to ask what it was she had discovered, but she wasn't about to show even the tiniest bit of interest in her ex-fiancé.

"Don't you want to know what I discovered?" she asked temptingly.

"Nothing about Jesse interests me," she stated on a note of boredom.

"Not even the fact that he doesn't have a steady girlfriend?"

Annie tried not to show any emotion when she asked, "Is that what Hank told you?"

"Yes."

"And you believe him?"

"Why would he lie to me about it?"

She shrugged. "It doesn't matter. I don't care if Jesse has a dozen women in his life. There's only one reason why I'm even on speaking terms with him and that's because of my dress."

Her mother arched one pencil-thin eyebrow. "If you say so, dear."

"I do. And if you know what's good for you, you'll keep away from Hank Conover. Those Conover men are nothing but trouble." As soon as she had uttered the words, Annie gasped in horror. Her worst nightmare had come true. She had heard her mother's words come out of her mouth.

JESSE HAD JUST FINISHED shaving when Hank arrived, which was why he opened the door in his T-shirt and had a navy blue towel draped around his neck.

"I came to show you my new truck."

Jesse glanced outside and whistled through his teeth. "Looks pretty good. Let me get dressed, and I'll come outside and take a look."

"I'm glad you're home. I need to talk to you," the

older man told him as he stamped the snow from his boots. He removed his coat and hung it over a newel post on the staircase, but left his baseball cap in place.

"Come on upstairs while I finish getting dressed," Jesse instructed, gesturing for his uncle to follow him. Hank kicked off his Sorrels and padded in his stocking feet up the stairs.

"By the way, where were you all day? I thought I told you to take the day off. You know, put your feet up, watch a little football," Jesse said as he led him to the master bedroom on the second floor.

"What makes you think I didn't?"

"I've been calling all afternoon."

"I had to check to make sure that the guys had done their job with the snow removal," he answered, tugging on his right earlobe. "Then I stopped in and had a couple of beers with an old friend."

"That's good to hear. You put in enough hours during the week. You don't need to work Saturdays." As an afterthought he added, "Or Sundays."

"Yes, boss." Hank grinned as he tipped his hat.

"So what did you want to talk to me about?" Jesse asked.

"Have you seen Roxy today?"

"Nope. It's Saturday. I imagine she's with Fred," Jesse answered, tossing the hand towel aside.

"Then you haven't talked to her since she went to see Annie?"

Jesse paused in front of his closet. "She went to see Annie?"

"To apologize for what happened to the wedding dress," Hank answered, watching Jesse pull several shirts from his closet and lay them across the king-size bed.

"Has there been any news from the police?"

"Not yet."

"So what did you want to talk to me about?"

"Roxy and I thought it might be a good idea if you…" He trailed off.

"If I what?"

He cleared his throat. "If you offered to pay Annie for the dress. It's not like you'd be giving it away. Once the insurance money comes through, you'd get it all back."

Jesse picked up an off-white banded-collar shirt. "And just what made you and Roxy come to this conclusion?" he asked, pushing his long arms into its sleeves.

"We found out Annie's hurting for money thanks to that no-good bum she almost married. Apparently he ran up all kinds of bills before the wedding and then left her holding the bag."

The idea of another man taking financial advantage of Annie irritated Jesse. Actually the thought of her being taken advantage of under any circumstances was like pouring salt on an open wound. He felt a surge of anger toward the unknown ex-fiancé, then quickly reminded himself that Annie wasn't exactly the helpless type.

"Nobody forced her to spend eighteen hundred dollars on a dress," Jesse argued, buttoning the front of the shirt.

"She was in love. That can make people do some pretty stupid things," Hank stated with the wisdom of someone who knew from experience how true it was.

That brought a grimace to Jesse's face. He didn't want to think of Annie being in love with anyone else. "I wouldn't know," he said stiffly. He pivoted in front of the full-length mirror, then impatiently undid the buttons of his shirt and peeled it off.

"What's wrong with the shirt?" Hank asked as Jesse tossed it aside.

"It was too tight around the neck," he answered, and

picked up a blue-and-white-striped oxford and quickly buttoned it. After a look in the mirror, the shirt met the same fate as the previous one.

Watching curiously, Hank asked, "Where are you going that you're so worried about what you wear?"

"I'm not worried about how I look. I just want to be comfortable," he explained as he tried on the third shirt, a dark burgundy silk. He adjusted the cuffs, then ran his fingers in between the collar and his neck.

"You got a date or something?" Hank asked as he watched him preen in front of the mirror.

"Business meeting," Jesse answered.

One of Hank's eyebrows lifted as Jesse liberally splashed on after-shave. "What about the business of Annie?"

"What about it?"

"Are you going to give her the money?"

"Eighteen hundred is a lot of money for a dress," Jesse reminded his uncle, although he wasn't sure why he needed to remind him. After all, Hank was the one who shopped the discount stores regularly.

"You're not still holding a grudge against her because she sent you that Dear John letter, are you?" he asked, rubbing his chin thoughtfully.

"No, Dr. Freud, I'm not," Jesse answered dryly.

"Good. Just because she didn't want to marry you doesn't mean you should withhold the money from her now," Hank told him. "You should let bygones be bygones."

Jesse stared at his uncle contemplatively. It wasn't like Hank to suggest that he part with money, especially not to a woman who had once been his stepdaughter. A woman Hank had made no bones about comparing to her mother, whom he had described as a conniving, selfish woman whose sole purpose in life was to send a man to an early grave without a penny in his pocket.

"So your advice to me is to pay her off and get the money back when the insurance payment comes through." His eyes met Hank's in the mirror.

"That's what I would do," his uncle contended.

Jesse had to suppress the chuckle of disbelief that threatened to spill out. He wondered if he should remind his uncle that one of the reasons his marriage to Annie's mother hadn't worked out was because of Hank's tendency to pull her purse strings tight.

"I'll tell you what. I just might consider taking that advice." Jesse opened his closet door and pulled out a black-and-gray herringbone sport coat that had just a hint of burgundy in its tweed.

Hank clapped him on the shoulder. "It's probably the fair thing to do—considering the circumstances and all. Well, I'd better let you finish getting ready for your business meeting." He started to leave, only to pause in the doorway. "One more thing. Caroline asked me to mention to you about the clothes you said she could have."

"Clothes?"

"You know, for that charity project she's working on. She said you told her you had some things to donate."

Jesse remembered briefly discussing it several weeks ago. "I do. I have a couple of pieces of old luggage she can take, as well. When does she need it?"

"I think she wants to stop by on Monday and get it."

Jesse shrugged. "No problem."

"I'll pass on the word," Hank said, and again started to leave. This time Jesse stopped him.

"I thought you came over to show me the pick-up."

"You got the time?" He gave him a sly grin. "With your date and all?"

"I told you it's business," Jesse retorted, then followed him outside.

IT FELT LIKE A DATE. As Jesse parked his car outside Annie's apartment building, he had the same rush of adrenaline he experienced whenever he went to pick up a beautiful woman. And Annie was gorgeous.

When she opened the door to him, he had to clamp his lips together to keep his jaw from dropping open. With her long blond hair flowing about her shoulders and her head cocked to one side, she looked like an ad out of a fashion magazine. She wore a red double-breasted suit with a pleated skirt that stopped several inches above her knees, exposing legs that were slender and shapely.

"Come on in. I'll get my coat," she said flatly. She dismissed him with barely a glance in his direction, as if he were a maintenance man, not her date.

Again Jesse had to shake himself mentally. She wasn't his date. When she picked up a gray trench coat from the back of the sofa, he quickly took it from her and held it open. For a moment he thought she was going to snatch it from him, but she turned her back to him and slid her arms inside, muttering a thank-you in the process.

Jesse had to fight the urge to wrap his arms around her and nuzzle kisses against her neck. She smelled like an exotic flower. As she pulled on a pair of gloves and reached for her shoulder purse, he shoved his hands in his pockets.

"Okay. I'm ready," she announced.

He glanced down and noticed she was wearing a pair of red tennis shoes covered with sequins. "What about your feet?"

"They're ready, too."

"Aren't you going to wear some boots or something?"

"Nope. I figure if Cybill Shepherd can wear tennis shoes to dinner in Hollywood, I can wear them to dinner in Minnesota."

He shrugged. "They might get wet."

"Does it bother you that I'm wearing them?"

"The only thing that's bothering me right now is your perfume. If its purpose is to incite a man's hormones, it's working."

That brought a rush of color to her cheeks. She marched over to the door and held it open, indicating he should walk through.

While he waited for her to lock up, he said, "You don't need perfume to get my hormones going."

She ignored the comment. As he escorted her outside, he kept one hand on her elbow.

He had been lucky enough to find a parking place at the curb. When he unlocked the passenger-side door, she asked, "Is this your truck?"

"All mine," he answered, offering his hand so that she could step over the slushy snow at her feet.

"So you're a pick-up man, too."

"You don't have to make it sound like it's a handicap," he joked.

He could see that she wasn't in a talkative mood. He attempted to make conversation, but she gave him curt answers or no reply. The entire time they were in the pick-up, she sat staring out the window at the passing scenery.

He was glad he had decided to take her to a quiet restaurant on the outskirts of the city. Alfred's was an old establishment with high ceilings and glass chandeliers, a place known for its intimate atmosphere and excellent cuisine. White linens covered the tables, with long-stem roses and candles providing an elegant setting for silver and crystal. Individually lit works of Impressionist art lined the walls, and a string quartet played background music as tuxedoed waiters discreetly saw to their guests' needs.

After checking Annie's raincoat, they were led to a booth padded in dark green velvet. The bench seat was actually a semicircle, allowing patrons to sit side by side if they chose. Annie deliberately sat at the far end of the arc, indicating she wanted to be across from Jesse, not next to him.

Separated from the main part of the restaurant by a drape that could be pulled to the side or closed, the booth made the perfect setting for lovers. It was just the kind of restaurant Jesse would have liked to have taken Annie to seven years ago. Only back then he couldn't afford it. At that point in his life, he had been lucky he could take Annie out for fast food. Today he had the money to bring her here, only now there was no need for the intimacy.

After taking the waiter's suggestion that they order a bottle of the house wine, Jesse focused his attention on Annie. She stiffened as the waiter let the velvet drape close behind him, leaving the two of them alone in a glow of candlelight.

She had never looked more beautiful to Jesse. He wanted to hate her for hurting him the way she had, but he couldn't. "Why did you do it, Annie?" he asked, unable to stop himself.

She flashed her innocent eyes at him. "Do what?"

"Destroy all of our dreams."

She shifted uneasily. "Is that why you brought me here? To dredge up the past?"

"I don't want to, but I can't look at you and not think about what happened between us."

She reached for her purse. "I don't think this dinner is a very good idea. I'll catch a cab home."

"Wait." He slid closer to her and put a hand on her wrist. "I don't want you to leave."

Just then the waiter reappeared with the wine. He displayed the bottle for Jesse's approval, then uncorked it and poured a small amount in Jesse's glass for him to taste. As soon as Jesse had given his approval, he filled both glasses, then just as discreetly as he had appeared, he left.

"I don't want to talk about the past, Jesse," Annie told him, fidgeting with the silverware beside her plate. "Seven years is a long time. A lot has happened. We're not the same people we were back then."

"We felt like the same two people when we kissed last night."

Her cheeks reddened slightly, and she lowered her eyes to sip her wine. She hadn't been unaffected by their kissing last night. The thought made him press on.

"But then physically, we always were a perfect match, weren't we?"

She kept her eyes on her wineglass, saying nothing.

"I thought we were suited in every way necessary to make a marriage work, but apparently you didn't feel the same way. Just what part of our relationship was it that caused you to break off our engagement?"

"I did it because you weren't ready to settle down, Jesse...no matter what you said." She finally looked up at him, a wounded look in her eyes that made his insides soften.

He couldn't believe what he was hearing. She was the one who had jilted him, yet she wanted him to believe it was for *his* benefit. "Are you telling me you sent me that letter as a favor to me?"

"Yes."

He could see she held her emotions closely in check. "Maybe you better explain this to me."

"I really don't see what good it's going to do to rehash all of this."

"We never hashed it out in the first place, Annie. All I have is a letter that says you couldn't go through with our marriage because you couldn't trust me. I tried calling you, you wouldn't come to the phone. I wrote you letters, you sent them back unopened. When I finally made it back home again, you were gone."

"I went to cooking school in Chicago." Again she avoided his eyes, focusing on her finger circling the rim of her wineglass.

"Is that why you broke our engagement—because you wanted to be a cook instead of a wife?" he asked, wondering why she couldn't have done both.

"No, that's not the reason," she denied hotly.

"Then what was it? Was my uncle Hank right?"

"Right about what?"

"That you Jamison women are fickle. You can't make up your mind what it is you want. One minute you want marriage, the next you don't," he said derisively.

"That's not true!" she vehemently denied.

"Then why aren't we married?"

"Because I wasn't willing to share my husband with other women!" Finally there was some emotion in her voice, some fire in her eyes.

"What other women? Annie, from the day I met you, I didn't look at another woman. I know in the past I didn't exactly have the reputation for being the nicest guy in town, but that all changed the day I fell in love with you."

"Is that why you would drop me off at midnight, then rush to another girl's arms?" she demanded, her eyes full of accusation.

Perplexed, he asked, "What are you talking about?"

"I know about Roxy. I saw you with her the night before you left to go back on duty." Again a hurt look shadowed her face, giving her a fragile appearance.

"Saw me with her where?"

"You told me you were going to play cards with your guy friends after you dropped me off that night." Her voice shook as she spoke. "Well, I followed you and you weren't playing cards. You were with *her*."

"And you thought I was having an affair with her?" Disbelief raised the pitch of his voice.

"Your car was still at her house when I drove by the next morning."

"Because I stayed up all night playing cards with my cousin and some friends. Roxy's been a friend of our family for a long time. She was only there because she brought over some food for us to eat." He could see the skepticism in her face. "Annie, after everything that had happened between us, how could you think I would cheat on you?"

"Hank had told my mother you couldn't stay faithful to one girl," she said in a small voice.

"That wasn't true. I was faithful to you." He held her gaze, trying to convey that sentiment to her, but he could see the confusion in her eyes.

"Look at the mess Hank and my mother made of their marriage. I didn't want that to happen to us," she said soberly.

"It wouldn't have," he insisted, reaching across the table to take her hand in his. "Why couldn't you have trusted me?"

She pulled her hand away from his. "It doesn't matter now. That's the past. Things have changed...we're different."

He wanted to tell her that nothing had changed as far as he was concerned. He still wanted her just as badly as he had back then. In seven years he had met no woman who could make him forget what they had together.

That wasn't true for her, however. She *had* met someone who had made her forget that she had ever loved him. The ex-fiancé who wasn't a masterpiece. The thought stuck in his craw like peanut butter sticks to the roof of a mouth.

"So what does the 'new' Annie want from life? The party life aboard a cruise ship?" He couldn't keep the disdain from his voice.

"There's nothing wrong with having fun," she said defensively.

"You never used to be the party type, Annie."

She took a sip of her wine. "I told you. I've changed."

"I guess so. The Annie I knew only wanted one thing— to get married and have a family. Now all you want is enough money to get out of town." He wanted to believe that somewhere inside her was still a part of that young woman he had fallen in love with. He wished that she would contradict him, tell him that she still wanted the same things as he did—a family, a home.

She didn't.

When the waiter appeared with their dinner, they stopped talking about the past. It was fine with Jesse. What he wanted was to hear what Annie was doing now.

"I was surprised to see you still working at the diner," he commented in between bites of his prime rib.

"Actually I only help out in a pinch. For the past three years I've run my own catering business," she told him.

"And did you like that?"

"Yes, I did. Especially the variety. Every job was different, which made it rather fun." Her eyes lit up as she talked about her work, and Jesse felt her enthusiasm flow into him.

"What about you? Do you like building homes?" she probed.

"Yes, for a lot of the same reasons you enjoy catering. Each house is a little different. It's nice to be able to create something from scratch for other people's pleasure."

"I'm surprised you ended up on the contracting end of things. You always talked as if you'd work the construction business with your uncles."

"When I came home from the service, I knew I wanted to be my own boss. So I went back to school, learned the tricks of the trade and went into partnership with my brother, Todd," he explained.

"It sounds like it's a successful partnership," she remarked.

He didn't miss the hint of admiration in her tone. "Yes, it's worked well for both of us."

Throughout dinner Jesse found himself wanting to slide closer, to put his arm around her. He didn't. He was discovering that the twenty-six-year-old Annie was every bit as intriguing as the nineteen-year-old had been. By the time they arrived back at her apartment, he had come to the decision that he needed to see her again. For his own peace of mind.

When she would have shut the door without inviting him in, he said, "Do you want me to leave?"

"I'm really tired, Jesse."

She did look as if a light breeze could knock her off her feet. He wanted to wrap her in his arms and cuddle her. He shoved his hands in his pockets to keep from doing just that. "Maybe we should talk about the money."

Reluctantly she opened the door and gestured for him to come inside. As she stepped into the living room, she switched on a lamp. "Do you want some coffee?" she asked as she removed her coat.

"A brandy would be nice."

She smiled apologetically. "Sorry."

"I'm fine. We probably drank enough coffee at the restaurant," he heard himself say, even though he was looking for any excuse to prolong his visit.

When she didn't take a seat, he remained standing, too.

"I want you to have the money for your dress, Annie," he said softly. "You can pay me back when the insurance claim comes through."

She smiled gratefully. "Thank you."

"The only problem is you'll have to wait until Monday, when I can get the cash," he told her.

"That's all right." She clasped her fingers together in front of her. "I want you to know that I really appreciate you doing this." A smile creased her cheeks.

He tugged on one ear. "I guess I should have told you there's one condition."

The smile slid from her face. "What's that?"

It was blackmail. He knew it but he didn't care. One way or another he would get what he needed from her. "I want you to spend the day with me tomorrow."

Chapter Nine

The following morning Annie found Joni sitting at the kitchen table, her face a picture of concentration as she balanced her checkbook. When she noticed Annie, a smile softened her features.

"Good morning. What's up?"

"My body wishes it wasn't." Annie grimaced as she stretched, rubbing the muscles on either side of her neck. "One of the waitresses called in sick yesterday, so I was on my feet nearly nonstop."

"I came home around eight, but you were out." Joni reached for a coffee mug that had a cartoon drawing of a woman eating a box of chocolates with the caption Life's Too Short To Spend It Dieting.

"I had a business meeting." Annie opened the cupboard and pulled out a bottle of aspirin.

"On a Saturday night?"

"Mm-hmm." She popped two tablets in her mouth and washed them down with a glass of water. "I met with Jesse to discuss the business of my missing wedding dress."

Joni looked at her over the rim of her mug. "And what happened?"

Annie sank down onto a chair. "He's going to give me

the money. Tomorrow morning as soon as the banks open.'' She gently massaged her temples, hoping to ease the headache thudding dully behind her eyes.

"Does this mean he isn't such a jerk after all?"

Annie lowered her eyes. "I didn't say that."

"So where was this business meeting?"

"At a restaurant.'' She saw the curious gleam in her roommate's eye and asked, "Why are you looking at me like that?"

"Like what?" Joni asked innocently.

"Like you think there's something going on between me and Jesse."

Joni leaned forward and grinned slyly. "Is there?"

"No." Annie got up to make herself some toast. As she plopped two slices of whole-wheat bread into the toaster, she said, "All we did last night was talk."

"About the past or the present?"

"Both. He told me he never cheated on me."

"What about Roxy?"

The bread popped out of the toaster, and Annie quickly spread jam on the slices of toast. "She was only at the poker party because she had brought over food for them."

"And you believe him?"

Annie shrugged. "It doesn't matter. Jesse and I aren't going to discover that we made a mistake breaking up seven years ago."

"If it's the way Jesse claims—that Roxy wasn't the other woman—then I'd say he didn't make the mistake. You did,'' Joni contended. "You're the one who called off the engagement."

It was that possibility that had kept Annie awake half of the night. Ever since her dinner with Jesse, she had been wondering if what he said hadn't been the truth. Had she jumped to the wrong conclusion about his relationship with Roxy? Had she made a mistake in calling off the engagement?

"There's not much point in speculating about it, is there?" she said dispiritedly. "What's done is done."

"Judging by the way he looks at you, I'd say you wouldn't have to work very hard to get him interested a second time."

"Who says I want him interested in me?" Annie tried to be cool about the subject of Jesse Conover, but she couldn't suppress the tiny tremors of excitement that ran through her every time she thought of him.

She was falling for him again and faced the risk of making the same mistake twice. As much as she hated to admit it, she had enjoyed dinner with him. For years she had tried to paint him as a lying, cheating kind of guy, but last night she had seen he could be the kind of man she had always dreamed of finding—kind and sensitive, yet passionate.

Joni didn't press the issue. She took another sip of her coffee, then said, "So you met with him last night, and he agreed to fork over the money." She snapped her fingers. "Just like that?"

"Not exactly," Annie took a bite of her toast, which she thought tasted like cardboard. She quickly washed it down with a sip of orange juice. "There was a condition."

"Which is…?" Joni leaned on her elbows, eagerly waiting for her answer.

"I have to spend the day with him today."

Joni's mouth dropped open, and she slapped her palms on the table. "I knew it. I could tell by the way he looked at you."

"Could tell what?"

"That he wants you," Joni exclaimed, her eyes dancing.

Annie couldn't prevent the blush.

"Did he kiss you?" Joni asked.

Annie's blush deepened. "Not last night."

"But he has other times, hasn't he? This is getting better by the minute. Tell me more," she demanded, her eyes glowing.

"There's nothing to tell," Annie insisted.

"Annie, the guy's hot for you. Why else would he want you to spend the day with him?"

Annie had been pondering that question half the night herself. She figured it was for one of two reasons. Knowing how uncomfortable she was with him, he wanted to punish her for walking out on him seven years ago. Or was he trying to make a move on her?

The second possibility sent a shiver of excitement through her. The thought of Jesse wanting her as a woman awakened emotions that had lain dormant for a long time. Desire stirred inside her, reminding her that what she shared with him was more than memories. She wanted him to want her. Despite everything that had happened between them, she still craved his touch. And it frightened her. She didn't want to be excited by Jesse Conover.

"I don't know and I don't care," she told Joni, although she knew it wasn't quite the truth. "I'm spending the day with him so I can get my money, and then I'm going to go to Florida. End of story." She dumped the remainder of her half-eaten toast in the garbage.

"He's awfully cute," Joni said in a singsong voice.

"So are puppies, and they're a whole lot less trouble." She rinsed out her glass and set it on the drainer.

"So where is he taking you today?"

Annie shrugged. "I didn't ask. All he said was that I

should wear old clothes—'the rattier the better,' were his words.''

"Where would he be taking you on Sunday dressed in old clothes?" Joni wondered aloud.

"Maybe we're going to the farm." When Joni shot her a quizzical look, she explained, "His grandfather lives on a farm near Hastings. We used to go there to..." She trailed off, not wanting to remember their favorite spot had been a shady patch of grass next to a bubbling creek. They'd take a picnic basket, wade in the cool, clear water and then make love on a blanket.

"To what?" Joni asked when she didn't complete her train of thought.

"To help his grandfather with the chores," she answered, avoiding her roommate's eyes. She glanced at the clock. "I'd better get dressed, or the next thing I know he'll be pounding on the door."

Jesse arrived a few minutes after eleven, wearing faded denims with holes in both knees and an old flannel shirt that had a frayed collar. When he saw Annie's crisp twill pants and navy blue henley, he told her she looked too good and sent her to change. She returned wearing a pair of tattered jeans and a sweatshirt that had once been gray but was now a rosy pink thanks to getting tossed in the washer with a red beach towel.

Joni tried to get Jesse to tell her where it was he was taking Annie. With a polished charm he evaded answering her questions, steering the conversation toward her job at the temporary service.

Annie, too, was curious to know where they were going, but she feigned indifference as his pick-up headed toward the inner city. When he turned onto a residential street in one of the oldest sections of St. Paul, her curiosity grew. Most of the buildings had stood since the turn of the century, with many of them boarded up and uninhabitable. Soon, however, they came to a block where new homes marked an area of redevelopment. Across the street was a park where children skated on an ice rink.

Jesse parked in front of one of the brand-new homes, a white split-level with a tuck-under garage. A huge sign in the front yard said Project Friendship Homes. Annie looked at Jesse with a question in her eyes.

All he said was, "We're here."

Anyone who watched the TV regularly or read the newspaper knew that Project Friendship Homes was an organization that used volunteer help to build shelters for those unable to obtain the funding to buy a house. Annie knew that many local businesses donated materials to make the houses affordable to the poor. She could only assume that Jesse was here to donate building supplies.

He climbed out of the pick-up and went around to the back. He pulled out two large buckets filled with paint supplies—rollers, brushes, masking tape and sponges. He handed one to Annie, saying, "For you."

It didn't take a genius to figure out that they had come to the house to work. "You want me to paint?" she asked, hoping she had misread the situation.

"Consider it interest on the money I'm going to loan you." He closed the back of the truck, locked it and slipped the keys into his jeans pockets. "Ready?" He didn't wait for her answer, but ushered her up the sidewalk toward the house.

The door opened, and they were greeted by a woman holding a paint roller.

"Hey, Jesse. How's it going?"

Annie's first thought was that the woman could be the prototype for Painter Barbie. Although she had on bib-front coveralls, they looked as if they had been tailor-made to emphasize every curve of her figure. With a professionally made-up face and not a hair out of place, she made Annie wish she had taken more time with her own hair.

"Pretty good, Gail." He nudged Annie forward and said, "This is Annie. She came to help."

Gail looked Annie over thoroughly. "Good. We can always use another pair of hands."

"I thought she could help you with the walls in here. I'm going to work on the ceilings in the kitchen." He flashed Gail one of his heart-stopping smiles, and Annie felt a tiny twinge of jealousy. "Can you get her set up?"

Annie wanted to say she didn't need anyone to set her up with anything, but bit her tongue. She had an idea that revenge motivated his interest in her today. He wanted to irritate her. She decided she wouldn't give him the satisfaction of showing him he had succeeded.

"Sounds like a good plan to me," the bleached blonde answered. "Betty's painting the bathroom, Larry and Connie are doing the smaller bedroom and Greg's taking care of the closets. I'm expecting Anita and Ray, too."

Jesse looked at Annie and said, "I'll let you get started. I'll be in the kitchen if you need me." Then he disappeared, leaving Annie alone with Painter Barbie.

She thought it was rather interesting that there wasn't so much as a drop of paint on Gail's hands. Annie soon learned the reason why. Gail didn't exactly paint, but was more of a gofer, getting supplies and going from room to room to see how everyone was doing.

Annie spent most of the time in the living room by herself until two more volunteers showed up to lend a hand. They were a middle-aged couple named Ray and Anita, and told Annie that this was the fifth Project Friendship Home they had been involved in putting together. They explained how all the labor on the home came from volunteers like themselves. When they heard that Annie had come with Jesse, they regaled her with stories of his generosity.

As the final coat of the living-room paint was being applied, Jesse came to check on her. "Getting hungry?"

"A little," Annie answered, ignoring the growls her stomach made. "Gail brought around sodas for everyone."

"If you two want to leave, Anita and I can finish up here," Ray offered.

While Jesse checked with the other workers, Annie washed up in the bathroom. On her way back to the living room, she met Gail, who stopped her in the hallway.

"Have you known Jesse long?" The life-size Barbie asked.

"Seven years," Annie answered honestly.

"You're kidding! I'm surprised I haven't seen you around before now."

Annie didn't know what she was implying with that remark. Of one thing she was certain—curiosity was written all over the other woman's face. She wanted to know just what Annie's relationship was to Jesse.

It would have been easy to tell her the only reason she was with Jesse had to do with a loan he was going to give her and his requirement that she put up collateral—her services. But something inside her wanted to let Gail believe that she was more than an old friend of his who just happened to lose her wedding dress and had to borrow money from him before she could start her new job.

She was saved from having to say anything by the appearance of Jesse, who ushered her out the door and into his pick-up.

When they were once more heading down the freeway,

he finally spoke. "Ray said you were pretty good with the paintbrush."

"He said the same thing about you—among other things."

Jesse cast her a sideways glance. "What things?"

"That you just don't donate your time to the project. He says you're one of the biggest benefactors."

"And that surprises you?"

"No." It was a lie and they both knew it. "All right. So I didn't expect you'd be involved in something like Project Friendship Homes. You never approved of my working at the soup kitchen."

"That was because I worried about you going into that section of town alone at night."

His protectiveness struck a tender chord. He was the kind of man who would always make a woman feel safe. "I wasn't alone," she reminded him. "I always went with another volunteer."

"Two women alone isn't much better than one. Do you still help out at the soup kitchen?" There was an honest concern in his eyes that made her wish that she could have said yes.

"Uh-uh." She felt the need to justify herself. "I haven't had much spare time lately." She didn't want to tell him that after she had broken off her engagement to Richard, it had been necessary to work a second job to pay off the debts left behind. It was too embarrassing to admit that she'd been foolish enough to spend money on a wedding that never took place. "I've been working too many hours lately."

"Saving up all that money so you can go cruising," he said disapprovingly.

"You make it sound as if I'm taking an extravagant vacation."

"I've been on a cruise ship before, Annie, and I know why the jobs are so popular. It's one big party."

"Maybe for the passengers, but not for the employees."

"Ha!"

She decided it was no good to try to convince him otherwise. Besides, she was tired of defending herself. And what did it matter to him what job she took?

They rode in an uncomfortable silence until finally he said, "Are you ready to eat?"

She looked at her paint-stained jeans. "I'm not exactly dressed for dinner. I think I might have paint in my hair."

He slanted her a look and grinned. "You do. Right on top there's a big gob of it."

She pulled down the visor and looked in the mirror. "If you're going to insist on dinner, I'd like to go home and change first."

"Don't worry. Where we're going, no one's going to notice you have paint in your hair."

"And just where is that?" she asked.

"You'll see," was all he said, and continued to their destination in silence.

Unlike the previous two days, when gray skies and a cold northwest wind had kept the temperature below freezing, today the sun shone brightly, melting the snow from rooftops and sidewalks. As they headed south away from the city and into the rolling meadows of the southern suburbs, Jesse opened a compartment beneath the dash and pulled out several CDs.

"Here. Pick the one you want."

All of them were country-western albums. "Don't you have any alternative?"

"Alternative what?"

"Music."

"Nope."

Annie read the unfamiliar titles and picked Shania Twain's *The Woman in Me*. She popped it in the CD player.

"Good choice," Jesse told her as music filled the cab.

Again they rode in silence except for the music playing softly. When Jesse turned off the main highway onto a county road, Annie suspected they were headed for his grandfather's farm.

Her suspicions were confirmed when he took a left and drove through an open gate that had Conover Creek in iron letters. How many times had they traveled down that road? she wondered as the truck bounced along the ruts created by melting snow. When she was nineteen, she had sat close to him, trying to distract him with kisses as he drove. She wondered if he were remembering the same thing, for there was a look in his eye that told her whatever it was that was going through his mind, it involved her.

What had been rows of corn-lined fields during most of Annie's visits were now covered with snow. A wooden fence bordered the driveway leading to the two-story farmhouse. Smoke curled from the chimney, and a big black dog barked as he raced back and forth in front of the barn, anticipating their arrival.

"Your grandfather still lives here?" she asked as he parked next to the house.

Jesse chuckled. "I couldn't get him to move if I tried." He slid out of the truck and came around to open her door for her. "Watch your step. It's muddy."

Annie carefully stepped around the melting patches of snow, avoiding the mud as much as possible. The large black mutt brushed his nose against Annie's thigh.

"That's Geezer," Jesse informed her.

Annie rubbed the dog's chin until Jesse chased him back to the barn. At the back door of the house, he motioned for her to go in ahead of him.

Annie could smell something cooking as she stepped into the kitchen. A glance at the stove told her someone had been at work. She soon discovered who it was. A gray-haired woman with rosy cheeks and wearing a bibbed apron over her flowered housedress waddled out to greet them.

"Well, there you are. We were wondering if you were going to make it today." She greeted Jesse with a grin. As soon as she spotted Annie she said, "You must be Annie. I'm Grace. Come on in. We've been waiting for you."

She waved for them to follow her into the living room, where Jesse's grandfather sat in a leather recliner watching a football game on the TV. Except for the thinning of his hair and a few more crevices in his weathered cheeks, he hadn't changed much since the last time Annie had visited him. He smiled when he saw her and rose to his feet.

"Jesse said he was bringing you out to Sunday dinner, and I didn't believe him," he told her as he gave her a hug. "How come you haven't come to see me? Just because you don't want anything to do with my grandson doesn't mean you have to ignore me."

"Grandpa, you're embarrassing her," Jesse scolded gently.

He dismissed his chastisement with a wave of his hand. "Annie understands me. That's why I like her." He jabbed a finger at the sofa, saying, "Sit down and tell me why a pretty thing like you isn't married and raising a family."

Annie's eyes met Jesse's. She saw the same question there.

"I haven't been able to find anyone who's as handsome as you." Her response brought a chuckle from Jesse's grandfather. To her relief Jesse steered the conversation away from her personal life, encouraging his grandfather to talk about the farm. It wasn't long before Grace announced that dinner was ready. Jesse helped his grandfather, who, Annie noticed, had a slight limp and relied on the support of a cane.

Grace joined them at the big oak dining-room table, serving pot roast with mashed potatoes and gravy, steamed vegetables and coleslaw. "Comfort food," Jesse murmured in Annie's ear as he pulled out her chair for her.

"It looks delicious," Annie said sincerely.

During dinner Annie learned that Jesse came to the farm every Sunday and seldom brought a guest. The latter piece of information gave Annie a sense of satisfaction. She knew the farm held special memories for the two of them—she didn't want to think that he had brought other women here.

When they had finished eating, Grace refused to let Annie help her clean up. She insisted that Jesse take her out to the barn to see the newest addition to the family. The sun was close to the horizon as they stepped outside, the barren trees a sharp contrast against the pink sky. Annie knew that beyond the trees was the creek where she and Jesse had waded in the summer.

"It's beautiful out here at sundown," she commented as they walked the short distance to the barn.

"Even more beautiful at sunrise," he answered.

Annie was grateful he couldn't see her face flush at the memory of the evening they had stayed awake all night making plans for their future. "You don't see sunsets like this when you live in the city."

"That's why I wanted to build you a house in Dakota County. Away from all the glass and metal that makes people forget there's nothing behind a sunset but darkness."

She swallowed back the lump in her throat. "You live in the city."

"It's convenient for now."

The barn was actually a metal shed that housed farm implements. As they stepped inside, Jesse flipped a switch that created a burst of light. Annie looked around and saw that the barn was just as she remembered it. It was only when she heard the whimpering that she realized what Geezer had done.

Lying on an old blanket was a German shepherd– Labrador mixed breed and her recent litter. "Meet Geezer's better half, Zelda, and their family," Jesse said as Annie gushed over the puppies.

She knelt down beside them. "Can I touch them, or will she get upset?"

"Go ahead. They're old enough now that she doesn't mind," he told her, hunkering down beside her.

There were two black and three multicolored pups. All but one was huddled close to Zelda's milk supply. Annie reached for the loner.

"Aren't you precious," she crooned as the tiny black puppy with paws that looked too big for his scrawny legs licked her hands with his tiny pink tongue. "What's your grandfather going to do with them?"

"Give them away. Do you want one?"

"I can't have a puppy. Not where I'm going," she reminded him.

"What if you weren't going?"

"I still couldn't take one. My apartment building doesn't allow pets." Reluctantly she returned the puppy to the litter. "What about you?"

"I don't think Sheba's ready for another dog in the house."

She debated whether she should ask. "Sheba?"

"My dog. She's part golden retriever, part golden Lab. She's a stray I picked up from the humane society a while back. Apparently the previous owners abused her, so she's a little skittish around strangers—animals and humans."

"How can anyone abuse a golden? They're such gentle creatures," Annie remarked.

Jesse didn't answer, but glanced at his watch. "We need to get going. I want to show you something before it gets dark."

The something he wanted to show her was a large house under construction just down the road from his grandfather's. It sat atop one of the rolling hills, rising like a fortress in the barren countryside.

"Is your construction company building this?" she asked as he parked the truck in the U-shaped driveway in front of the house.

"We started it last spring. Unfortunately this is as far as we got." He unlocked the double oak doors and gestured for her to step inside. "You have to use your imagination a bit."

Annie could see why. There were no walls, only two-by-fours separating the rooms. Solitary light bulbs hung from the rafters, and plywood subflooring echoed beneath their feet as he gave her a tour. Annie soon discovered, however, it wasn't the interior that would be its best selling feature. Nearly the entire back side of the house was glass, providing a spectacular view of the sunset on the river.

"Oh, my gosh! This is gorgeous!" she crooned, walking over to the plate-glass windows.

"The view is definitely the best feature at this stage of construction," Jesse agreed.

"The people you're building this for must be anxious to move in," she remarked, gazing at the vaulted ceilings.

"Actually they're not. The man who bought the house died, and his widow doesn't want to go through with the purchase," Jesse explained.

"Oh, how sad," she commiserated. She looked around, spreading her hands expressively. "To have all of this and not be able to enjoy it. Were they a young couple with children?"

He shook his head. "No, their children were grown, which is why his widow doesn't want to live this far from the city by herself."

Annie nodded in understanding. "This house should have kids in it."

He came to stand behind her as she gazed at what remained of the spectacular sunset through the plate-glass window. "Look." He tucked his head close to hers and pointed his arm over her shoulder. "There's a small pond that'll freeze over in winter for ice-skating. And see that gnarly old oak tree down by the river? Wouldn't that make a good spot for a rope swing?"

"Mm-hmm. And there's a clearing on the bank of the river that would make a perfect place for a breakfast..." She trailed off as she realized she had nearly said *breakfast picnic*. One of her and Jesse's favorite dates had been to get up before sunrise, pack a cooler with fruit and bagels and head down to the river to watch the sunrise. The memory was enough to bring a lump to her throat.

"You're right. It is the perfect spot for a breakfast picnic.'' She could feel him move closer to her, until the scent of his after-shave filled her nostrils.

More than anything, she wanted to be enveloped by his thick, muscular arms. To snuggle into an embrace with all of her senses focusing on the man holding her. But he made no attempt to reach out to her.

''I've had this land for six years, Annie. I bought it with my severance pay from the military.'' His voice was low, as if it were full of regret.

Annie didn't turn around. She couldn't. Her heart was beating so fast she thought he would see it thumping in her chest. Regret washed over her. This would have been her house had they been married.

Jesse's voice dropped even lower, and she could feel him move closer to her. The next time he spoke, she could feel his breath on her hair.

''I thought that once I came home from the service, you'd tell me that your Dear John letter had been a mistake. But that never happened, did it?''

He waited for her to answer, but self-preservation had Annie remaining silent. She was dangerously close to falling in love with him all over again. Could she risk letting him know?

Finally she turned to face him. ''Why did you bring me here, Jesse? To show me what I missed out on?'' She needed to think the worst of him. Otherwise she would give in to the emotions that were ready to come rushing to the surface with a force greater than ever.

He studied her face. ''No. I guess I wanted to see if you remembered that this was the kind of house we had dreamed of sharing.''

The look on his face told her it was too late for that dream. Annie's heart swelled with sadness. ''It was a long time ago, Jesse. We were just kids,'' she managed to say.

He traced her jaw with his fingertips. "Maybe, but we were kids with dreams." His voice filled with emotion as he said, "We had so many dreams, Annie."

He lifted her chin and gazed deep into her eyes, as if he could see into her very soul. The same desire that glazed his eyes stirred inside her, spreading heat to her most intimate parts. He wanted her—plain and simple. She could pretend all she wanted that she had no feelings for him, but she knew it wasn't true.

She went into his arms without another word. She had shoved her hands in the pockets of her anorak to keep them warm, but before she knew it they were wrapped around his neck, pulling his mouth to hers. He kissed her with deep strokes of his tongue, awakening the feminine side of her in a most provocative way. Need swelled inside her, demanding to be assuaged.

With an equal passion, she kissed his mouth and his neck, tasted his skin and inhaled the tantalizing scent of him. This was her Jesse, and she wanted to surrender to the feelings he aroused in her. Exploring first the warm, silky hair on his head, her hands became instruments of her passion, enjoying the solid, strong muscles of his chest as they pushed inside his leather jacket.

Despite the chill in the house, Annie's flesh burned with yearning. Jesse's strong, callused hands slid beneath her sweatshirt to release the clasp on her bra. She moaned as his fingers found the silky warmth of her skin. When his lips traced a path across her breasts, delightful tingles shot through every nerve in her body.

She wished he would tear her clothes right off and kiss every inch of her with those magnificent lips. Unable to stop herself, she slid the tips of her fingers into the waistband of his jeans. She became oblivious to their surroundings, thinking of nothing but the exquisite sensations her body was experiencing.

Caught in a sensual spell, she felt bereft when Jesse pulled away from her. He raked his hand through his hair, turning his back to her momentarily.

With fumbling fingers, she reached under her sweatshirt to hook her bra. The only other sound in the room was their heavy breathing. When he turned to face her, there was an unreadable expression on his face.

Seeing her shiver, he said, "There's no heat in this place. We'd better get going before it gets any colder in here."

On the way home he was quiet. Annie wanted to know what he was thinking. What had those kisses meant to him? Since he had been the one to put a stop to their lovemaking, she had no way of even guessing what was running through his mind.

She knew they should talk about what had happened, but she was afraid she might not like what she heard. The choice was taken from her, for when they arrived at her place, he mentioned what had happened between them.

"I still want you, Annie, and I know you want me," he said to her as they sat in his pick-up, staring out the front window.

She knew there was no point in denying it. She also knew there was no future for them. "Jesse, I'm leaving in three days."

"You don't have to go."

"Yes, I do." She didn't want to utter the words, but they came out without any effort on her part.

"Right." He climbed out of the cab and came around to her side of the truck. Silently he walked her to her door. She thought he might leave without saying another word, but then he surprised her.

"If you want to talk to me later this evening, I'll be playing broomball at the ice arena in Cottage Grove."

Annie knew there was an unspoken message in his words. "I can't come watch you play, Jesse. I have to check on my mother."

"Is she ill?"

"Hank didn't tell you?"

He frowned in confusion. "Tell me what?"

"My mother slipped on the ice outside your office yesterday. Fortunately Hank was there and helped her to the doctor. She has a sprained ankle," she explained.

Jesse shook his head in disbelief. "No wonder he—" he broke off.

"No wonder he what?" she asked.

"Nothing." He changed the subject. "Is she going to be all right?"

"She says she is. I'm surprised you didn't know about it."

His eyes narrowed. "What was she doing at C & C Homes?"

"She hoped to convince you to give me the money for the dress," Annie admitted with a bit of embarrassment. "I didn't know she was going to see you."

"It must have been a little awkward for her—running into Hank and all." He dangled the question, waiting for Annie to elaborate.

"I think it went okay," she said evasively.

"Well, I better go." He looked as if leaving was the last thing he wanted to do.

Annie didn't stop him. In three days she would be gone. To get involved with Jesse a second time would be a very foolish thing to do. She kept telling herself that over and over as she stood at the window and watched his truck disappear down the street.

Chapter Ten

As Annie waited for the left-turn arrow to turn green, she saw a man leave her mother's house, climb into a pick-up parked at the curb and drive away. Although she was a couple hundred feet away, she had a pretty good idea that the man behind the wheel was Hank Conover.

That's why she had a frown on her face when she entered her mother's living room and found Margaret sitting on the sofa in purple satin lounging pajamas, her hair swept up into a French twist. On her wrist was a gold bangle bracelet, and gold hoops dangled from her ears. When she saw Annie, she shifted nervously.

"You're early. I wasn't expecting you until seven."

"It's a quarter to— Did I interrupt something?" Annie asked, giving her mother the perfect opportunity to confess that Hank had been there. She didn't.

"No." Margaret looked as innocent as a six-year-old caught with a hand in the cookie jar.

"Good. How's your ankle?" Annie asked, pulling off her anorak. After washing away the traces of paint in her hair, she had put on a clean pair of denims and a long-sleeved shirt. She pushed up the sleeves and shoved her hands to her hips, ready to help her mother in any way necessary.

"It's still sore, but I think it's better," she said cautiously.

"Are you having trouble getting around?"

"I'm using the crutches."

Annie hadn't noticed the wooden crutches yesterday and wondered if Hank had brought them to her. "Would you like me to make you something to eat?"

"No, I already ate dinner."

With Hank, no doubt, Annie figured. "Then how about a cup of coffee?"

"No, I'm fine," she said, gesturing to a glass of iced tea that was on the end table.

Annie couldn't figure out why her mother was so nervous. For someone who was fine, she was fidgeting an awful lot. When her mother's eyes darted nervously toward the dining room, Annie turned to see the reason why. A bouquet of flowers graced the pedestal oak table. Tiny pink roses and white carnations spilled over a tall, slender white vase.

Annie arched one eyebrow. "A get-well wish?"

Margaret wet her lips before answering. "They're from Hank."

"He must be worried you're going to sue," Annie said dryly, then walked over to the table to read the card. "To my little Margie...cheer up."

She looked over at her mother. *"My little Margie?"*

"That's what he used to call me when we were married."

Annie disliked the wistfulness in her mother's voice. "You mean when he wouldn't show you what the balance was in the checkbook?"

Margaret waved her hand and said, "That's all water under the bridge."

"Maybe the water upstream is just as muddy," Annie suggested.

Margaret scowled at her. "You don't have to be so hard on the man just because you hate his nephew."

Annie gasped in indignation. "My feelings for Hank have nothing to do with my relationship with Jesse! Mother, your marriage was only six weeks old when the man walked out on you—or have you conveniently forgotten that?"

"It was a long time ago, and you don't know the whole story," her mother said quietly. "I know you're probably not going to understand this, but—" she began, only to have Annie interrupt.

"Ma, stop! If you're going to tell me the reason he left you seven years ago was your fault, I don't want to hear it."

Margaret sighed. "Oh, Annie. It's seldom one person's fault when a marriage fails. Both of us were to blame. It takes two people to make a marriage work and two to break it."

"So what *are* you trying to tell me? That you can forget all the heartbreak you suffered and give Hank another chance?"

"It's not like that at all," she said a bit impatiently.

"Then what is it like? Yesterday I find you drinking beer and giggling like a schoolgirl with him. Today he's bringing you flowers and sneaking away before I get here."

"He didn't sneak away."

"I saw him leaving as I pulled around the corner, Ma."

"He had to be somewhere by eight. He only stopped by to bring me the flowers," Margaret said, tugging on the V-neck closing of her pajamas.

"Yeah—it saved him the five-dollar delivery charge," Annie said with a snicker.

Margaret huffed indignantly. "It was a nice gesture!"

"Nice and calculated," Annie said shrewdly.

Margaret waved her fingers, dismissing her remark. "There's no point in discussing this with you. It's obvious you don't want to understand."

Annie groaned. "Mother, I can't believe you're behaving like this!"

"Like what?"

"Like Hank Conover is a long-lost friend who's just returned from the dead," she said on a note of exasperation.

"Because he's a nice man."

Annie could only stare at her in disbelief. "You're not falling for him again, are you?" she asked warily.

"Just because I'm polite to my ex-husband doesn't mean I still carry the torch for him," she said in her annoying I'm-your-mother-and-I'm-right voice.

"Good, because technically you're still married to Neil," Annie reminded her.

"I know that," Margaret snapped a bit impatiently. "Hank and I have talked, that's all. We agree that seven years ago we both made mistakes."

"Yes. Yours was that you married a Conover."

Margaret ignored her comment. "Hank was fifty-four years old when he married me and he had never been married before. Do you understand what kind of an adjustment that must have been for him?"

The sympathy in her mother's voice grated on Annie's nerves. "Is that why he wouldn't give you any money?"

Margaret heaved a sigh of impatience. "There's more to it than that, Annie. He's not a selfish man."

Annie didn't respond, but simply raised her eyebrows dubiously.

"It's true he's cautious with money, but only because he's had to work hard for it all his life," she defended the older man.

Annie rolled her eyes. "Are you sure you haven't taken one too many pain pills?"

Margaret glared at her daughter. "Just because you and Jesse can't get along doesn't mean Hank and I have to snarl like a couple of lions every time we see each other."

"I get along with Jesse," Annie insisted, remembering all too clearly just how well they had gotten along that day. The more she thought about it, the more guilty she felt at jumping on her mother's case regarding Hank Conover. After all, who was she to criticize? All it had taken was for Jesse to lead her on a trip down memory lane, and she had fallen back into his arms.

She winced when her mother asked, "Where were you all day? I tried calling you several times, but there was no answer."

"I was earning my loan." Annie dropped down onto the green brocaded wing chair across from the sofa and sighed.

"What do you mean?"

"Jesse agreed to give me the money—but on one condition. I had to spend the day with him." She studied her mother's face to gauge her reaction. It was as blank as if she had said she'd had a hamburger and fries for dinner.

"I see."

"Aren't you even a little bit surprised?"

"Frankly I'm not, dear. Hank told me he had put in a good word for you. Instead of mocking him, you should be thanking him. He talked Jesse into giving you the money."

It was not what Annie wanted to hear. She didn't want to know that Jesse had needed some prodding to cough up the money for the dress. She had thought he had made the offer because of... She quickly squelched the idea. He didn't still harbor feelings for her, and it was foolish to fantasize that he did.

"You look disappointed," her mother said astutely.

"Why would I be? It doesn't matter why he's giving me the money," she stated nonchalantly. "At least he's agreed to help me out." She decided it would be wise to shift the focus of the conversation away from Jesse. "So what did you and Hank talk about while he was here?"

"Oh, this and that," Margaret answered evasively.

It was obvious that Annie's mother was not going to tell her any more about Hank's visit. They discussed the running of the café, and Annie promised her mother she'd check on the place tomorrow to make sure everything was going smoothly without Margaret's presence.

On the way home Annie thought about the irony of their situation. It was because of Hank and her mother's marriage that she had met Jesse in the first place. Now, because Jesse's and her paths had crossed once more, her mother and Hank had been thrown together.

Annie knew that as much as her mother wanted her to believe that her interest in Hank was purely platonic, there was something going on between the two of them. She had heard the lilt in her mother's voice when she spoke of him, and she had seen the sparkle in her eyes whenever she looked at him. And then there was her hair. The only time her mother put her hair up in a French twist was when she was on a manhunt.

Annie had seen the signs once too often. When one husband left, her mother would immediately go in search of another. What worried Annie was that Hank could simply be sweet-talking her mother to keep her from making any trouble for C & C. If that was the case, she needed to do something. She couldn't let her mother be hurt by a Conover again.

That's why when she got back to her apartment, she was relieved to find Joni didn't have a date. "Oh, good. You're home."

"Keith's working tonight," Joni told her. "What's up?"

"Have you ever been to a broomball game?"

"You know I'm not big on outdoor sports." She shivered at the thought.

"This one's indoors at the Cottage Grove ice arena. Want to go?"

"To play?"

"No, just to watch."

Joni eyed her suspiciously. "And who would we be watching?"

"Jesse."

"Ah." Her curls bounced as she plopped down onto the sofa.

"Ah nothing. It's not what you think," Annie protested, standing over her.

Joni flashed innocent eyes at her and asked, "And just what was it you did today in your old clothes that makes you want to go watch him play broomball tonight?"

"He put me to work painting." She went on to tell her about their trip to the farm, finishing with her visit to her mother, where she'd found Hank Conover leaving just as she was arriving. "So you see, I need to talk to Jesse."

Joni raised one eyebrow. "To let him know his uncle can't sweet-talk your mother into signing anything that would absolve C & C Homes of liability for her accident?"

Annie nodded. "Yes. What else would it be?"

Joni rolled her eyes and groaned.

"So, will you go with me?" Annie pleaded.

"I'll go." She jumped up from the sofa.

When Annie went to grab her keys, Joni stopped her. "Why don't we take my car? I need to get gas anyway."

Annie didn't protest.

When they arrived at the arena, her eyes automatically went to the ice, where the game was already in progress. All the players wore either white or blue jerseys. She spotted Jesse in blue with matching shin pads and a pair of white gloves. In his hands he wielded an orange-and-white broom.

"What's the object here?" Joni asked as they sat down on the bench seat.

"I think it's like hockey except instead of a little black puck they use that orange-and-black ball," Annie answered.

Instead of skating, the players ran across the ice. Annie watched them slip and slide as they whacked the ball with their brooms in an effort to get it into the netted goal. Many comic slides and spills later, there was a break in the action. As Jesse headed for the sidelines, he noticed Annie sitting in the bleachers and waved.

"I think they want us to come down," Joni remarked.

Annie realized why her roommate had said "they" and "us"—Todd Conover was right behind his brother. Before Annie could respond, Joni was on her feet and scampering down the bleacher steps.

"When did you get here?" Todd's question was directed at Joni, who didn't hesitate to lean over the short wall separating the ice from the spectators.

Jesse diverted Annie's attention. "I'm glad you came."

He peeled off the white gloves, revealing tiny dark hairs on the backs of his hands.

"I wanted to talk to you." Annie swallowed hard as she remembered how good those hands could make her feel.

"I only have a couple of minutes now." His cheeks were flushed, his hair slightly damp from the physical activity. Never had he looked more attractive to Annie. "What about when the game's over?"

Annie chewed on her lower lip. "You want me to wait for you?"

"Yes."

His stare was so intense, Annie needed to look away. She looked at the scoreboard at the end of the arena. "Are you winning?"

He nodded. "Three to two." He followed the direction of her gaze. "We're the home team."

A buzzer signaled the action was about to begin. "How about if I meet you at the front door about fifteen minutes after the game's over?" Jesse suggested.

Annie nodded and watched as he put his gloves back on and headed toward the center of the ice. Jesse the athlete was every bit as attractive as Jesse the construction worker, which her body didn't hesitate to acknowledge. Tremors of excitement raced through her.

When she and Joni were once again seated on the bleachers, Annie asked, "Did you enjoy your visit with Todd?"

"Mm-hmm." Joni answered absently. "He gave me a crash course in understanding broomball."

Annie hadn't missed Todd's little touches on her roommate's arm or his engaging smile. "Oh, that's what you called it? An explanation of the rules of the game?" Sarcasm edged her words.

"What did you think? That he was asking me out or something?"

"The thought did cross my mind," Annie admitted. "He's not the kind to let the fact that a girl is engaged stop him."

"But I'm not engaged," she said irritably.

Annie shifted uneasily. What was it with these Conover men? First her mother, now her roommate. "Well, you won't ever be if you start seeing Todd," she warned.

"I'm not going to date the man. For cripes' sake. All I did was talk to him," she protested. A bit too strongly for Annie's peace of mind.

Both Todd and Jesse scored goals to make the final score five to three. A jubilant Todd was at Jesse's side when he met Annie out front after the game. In his hands were a broken broom and a deflated ball.

"A bunch of us are going over to the Forty Club for a little victory celebration. Want to come along?" Todd inquired of the two women.

Before Annie could refuse, Joni accepted. "Sounds like fun."

Jesse must have read the hesitation in her eyes, for he asked her, "Is that what you want to do?"

It wasn't what she wanted, yet she needed to talk to Jesse—something that wouldn't be easy to do in the lobby of the noisy ice arena. And then there was Joni, sending her a signal that begged her not to say no. Before Annie could open her mouth, Joni accepted for both of them.

Annie reluctantly agreed. "That's fine."

Joni smiled gratefully, her eyes sparkling. On the way to the bar, Annie again warned her roommate about Todd Conover. Joni assured her she had no interest in Jesse's brother, yet when they arrived at the Forty Club, Joni took the chair next to his.

As several tables were shoved together to accommodate the broomball players, Jesse put his head close to Annie's and said in a low voice, "Why don't we sit at the bar?"

Annie knew it would be easier to talk to Jesse away from the large group. She allowed him to lead her to the bar, where they sat side by side on a pair of high stools. Annie ordered a mineral water while he ordered a beer.

He was the one to break the ice. "So what did you think of the game?"

"There was an awful lot of shoving and laughing," she answered.

"You should see us when we're not in league play. It's a fun game. You ought to try it sometime." He reached for a handful of peanuts and popped them in his mouth.

"I don't think I could stay on my feet on the ice," she admitted as the bartender served their drinks.

"Sure, you could if you had a pair of broomball shoes. They look like tennis shoes, but they have holes in the soles to help grip the ice." The bartender set two glasses in front of them. "It's like hockey only you don't have to put on skates."

"I don't know the first thing about hockey," Annie confessed.

"I could teach you."

The warmth in his eyes telegraphed a message to her blood, and heat spread through her. She quenched the dryness of her mouth with a sip of the mineral water. To avoid his penetrating gaze, she busied her hands with squeezing the lime perched on the rim of her glass, then poking at it with her straw as it floated in the clear liquid.

"I'd like to teach you a lot of things, Annie," he said, an unmistakable note of longing in his voice.

Memories of what had happened earlier that day came to her mind. She closed her eyes, hoping to dampen the rush of excitement those memories evoked. She needed to move the subject away from their relationship.

"Jesse, there's something I want to discuss with you," she said, looking down at her glass. "It's about your uncle."

Puzzled, he frowned. "You mean Hank?"

She met his gaze once more, nodding. "He's been over to see my mother."

"I know. You told me he brought her home after she fell on the ice yesterday."

"Yes, but he was over there again today. He brought her flowers."

"They were probably from C & C Custom Homes. After all, she did get hurt on our premises. By the way, she should call Roxy and make sure all the proper forms get filed for insurance purposes," he informed her.

Suddenly the idea that Hank was sweet-talking her mother to avoid any monetary claim her mother might make seemed rather absurd. It was Jesse who was responsible, not Hank.

He stared at her blankly. "Is that what's worrying you? That your mother won't get reimbursed for her accident?"

"No, what bothers me is Hank's interest in her. I don't think he went to see her as a representative of your company."

"What else would it be?" When she didn't answer right away, he added, "You think he's interested in your mother romantically?"

He made it sound as if it were a preposterous suggestion. What did he think? That her mother wasn't attractive to men?

Annoyed, Annie asked, "Why wouldn't he be? She's a woman and he's a Conover."

"Well, contrary to what you and your mother believe,

we Conovers don't chase everything in a skirt." A tension inched its way into their conversation.

"Look, I don't want to argue with you. I'm simply telling you this because I'm concerned about my mother," she told him. "She's vulnerable right now, and I don't want to see her get hurt again."

His eyes narrowed. "What makes you think he's going to hurt her?"

"She was devastated when he left seven years ago."

She couldn't have destroyed the ambience more perfectly if she had tried. "Don't you mean when she kicked him out?" he asked with a scowl.

"Are you insinuating it was my mother's fault that the marriage didn't work?" Annie bristled at the accusation in his tone.

"No, but your mother wasn't the only one who suffered. I don't know what went wrong between the two of them, but I do know that Hank took it hard."

Annie guessed that her mother had said more about the divorce to her than Hank had told Jesse. Arguing with Jesse over the rights and wrongs of her mother's marriage to his uncle was not going to solve anything.

"So do you agree with me then that it would be disastrous for the two of them to resurrect those feelings?"

"If you're asking me whether or not I want to see Hank get involved with your mother a second time, the answer is no. But that doesn't mean I'm going to do anything to stop it." She detected a hint of a warning in his words.

"I'm not asking you to interfere."

He pinned her with a penetrating gaze. "What are you asking me to do?"

Annie wasn't sure she knew the answer to that question. At first she had wanted Jesse to ask Hank what his intentions were toward her mother. But the more she thought about it, the more ridiculous it sounded.

Feeling rather awkward about even bringing up the subject, she said, "I don't want you to do anything."

"Good. Because it's none of my business who Hank sees."

"And you don't think it's any of mine, either, do you?"

"Nope." He took another long swallow of beer, then let his mug hit the bar with a thud.

A silence stretched between them. Annie wanted to defend her interest in her mother's relationship with Hank, but every argument she came up with sounded lame to her ears. Maybe Jesse was right. After all, her mother was fifty-four years old and had been married five times. Who was Annie to give her any advice in the romance department?

She took a long swig of the water until all that remained was the slice of lime on a bed of ice cubes. Seeing her glass was empty, Jesse asked, "Do you want another one?"

"No. I think I'll go home." She glanced across the bar to where Joni sat laughing with the rest of the broomball team. She had the uneasy feeling that her roommate wasn't going to want to leave.

Jesse had followed the direction of her gaze. "I can give you a ride."

"Then Joni would have to drive home alone."

"I doubt that," Jesse remarked dryly.

Annie slid down off the high stool, giving him a scornful glance, then went to find out for herself. As she expected, Joni didn't want to leave. Several of the broomball players, including Todd, offered to see that she got home safely. Annie marched back to the bar and accepted Jesse's offer.

Little was said as they walked to the parking lot. Once they were seated in the truck and Jesse had pulled out onto the highway, he asked, "Is that why you came to the game tonight—to tell me about your mother and Hank?"

"Yes."

Her answer produced a sigh from him.

Annie realized that her presence at the broomball game had misled him. He'd thought she had come to watch him play because he had invited her. "I thought you should know about it," she said weakly.

"Thanks for being so considerate of my feelings," he drawled sarcastically. Annie had no response.

They finished the ride in silence. At Annie's apartment building, Jesse insisted on walking her to her door despite her protests that she'd be all right on her own.

"Thanks for bringing me home," Annie recited dutifully as they stood outside the door. She reached inside her purse for her keys, only to have him take them out of her fingers.

"Which one?" he asked, holding up the small collection of keys.

"The biggest one," she answered, then watched as he inserted a key into the lock and opened the door for her. Then he dropped the keys back into her open palm.

She stood with the door open, debating whether she should invite him in. He gave no indication that he wanted to come inside, but stood staring at her with an unreadable expression on his face. As she flipped the switch on the overhead light in the hallway, she noticed the shadows beneath his eyes.

"You're tired," she commented, her voice softening.

"It's been a long day," he agreed, rubbing a hand across the back of his neck, as if to ease aching muscles.

"Would you like me to make you a cup of coffee before you drive home?" It was an automatic offer to someone who appeared in need of a jolt of caffeine.

His mouth curved into a crooked grin. "You never used to drink coffee."

"I've grown up, in case you haven't noticed." A sparkle in her eye told him she was in a teasing mood as she ushered him inside. "Why don't you take a seat on the sofa and I'll brew some," she said as he removed his jacket.

While she went to the kitchen and filled the coffee maker, he sat on her sofa leafing through a travel magazine that he found on the coffee table. Before she joined him, she put a Kenny G CD on the stereo with the intention that the music would be relaxing. As she met Jesse's gaze, however, she saw that was not the effect it had.

"The coffee will be ready in a few minutes," she announced.

When she would have taken the chair across from him, he said, "Come sit over here."

"I think it's probably safer here," Annie answered, making herself comfortable in the chair.

"You don't need to worry, Annie. I got your message loud and clear."

"What message?"

"Every time I come within two feet of you, you bristle."

"I do not," she denied, although she knew that what he said was true. What Jesse didn't realize was that she tensed because of the effect his presence was having on her, not because she didn't want him to touch her.

He reached for his coat. "Maybe the coffee's not such a good idea."

"Why not? Because I won't sit next to you on the couch?"

He closed the distance between them, placing a hand on either side of her as he pinned her in place. He leaned close to her and whispered, "Because I don't know if I can be in the same room with you and keep my hands off that delectable body of yours."

She stared up at him, mesmerized by the incredibly sensual shape of his mouth. She wanted to hear him speak, to watch his lips move.

"The day you stepped in the concrete at my job site, I wanted to be angry at you for making my life miserable. I wanted to convince you that you had made a mistake breaking our engagement. That's why I took you to the farm, because I wanted you to remember everything we had meant to each other."

"I haven't forgotten." Her voice was like velvet.

His eyes raked over her as his breath caressed her face. The sounds of Kenny G's saxophone drifted around them with a sensual rhythm that matched the beating of their hearts.

"Dance with me," Jesse commanded, pulling her to her feet.

Annie went into his arms, nestling her head against his shoulder. Together they swayed and shuffled to the music, their bodies pressed close together. When Jesse brushed his lips against her neck, shivers of pleasure went through her.

"Do you recognize this song?" he whispered in her ear before nibbling at her lobe.

"Mm-hmm."

"Don't Make Me Wait for Love" had been a favorite of theirs seven years ago. He lifted his head to gaze into her eyes, waiting for the answer to his unspoken question.

He pulled her even closer, so that Annie could feel his arousal, his undeniable need for her. A wave of desire ricocheted through her, inciting feelings that both excited and frightened her.

"See how much I need you, Annie?" he murmured close to her mouth, then covered her mouth with his perfectly shaped lips in an intoxicating kiss that had her melting into him. He slipped his tongue between her parted lips, stroking and exploring with a familiarity that defied the passage of seven years. She returned his kisses with a matching passion, replacing all logic with emotion. It felt so good, so right, to be in his arms.

"Yes," she murmured, sliding her hand around to the front of his shirt. She undid the top button, then pressed kisses into the exposed V of his skin. From deep in his chest came a moan of pleasure, and Annie arched against him in an unspoken invitation, tempting and tantalizing him until he slid his hand down over her hip and cupped her buttock. A primitive thrill shot through her as he pressed his hard and urgent need against her belly.

He lifted his head briefly and looked into her eyes. "I've never met a woman who can make me feel the way that you do. I want you Annie and I want you now."

"Here?"

"Wherever you'll have me."

She framed his face with her hands and covered his lips with hers, kissing him deeply. Then she led him to her bedroom. As soon as she had closed the door, he stripped the blouse from her shoulders, tossing it across the room. He hooked his thumbs beneath the straps of her bra, gently easing them down until the fullness of her breasts was no longer hidden. Her breath came in shallow little gasps as his hands cupped her naked flesh.

"They're every bit as beautiful as I remembered

them.'' Tremors of desire rocked his body as he caressed her.

Annie tangled her fingers in his hair and reveled in the exquisite sensations his touch provided. Together they stumbled toward the bed, discarding the rest of their clothes in a matter of seconds, never taking their eyes off each other.

To see Jesse naked nearly took Annie's breath away. It was true that at age twenty-seven he was heavier than he had been at twenty, but in her eyes he was the perfect specimen of man. She had thought so seven years ago; she felt the same way now as she gazed at his perfectly sculpted muscles. Looking at his hard, pulsing erection, she trembled at the thought of being possessed by him.

And she knew she would be his lover. It was as if destiny had decreed it that day his phone number had been placed on her ad.

She moaned in pleasure as he pulled her back into his arms. He kissed her again and again, stroking her intimately, finding the heat of her desire. An incredible surge of sensation swirled through her as his hands and tongue explored every inch of her.

As her body signaled her readiness, he lifted his head and gazed into her eyes. ''I want to make this last, but it's been so long....''

She felt the same sense of urgency, and to pretend otherwise was ridiculous when her body was sending him every signal he needed to make love with her. She guided him inside her, wrapping her arms around his back, her legs around his hips. He groaned as she moved beneath him, tightening around him.

''You feel so good,'' he whispered throatily.

Annie couldn't speak. Emotion choked back every attempt she made to tell him how much she had missed this part of their relationship. Being with Jesse was unlike anything she had ever experienced. It wasn't simply a union of two bodies, but of two souls. They moved together in perfect harmony in a unique rhythm that wouldn't let go until they had surrendered completely. As their desire burst into a million waves of ecstasy, tears trickled down her cheeks.

Jesse mistook the reason for them. "I'm sorry. I didn't mean to upset you." He kissed the teardrops away.

"You didn't. I just can't believe what happened," she said, her voice choked with emotion.

Again he misunderstood. "I thought you wanted it to happen." He eased himself away from her, and she felt a tremendous sense of loss.

As he lay flat on his back beside her, she rolled over on top of him, her damp, warm flesh sticking to his. With her swollen lips she planted a tender kiss on his mouth. "I love what happened between us."

With her touch the uncertainty flowed out of his body. He smoothed the hair back from her face and studied her flushed features. "It was always special between us, Annie."

"I know," she said softly, gazing down into his face in wonder. "I never realized how special it was until you were gone." This time, instead of kissing his lips, she traced them with her fingertips. Then she nuzzled his neck and slid in beside him, pulling the sheet up around them.

His arm automatically encircled her, pulling her into the crook of his arm where she nestled contentedly. They lay quietly in the afterglow of passion, waiting for their hearts to return to normal tempo.

It was just like old times, Annie thought. They hadn't needed any words between them, just the rhythm of their breathing, the feel of warm skin and the taste of passion lingering in their senses. And for the first time in seven years, it felt right to sleep in a man's arms.

Chapter Eleven

Jesse was a light sleeper. That's why when a door creaked, he awoke with a start. His first thought was that someone was in his house, which made him wonder why Sheba hadn't barked. Then he realized that he wasn't in his own bed. Warm breath fanned his back, bare legs entwined with his and a slender arm hung over his midsection. He was with Annie.

The squeaky door reminded him that although they were alone in her bed, they were not alone in the apartment. Joni had the bedroom next door. Jesse glanced at his watch. It read 2:30.

He rolled over onto his back, carefully shifting Annie so that her head rested in the V created by his arm and shoulder. When she made a soft sound of protest, he kissed her forehead and cuddled her.

It felt so right to have her sleeping beside him. While she slept, he studied her face. It was a face he had committed to memory, a face that had gotten him through the months of regimented daily life in the military. A perfectly shaped nose, a defiant little chin that had a way of tilting stubbornly when she didn't get her way and a heart-shaped mouth he couldn't resist.

Carefully he shifted her head onto the pillow at his

elbow. When he tried to extricate his legs from hers, she stirred. As he was slipping a leg into his jeans, she awoke.

"Jesse? Where are you going?" Annie stared at him. She hadn't expected he would leave in the middle of the night. She wanted to cook him breakfast and talk about what had happened between them.

"I have to leave, Annie."

"Why?"

"Because I have to work in the morning. Besides, you have a roommate." As soon as he had zipped his jeans, he sat on the edge of the bed. "I don't want to go," he told her, caressing the bare shoulder peeking out of the covers.

Immediately doubts began to cloud her happiness. She sat forward, wrapping the sheet around her. Was that all it really was? A matter of obligations and privacy?

Some of her insecurity must have shown, for he said, "I'd ask you to come home with me, but it's almost three o'clock in the morning. By the time I get there, I'll only have a couple of hours before I have to get up. I have a very busy schedule tomorrow." He kissed her slowly and deeply. "I would rather you spent tomorrow night with me—then there won't be any interruptions."

She nodded in understanding, although she wasn't really sure.

He gave her lips a quick kiss. "How early can I pick you up tomorrow night?" he asked.

"You name a time," she suggested.

"Maybe we should make it eight. I have an appointment in Rochester tomorrow afternoon, and I want to make sure I'm back in time."

"All right."

With one last kiss, he said goodbye. As Annie watched him leave, feelings that had seemed so clear in the aftermath of their lovemaking now seem muddled. As she fell back against the pillows, she wondered just what it was that was happening between her and Jesse.

"DID YOU KNOW you left the coffeepot on last night?" Joni announced when Annie padded into the kitchen the following morning.

"What time did you get home?" Annie asked, opening the refrigerator to get the carton of orange juice.

"A little after midnight," Joni answered. "Your door was closed, and I didn't think I should interrupt."

Annie poured herself a glass of juice. "You saw Jesse's truck out front."

"Is everything okay?" Joni asked cautiously.

Annie sat down at the table. "Everything's okay." She took a sip of her juice, then grinned like a Cheshire cat. "Everything's wonderful."

"Then you got this business with your mother and Hank resolved?"

"No. Jesse and I decided that it was none of our business." She tucked her feet up on the chair so that she could wrap her legs inside the robe.

"Then I take it the wonderful stuff is what's happening between you and Jesse," Joni deduced with a sly grin.

Annie lifted her glass in a salute. "Bingo. It's like seven years hasn't passed. When we were together last night, everything clicked. You know what I mean?"

"I'm really happy for you, Annie," Joni said sincerely.

Annie noticed her roommate was not her usual perky self. "Do I want to know what happened between you and Todd last night?"

"Nothing happened," Joni assured her. "We talked, we laughed, we danced."

"Danced?"

"Yeah. He decided I needed to know how to line dance, so he put some country-western music on the jukebox—much to the dismay of the rest of the guys, who were trying to watch a football game on TV."

"What about Keith?"

Joni sighed and pushed her hair back off her forehead. "We've been going together three years with the understanding that we'll get married, yet every time I bring up the subject, he manages to avoid talking about it. I don't know what's worse—dating a guy who says he believes in marriage but refuses to be pinned down, or dating one who tells you up front there's no chance wedding bells are going to ring."

"Does that mean you're considering dating Todd?"

She shook her head. "Uh-uh. He's not my type."

"I agree." Annie pulled a banana from the bowl of fruit in the center of the table and started to peel it.

"So what happens next with you and Jesse?"

"I'm seeing him again tonight." At the thought, a grin lit up her face. "So if I don't come home, don't worry about me, okay?" She broke off a piece of the banana and popped it in her mouth.

Joni shook her head reflectively. "What a difference a day makes," she marveled.

Annie washed down the banana with a sip of juice. "I feel like I should pinch myself. Five days ago I didn't know Jesse was even in the same city. Now..." She trailed off on a dreamy sigh.

"And your paths probably wouldn't have crossed if you hadn't wanted to sell your dress," Joni remarked.

At the mention of her dress, Annie straightened. "That's right. I'm supposed to meet Jesse this morning to get the money."

"Are you still going to ask him for it?"·

"I don't know. I hadn't thought about it until now." It didn't take her long to say, "No, I'll wait for the insurance to pay for it." She got up off the chair and went to the phone. "I'd better call him before he leaves for Rochester."

After several attempts she said, "It's busy. Maybe I'll just run over and see him...bring him some bagels and cream cheese. I was looking for an excuse to see him today." She gave Joni a wink and went to get dressed.

JESSE HAD NEVER FELT better than he did that morning. As he showered, he savored the memories from the night before. After all these years he had finally found Annie again. She was in his thoughts as he got ready for work. It was a good thing he had a full schedule today. He needed time to pass quickly so he could be with her again.

After grabbing a quick cup of coffee, he was about to leave for work when the doorbell rang. When he went to answer it, he found Caroline on the front step.

"Hi, Jesse. I've come for the clothes."

For a moment he was puzzled, then he remembered his conversation with Hank. "You mean the donation for charity." He gestured for her to step inside. "I've put the stuff in a couple of suitcases. They're old but they're sturdy. I figured there's probably someone who can use them."

He retrieved the two pieces of luggage from the hallway closet. "If you'll get the door, I'll carry these out for you," he told Caroline.

"Great." She gave him a grateful smile as she held the door open.

ALL THE WAY OVER to Jesse's, Annie thought about what had happened between them last night. The closer she got to his house, the less confident she felt about their relationship. Last night they hadn't really talked about what would happen next. She had simply assumed that he wanted what she wanted—to be together. Yet now in the light of day, her doubts grew like ugly weeds in a flower garden.

After all, he hadn't even asked about her trip to Florida. Had he just assumed she wouldn't be going, or was he just taking what she had to give, knowing that in a few days she'd be gone? It was uncertainty Annie didn't need at the moment.

Maybe it was a good idea she was going to see him this morning. She could put to rest any fears she had that last night hadn't been as special for him as it was for her.

However, she never spoke to Jesse that morning. Just as she was about to turn into his driveway, she saw him come out of the house with a woman—a very attractive female with dark hair. She wore a white coat and had a red scarf wrapped around her throat. She smiled at Jesse as he carried two suitcases out of the house. Annie's stomach turned over. She slammed on the brakes and quickly took a left instead of a right. Across the street she sat, staring at the two of them in her rearview mirror.

She saw Jesse put the suitcases in the trunk of the woman's little red sports car. Then she saw the brunette give him a hug before climbing inside.

Annie felt sick to her stomach. No wonder he hadn't wanted her to come home with him last night. He had another woman staying in his house.

With tears pooling in her eyes, Annie moved her foot from the brake to the gas pedal. Without stopping to say a single word to Jesse, she drove back home. After years of fighting it, the inevitable had happened. She had become her mother's daughter.

IT WAS NEARLY NOON by the time Annie had pulled herself together and come up with what she thought was the perfect action to take. She called Jesse's office.

"Hi, this is Annie Jamison. Is Jesse in?" She had to struggle to keep her voice steady.

"Gee, I'm sorry, Annie, but he had to drive to Rochester today," Roxy said, confirming what she already knew.

Annie groaned. "Oh, no. I hope he didn't forget about my money." She was careful to make sure her tone held a helpless plea for sympathy, not a demand for attention.

"Are you talking about the money for your dress?"

"Mm-hmm. He told me Saturday that he would reimburse me for the loss of my dress first thing Monday morning. I've been waiting and waiting, and when I didn't hear from him I thought I'd better call. He didn't leave any money for me, did he?"

There was a pause as Roxy searched her desk. "No, I don't think so. I might be able to reach him by phone, although I have to warn you, it'll take a while."

She moaned lightly. "I only have until two o'clock to pay for my airline ticket or I'll lose the reservation." It was a fib, but a necessary one in Annie's estimation.

There was another short pause, then Roxy said, "I could get the money for you. I do all the bookkeeping for C & C."

"I don't want to get you into any trouble," Annie said hesitantly.

"You won't. I'm sure Jesse wanted you to have it. He probably just forgot to leave me instructions."

Annie grinned. "Why, thank you, that is so sweet of you!" she gushed.

"It's the least I can do, considering the dress wouldn't

have been stolen if I hadn't wanted to buy it," Roxy told her.

So Annie did as Roxy suggested. By the time she reached the offices of C & C Custom Homes, there had been no word from Jesse. Roxy handed Annie an envelope with an enclosed check and wished her good luck on her new job. Annie smiled and went home to finish packing.

IT WAS DARK by the time Jesse got home from Rochester. Roxy had already gone home for the day. The message light was blinking on his answering machine, which didn't surprise him. Roxy usually left a brief message before going home each evening. He grabbed a beer from the refrigerator, then sat down to listen.

"Hi, Jesse. I put your telephone messages under the crystal paperweight on your desk." Jesse's eyes automatically sought out the pink slips secured by the blue globe. "Mike Patterson called to say he had set a date for a closing on the Roberts place—November 30. I wrote it on your calendar." Jesse glanced at the calendar and saw the time and place written in red.

"Other than that, it was a pretty quiet Monday. Oh— one other thing. I gave Annie the money for her dress. I figured you had forgotten about it, so I took care of it for you."

Jesse nearly choked on his beer. He punched the Rewind button and replayed Roxy's message. "I gave Annie the money for her dress."

"What?" Confused, he sat forward. She had to be mistaken. Why would Annie want the money after everything that had happened last night? She wouldn't need it, not if she had decided against taking the job on the cruise ship. And certainly after their night together she wasn't going to leave on Wednesday. He walked over to Roxy's desk and pulled the drawer. It was locked.

He dug in his pocket until he found a small set of keys. He unlocked the drawer, then pulled out the ledger. It only took a matter of seconds before he found it. The carbon copy of a check written out to Annie Jamison for the amount of fifteen hundred dollars.

Pain knifed through him. How could she have taken the money after last night? Did this mean that nothing had changed between them…that she was still planning to take the job on the cruise ship? He needed some answers and he needed them now. He grabbed his jacket and flew out the door.

"I'M SPENDING THE NIGHT at my mother's," Annie announced to her roommate as she lugged a small suitcase from her bedroom.

"I thought you had a date with Jesse." Joni's brow wrinkled in confusion.

"It's off, and if he comes looking for me, don't tell him where I am," she instructed, tugging her anorak over her long-sleeved T-shirt.

"Wait a minute. You just can't go running out of here without telling me what's going on."

"I don't want to talk about it," Annie said stubbornly, pulling her hair out from the anorak and flipping it back.

"You can't expect me to lie for you without knowing why," Joni argued. "Come on, Annie. Tell me what's wrong."

Annie closed her eyes briefly, took a deep breath and said, "He's a jerk, that's what's wrong. Please don't ask me to talk about it." She struggled to swallow back the tears.

Joni's arm came around her protectively. "All right.

You don't have to talk about it, but do you think you should go to your mother's? I mean, what if Hank is there?"

"He's not. I already talked to my mom." Annie sniffled and Joni handed her a tissue.

"Are you sure this is how you want to handle this?"

Annie blew her nose. "I don't want to see him."

"Okay, but what if he's persistent? What if he won't leave when I tell him you're not here?" Her eyes widened at the thought. "What if I can't get rid of him?"

"Tell him I've left town," she said irrationally.

"Do you think he'll believe that?"

She shrugged. "Who cares?"

Joni eyed her suspiciously. "Are you still going to Florida?"

"Yes. I called the airlines and I have a seat on a flight Wednesday morning." Seeing the concern in her roommate's eyes, she added, "I'm doing the right thing."

"You're not going to leave without saying goodbye to me, are you?"

Annie shook her head. "I was hoping you'd take me to the airport. Or are you working?"

"No, it's not a problem. It's been slow at the temp service."

"What about the telegrams?"

"I have one tonight and one on Thursday. If I'm lucky, I'll be gone when Jesse comes looking for you."

Annie glanced at her watch. "I better go." She hugged Joni. "Thanks for being such a good friend."

"Call me, okay?"

Annie nodded and dragged her suitcase out the door.

JESSE TOOK THE STEPS to Annie's apartment two at a time. When he reached her door, he was breathing heavily. He wasted no time catching his breath before knocking.

He was taken by surprise when the door opened and Joni stood before him wearing a fairy costume. On her head was a wig of waist-length golden curls with a tiara perched at the crown. In her hand was a wand, and across her chest was written Fairy Godmother. If he wouldn't have been so angry, he could have laughed at the picture she made.

"Jesse, h-hi," she stammered. Seeing the expression on his face, she said, "I guess Annie didn't tell you I do singing telegrams, did she?"

He shook his head. "Where is she?"

"She's not here."

He looked past her shoulder, prompting Joni to say, "Would you like to come in and look for yourself?"

"No," he said dejectedly. "Do you know where she's at?"

She fidgeted with the wand in her hands. "She asked me not to tell you, Jesse."

He raked a hand across his hair and tried to maintain his cool. "Why?"

"Look, it's not fair for you two to put me in the middle of all of this," Joni pleaded for understanding. "And I really need to leave or I'm going to be late for work."

Realizing it would do no good to press the issue, he said, "Will you tell her I need to talk to her?"

"Sure. But I think you ought to know she's leaving for Florida on Wednesday."

"Not if I have anything to say about it."

ANNIE WAS STIR-FRYING vegetables in her mother's wok when the doorbell rang. Quickly she lifted the kitchen curtain and peeked outside. Her heart leapt into her throat at the sight of Jesse's truck in the driveway.

She hurried into the living room. "Mom, get the door. It's Jesse," she said in a frantic whisper.

"Annie, I have crutches!"

"I don't want him to know that I'm here."

"Your car's in the driveway."

Annie groaned and went to answer the door, her heart pumping wildly in her chest. Her mouth went dry, and she found it difficult to swallow.

"Annie, let me in. We need to talk," he pleaded when she opened the door but kept the dead bolt in place.

"Go away, Jesse. I don't want to see you."

"Why did you take the money?"

"You told me I could have it."

"That's not what I mean. Why do you need the money?"

"Because I'm going to work on the cruise ship. I leave Wednesday."

"Then Joni was right? You still plan to go?"

"Why wouldn't I?"

There was a long silence. "Didn't last night mean anything to you?"

She wanted to tell him the truth, that last night had been the first time in seven years that she had felt as if everything was truly right in her world. That making love with him made her realize that the answer to her dreams didn't lie on a cruise ship. Yet she couldn't.

Because she knew that to Jesse, last night had just been a physical experience. She had been an object for his pleasure, a way for him to prove that he could still get her back if he wanted her. She had wanted to believe him when he had said there had never been an affair with Roxy. This morning had proved how wrong she was to trust him. To place her future in his hands would be emotional suicide.

So instead of telling him she wanted to spend the rest of her life with him, she told him, "Sure. It was fun, but it doesn't change the fact that I have a job waiting for me in Florida." A stabbing pain knifed through her as she uttered the words.

"So last night didn't mean a thing except a good time to you?"

She sensed hurt in his voice and she almost retracted her words, but then she remembered the brunette coming out of his house with the suitcases. She said nothing.

He jiggled the handle. "Annie, why won't you open the door and look at me?"

The frustration in his voice caused her skin to tingle. "I told you. I don't want to see you. Please go away, Jesse."

To her surprise he did as she suggested, not uttering another single word. She heard his footsteps fade away. The sound of a car door slamming and an engine starting told her he was truly gone.

Wearily she padded out to face her mother, who gave her a look she remembered well from childhood. It said *I'm not pleased with the way you behaved.*

Annie held up her hands defensively. "Don't say anything, Ma."

Her mother didn't listen. "Don't you think that was rather childish?"

Annie dropped down on the sofa, clutching a throw pillow to her bosom. "I had to do it. It was the only way to get rid of him."

"Is that what you really want—to get rid of him?" Margaret asked gently.

"No." She tried to hold back the tears but couldn't.

Sobs racked her body as she cried. Her mother lowered herself beside her and gathered her into her arms, rocking her ever so slightly, smoothing her hand over Annie's hair as she had done so often as a child.

When the tears were spent, Margaret asked, "Do you feel like talking about it?"

Annie looked down at the tissue in her hand. "I love him, Mom, but I can't trust him."

Margaret sighed. "You can't get past what happened seven years ago?"

"I did get past that. It's what happened this morning." She told her mother about the woman she saw coming out of Jesse's home. "Nothing's changed, Mom. *He* hasn't changed."

"Well, you did say she was leaving…maybe after what happened with you, he asked her to leave," her mother said weakly.

"That's the whole point, Mother. Nothing should have happened with me if he was in a relationship with another woman. I mean, if he had her living with him, she must have been someone special to him." Her voice broke, and the tears threatened to fall again. She took a deep breath to fight them back. "I don't want a man like that in my life."

"No, and you deserve better."

She sniffed. She wrinkled her nose and sniffed again. Then she jumped up and ran into the kitchen to unplug the wok. "Just great. Burned stir-fry."

"Turn on the exhaust fan," Margaret called out from the other room.

Annie dumped the blackened vegetables into the garbage, then rummaged through her mother's refrigerator. With a sigh she returned to the living room. "It looks like we either order pizza or settle for soup and sandwiches."

Margaret patted the cushion beside her. "Come sit down, dear. We'll have something delivered."

Like a small child in need of comfort, Annie slid in beside her mother. She leaned her head back against the cushion and closed her eyes. "I should have known better than to trust a Conover."

Margaret reached over to pat her hand. "The truth is, Annie, men don't know how to be faithful."

"I know, Ma. It's a gender defect." She exhaled a long sigh. "There's got to be some men out there who are monogamous."

"Well, sure, there are," her mother retorted with a surprising touch of optimism. "Your father was." She sighed. "Maybe that's why none of my relationships have worked. I can't seem to find a man as good as he was."

Annie turned to face her mother. "He really was a good guy?"

"Of course he was. Why would you think he wasn't?"

Annie shrugged. "Maybe because I can't remember him. All I have are the pictures and the stories you've told me."

"The stories are true, Annie. Your father was a gentleman. The way he fussed over me!" She shook her head reflectively, a smile tugging at her mouth. "On cold days like this, he'd warm up the car for me, drop me off at the door of the grocery store then go park the car and pick me up when we were finished shopping." She chuckled. "One time he even carried me into the movie theater because it was slushy outside and I had worn my new shoes."

"You still miss him, don't you?"

"I do." She squeezed Annie's hand. "But I just have to look at you and I know that a part of him is still with me."

Annie reached over to give her mother a hug. "I love you, Mom." Then she sat back and stared at her pensively. "Do you know this is the first time you've ever really talked about the men in your life with me?"

"It is?" She seemed surprised by Annie's comment.

Annie nodded. "You always shut me out." A lump of emotion rose in her throat.

"I don't mean to," Margaret said gently. "It's just that I've made such a mess of my life, I didn't want any of that to rub off on you."

"Your life's not a mess," Annie contradicted her.

"The romance part is," she said with a mirthless chuckle. "I'm sorry it didn't work out with Jesse."

Annie shrugged. "It's not your fault."

"I'm not so sure that's true," her mother said uneasily.

"What are you talking about?"

"I haven't exactly been the best role model for you. I mean, look at my love life." She chuckled mirthlessly. "It's no wonder you picked the wrong men—I've been doing it for the last twenty years. And if I hadn't brought Hank home, you would have never met Jesse."

"Mom, about Hank..." she began, only to have her mother stop her.

"You don't need to worry about me and Hank. Nothing's going to happen between us."

"Are you sure?"

"He has a girlfriend."

"So you're not interested in him?"

Her mother sighed. "He's a nice man, Annie. I know your relationship with Jesse has made you think that all the Conover men are bad, but I'm not so sure that's the case with Hank."

Annie rubbed her forehead. "I really don't want to talk about the Conovers anymore, Mom. On Wednesday I leave for my job on the cruise ship. It's a new start for me.''

''And a good one.'' Again her mother patted her hand. ''If I were your age, I'd do the same thing. Have fun, travel, be carefree.''

In her present state of mind, Annie wondered if she would ever feel carefree again. She had a feeling the past would haunt her for a long, long time.

Chapter Twelve

Jesse glanced at the clock beside his bed and groaned. It was 3:17 a.m., and he was still awake. He punched his pillow with his fist and rolled over, trying not to think about Annie. It was impossible. For the past four hours he had done nothing but think about her, which was why he was still awake.

Over and over his mind replayed the events of the past five days. He had thought that by taking her out to the farm and showing her the house in Dakota County he could resurrect the old feelings they once shared. He wanted to convince her that the love they had once felt for each other had been too good to throw away, and he thought he had been successful.

Last night had been the most wonderful night of his life. He didn't want to believe that she could make love with him with such passion and not feel more than a passing attraction for him.

His body ached at the memory of how good she felt in his arms. With one simple touch she could create a fire inside him that made nothing else matter except that they spend the rest of their lives together. Lying in her bed last night had driven every rational thought from his mind.

Love *did* do crazy things to people. He was living

proof. All it had taken was one night in her bed, and he was ready to forgive anything she had done. He could forget that seven years ago she had tossed him aside as if he were nothing more than a pair of old shoes that no longer fit.

For he was in love with Annie. Despite all the heartache she had caused him, he hadn't stopped wanting her. However, there was one emotion that could match his love for her, and that was his pride. He wasn't going to let her make a fool of him again.

He would get over her. He had done it before; he could do it again. This time it would be easier. He was a man who learned from experiences. He would forget...he would...

The alarm woke Jesse two hours later. With a groan he crawled over to the edge of the bed and turned it off. For several minutes he sat with his head in his hands, willing the throbbing to stop. He pulled open the drawer on the nightstand and found the bottle of painkillers. He shook a couple into his hand and was about to go into the bathroom for a glass of water when the phone rang.

"It's Hank." Jesse heard the anxiety in his uncle's voice.

"What are you doing calling me at five-thirty in the morning?" he grumbled, grimacing as he worked tense neck muscles.

"They found the truck!"

That woke Jesse up in a hurry. "Where?"

"About forty miles north of the city. It was abandoned on some dirt road. A farmer spotted it and called the cops."

"Was Annie's dress inside?"

"I don't know. The police didn't say. I need to go get it. Can you give me a ride?"

"I'll be over in a half hour."

"GOOD GRIEF! They wrecked it!" Hank exclaimed in frustration when he saw the pick-up. "They must have hit a pole or something." He studied the smashed front end. "It's going to have to be towed back to town."

Jesse didn't bother to examine the damage done to the truck, but went directly to the passenger side and looked in the window. Annie's dress wasn't there.

He turned to the police officer who had accompanied them to the site and asked, "You didn't find a wedding dress lying on the front seat, did you?"

The officer gave him a sympathetic smile. "Sorry."

As soon as Hank had examined every wheel on the truck, he walked over to Jesse and said, "I guess it could be worse." He removed his baseball cap and scratched his head.

"The wedding dress isn't in the cab," Jesse stated.

"Why would it be?" He crooked a finger for Jesse to follow him. "I put it in the back."

Jesse followed him to the rear of the truck, where Hank unlocked the topper. The hinges squeaked as he raised the hatch and lowered the tailgate.

"Look. They didn't touch anything back here," Hank said, sifting through a pile of building supplies. "They must have been kids out for a joyride." He crawled up on his knees to reach the plastic dress bag that had slipped behind a stack of boxes.

He held the garment bag up for Jesse's inspection. "Is this what you're looking for?"

Jesse unzipped the bag and looked inside. It was Annie's dress, all right, and not a mark was on it. He leaned a hip against the tailgate and shook his head. "Do you know how much trouble this one dress has caused me?"

Hank rubbed his chin thoughtfully. "What are you going to do with it?"

"Give it back."

"But you said you already gave her the money."

"I didn't *give* her anything. She *took* it," Jesse snapped irritably.

Hank slowly shook his head back and forth. "Are you telling me you let that little slip of a thing get the better of you?"

"Before you start dishing out any advice in the romance department, I suggest you practice what you preach," Jesse advised him.

Hank stared at him with an innocent look on his face. "What's that supposed to mean?"

"I heard about your little visits to Margaret," he said dryly.

"It's not what you think," his uncle said, rushing to the defense. "I was just making sure she was all right."

"And does Margaret know that's what you were doing?"

"Yes. I told her about Caroline," he stated calmly, although Jesse guessed from the sparkle that came into his uncle's eye at the mention of Margaret Jamison's name that he wasn't totally immune to his ex-wife.

"She's had another husband since you," Jesse told him. "That makes five, doesn't it?"

"Yup. She goes through men faster than this old truck burns oil," Hank commented. "That's why I warned you to stay away from Annie. Those Jamison women are fickle."

Jesse grimaced. He didn't want to think that Annie was like her mother. "So what do you suppose I should do with this?" He gestured to the plastic dress bag.

"You gotta give it back."

In the mood Jesse was in, the last thing he wanted to do was go see Annie. However, after the way she had treated him, maybe she deserved to have another kink tossed into her plans. He wondered what she'd do if he did ask for his money back.

Jesse shrugged. "She's probably already spent the money."

"Well, then she better hope she can sell the dress, because the insurance company won't pay off now that it's been found."

Jesse knew his uncle was right about the claim. And then there was the fact that Annie hadn't hesitated to connive him out of the eighteen hundred dollars. Maybe he should give her a taste of her own medicine.

"I doubt she's going to find anyone who'll pay eighteen hundred for that." Jesse glanced at the plastic garment bag with distaste.

"So what are you going to do?"

"I suppose I should do what every good businessperson would do...foreclose on the loan if there isn't sufficient collateral," he told his uncle, squinting as the sun broke through a bank of gray clouds.

"You want me to take care of it?" He stood tall, pulling up on the waistband of his jeans and pushing out his chest.

Jesse stood. "You don't mind?"

"Consider it done, boss."

ALL MORNING LONG Annie expected Jesse to show up at her mother's house. He didn't. As she washed up the dishes for her mother, she heard a car pull up into the driveway. It wasn't a car but a pick-up—Hank's. She glanced out the window in time to see him jump down from the cab.

Wiping her hands on a towel, Annie went to get the door.

"Hi, Annie," Hank greeted her with a guarded smile.

She didn't want to invite him in, but her mother had already seen his truck. Annie worried that if she sent him away, her mother might beat her with a crutch.

"Mom's in the living room." Annie gestured for him to take a seat.

"Hi, Margie. How's the ankle?" he asked with a twinkle in his eye that reminded Annie of the gleam Jesse flashed at her.

"It's better, thanks," her mother answered like a schoolgirl waiting for a date for the prom. "I'm surprised to see you here. I thought you'd be working."

"I am," he told her. "I'm here on official business."

That brought a frown to Margaret's face. Annie decided it was time she left. "I'll be in the kitchen making coffee." She started to leave, but Hank stopped her.

"No, wait. You're the one I came to see."

Annie knew the puzzled look on her mother's face was mirrored on hers. "Me?"

"Jesse wanted me to tell you—" he began, but Annie cut him off.

She raised her hands defensively as if she were a cop stopping traffic. "I don't want to hear anything that Jesse has to say," she told him in no uncertain terms. "If you came to plead his case, you've wasted your time."

"This isn't about your love life. It's business," he said bluntly. "My stolen pick-up has been found."

Annie felt ridiculously small. She could feel a blush spread over her face. She had thought Jesse had sent his uncle to try to patch up things in their relationship when the only reason he had come was to tell her the stolen pick-up had been recovered.

Hank stood staring at her, waiting for her reaction. Suddenly she remembered the reason why. "Are you saying that my dress has been found?"

Hank grinned. "It has. Wait here and I'll go get it."

Annie wanted to ask what kind of shape the dress was in, but he was gone before she had the chance. When he returned, he carried the plastic garment bag in his hands, an even bigger grin on his face.

Annie took it from him and draped it over the dining-room table. With trembling fingers she unzipped the bag and pulled out the dress. She held it up, examining it carefully.

"Not a thread's been touched," Hank boasted proudly. "You know what this means." It wasn't a question, but a warning.

It didn't take Annie long to figure out the message behind the sinister grin. "Jesse wants his money back?" she asked weakly.

"He says you can keep the three-hundred deposit because of all the inconvenience you've been through," Hank answered. "You do have the rest of it, don't you?"

Anger swelled in Annie, destroying any hope that she would be logical about the situation. Who did Jesse Conover think he was, sending his uncle over to do his dirty work for him? She carefully set the wedding dress down and turned to face Hank.

"You tell Jesse that if he wants it, he can come get it," she snapped irritably, forgetting that only last night she would have done anything to avoid seeing her ex-fiancé. "He gave the money to me as a loan, which I could repay in thirty days. You tell him I'll have the money back to him then and not one day before."

Hank tugged on his ear, saying, "The way I understand

it, it wasn't exactly a loan.'' He let the innuendo drop, deliberately raising Margaret's curiosity.

"What's he talking about, Annie?'' her mother asked, worry lines crinkling her face.

"It's nothing, Ma. I can handle this,'' Annie answered.

Hank wasn't about to let her sidestep the issue. "Jesse didn't exactly *loan* her the money.'' In an aside to Annie he said, "Do you want to tell her or should I?''

"Jesse said I could have that money,'' she stated firmly, her arms folded across her chest.

"That's not the way I heard it. I heard that when Jesse was out of town, you snuck over to the office and soft talked Roxy into giving it to you,'' he accused. "Boy, you must be pretty good if you can get Roxy to disburse unauthorized funds.''

"Annie! Is this true?'' her mother demanded.

"It's not what it sounds like, Ma. Jesse told me I could have the money.''

"We're getting off track here,'' Hank interrupted their discussion. "The point is, your collateral for the loan has disappeared.''

"No, it hasn't,'' Annie retorted. "It's right here.'' She gestured to the wedding dress.

Hank shook his head. "The loan was based on the insurance-policy claim—that was sure money. You selling that wedding dress isn't.''

"I can sell this dress,'' Annie stated confidently.

Hank's look told her he thought the chances were slim or next to none.

"I can!'' she insisted. "Then I'll pay back Jesse every penny I borrowed—even the three hundred he left as a deposit.'' In a grand, dramatic gesture she marched over to the front door and held it open. "Now I'd like for you to leave," she said with her chin held high.

Annie half expected her mother to stop Hank from leaving. To her relief she didn't. As soon as he had stepped out the door, Annie slammed it shut. She stomped into the spare bedroom, grabbed her suitcase from under the bed and shoved her clothes back inside. There was no longer any need to hide from Jesse.

Quite the opposite. She was going to be in his face so badly he was going to wish he had never sent his uncle to see her.

ANNIE SCRAPED together the money. It helped that she hadn't picked up her airline ticket yet. All she had to do was deliver the money to Jesse.

At five o'clock she pulled up outside the offices of C & C Custom Homes. When she went inside, she found Roxy at one of the desks. She smiled when she saw Annie.

"This is a surprise. How are you?" Roxy asked.

"I'm fine," she answered politely.

"I heard they finally found your dress."

Annie could see the relief in the other woman's eyes. "Yup, it's back."

Roxy acted as if she didn't have a clue what had gone on between her and Jesse. Annie gave her the benefit of the doubt and said, "I need to see Jesse. Do you know where I can find him?"

"I believe he's out at the St. Michael site. I'm not sure when he'll get back."

"Would it be all right if I waited?"

Roxy hesitated briefly, then said, "Sure. There's coffee

if you'd like some.'' She glanced over to a small alcove where a coffee maker and a stack of foam cups sat.

"None for me right now, thanks."

They made small talk for several minutes, then Roxy had to excuse herself to answer the phone. Annie picked up a magazine from the stack on the coffee table in the waiting area and began to thumb through it. It was filled with pictures of new homes and remodeling ideas.

"I'm really sorry, Annie, but I have to leave," Roxy announced as she put down the receiver. "I have a night class I have to attend. You're welcome to stay and wait for Jesse, but I'm not sure how long that's going to be."

Annie had the feeling that she hoped she wouldn't take her up on her offer. "I don't want to create a problem for you."

"Oh, it's no problem. I just hate to see you sitting here all alone."

A pair of headlights shone through the plate-glass windows. "Maybe that's Jesse now." Roxy walked over to the windows.

Annie's heartbeat increased.

"It's him." Roxy breathed a heavy sigh of relief. "Now I don't need to feel badly about leaving."

Annie's breath caught in her throat when he stepped through the door. With a five-o'clock shadow darkening his jaw and a baseball cap cocked at an angle on his head, he looked dangerously attractive. Was it any wonder she had fallen into his arms so easily for a second time?

When he saw Annie, his eyes darkened. Roxy didn't miss the looks that passed between the two of them. If she had any business to discuss with Jesse, it wasn't a priority. She made as quick a departure as possible, leaving the two of them alone.

"I didn't expect to find you here," Jesse said as he shrugged out of his work jacket.

"What did you think? That you could send your gorilla to get rid of me?"

He walked over to her, an ominous look in his eyes that had her rising to her feet. She wouldn't give him the advantage of being able to look down at her.

"I think you've got it backward. You're the one who wanted to get rid of me. Remember?" he said, his face only inches away from hers. "What did you expect me to do? Come running after you a second time so you could slam another door in my face?"

Annie felt a twinge of guilt, but that quickly disappeared when she thought about the brunette she had seen leaving his house. "What was I supposed to do? Welcome you with open arms and thank you for getting rid of your other girlfriend so you could make room for me?" she asked snidely.

He shoved hands to his trim waist. "And just what does that mean?"

"I'm talking about the brunette who's been living with you, the woman you conveniently forgot existed when you hopped into bed with me," she said derisively.

"I live alone," he told her, a dangerous glint in his eye.

"Don't try to pretend like you don't know what I'm talking about. I saw her with my own two eyes."

"Saw whom?"

"Your girlfriend. Yesterday morning. I came over. I wanted to—" She almost said *I wanted to see you*, but caught herself. "I wanted to bring you some bagels. Only when I got there, I saw you and your bimbo girlfriend coming out of the house. You had two suitcases that you put in the trunk of her car," she said angrily.

"And that's why you wouldn't speak to me last night? Because you thought I was having an affair with Caroline?" His mouth dropped open in disbelief.

"Maybe some women think it's flattering to have a guy send a woman packing for them, but I find it disgusting! How could you make love with me when she was living with you...?" She trailed off as tears threatened to fall.

"She wasn't living with me. She never has and never will. And she's definitely not my girlfriend. She's Hank's."

This time Annie was the one who gave him a look of disbelief.

"Her name is Caroline. She only came by to pick up some clothes I was donating to charity. They were in the suitcases that I put in the trunk," he explained. "Good grief, Annie. Do you think we could have made love the way we did if I were involved with someone else?"

Suddenly Annie remembered her mother saying that Hank was involved with another woman. "I thought..." she started to speak, but emotion blocked her throat.

"You thought what, Annie?" He shook his head in regret. "This is the second time you've jumped to the wrong conclusion about me."

"I'm sorry, Jesse." She reached out to him, but he backed away.

"Seven years ago we were both young and unsure of ourselves. There were so many circumstances working against us—Hank and your mother's divorce, the distance separating us, I can understand how something like the incident with Roxy could drive us apart. But now—" he raked a hand through his hair "—we're adults, Annie. In the past six days I've done everything I can to convince you to give us another chance. I thought that when we made love, you were telling me yes, that you wanted to try again."

"I do." She swallowed back the lump in her throat and tried to still her racing heart.

He heaved a long sigh. "It's not going to work, Annie."

"Don't say that, Jesse," she said, on the verge of tears.

He shook his head. "It might work for a while, but then another Roxy or Caroline would show up and send you off packing."

Annie felt as if a blow had been delivered to her solar plexus, knocking all the air out of her. She needed to convince him he was wrong, but she couldn't speak. She took several deep breaths, trying to control her emotions.

"It's over, Annie."

She didn't want to believe him, but there was a finality in his voice that warned her not to try to convince him otherwise.

She fumbled with the clasp on her purse, then reached inside for the money. "Here." She stuck it in his face. "Every penny...even the three-hundred deposit."

He took the envelope from her. "I told Hank you could keep the three hundred."

"I don't want your money, Jesse. I don't need it," she said with a lift of her chin.

He quirked a dark eyebrow. "You sold the masterpiece?"

"No, I canceled my trip to Florida." She hoped that with that announcement he would have a change of heart.

He didn't. She turned around and started for the door.

"I'm so sorry your party plans had to be put on hold," he said with mock sympathy.

She spun back around to face him, her eyes flashing. "I told you. It was a job—a job I needed. But thanks to you and your uncle's stupid pick-up, I'm unemployed. I now have no job, no money and no buyer for my wedding dress!" She grabbed her purse and started for the door.

She intended to have the last word, but as she had her hand on the doorknob he said, "No wedding dress is worth that kind of money."

Annie's only answer was to slam the door on her way out.

Chapter Thirteen

Jesse felt like a caged animal. He paced back and forth in his office, trying to convince himself that he had done the right thing telling Annie there was no future for them. The problem was, if it was the right thing, then why did he feel so rotten?

Maybe it was because he had a guilty conscience. As hard as he tried, he couldn't ignore the fact that he was partly to blame for her losing the opportunity to work on the cruise ship. Even though she had gotten herself into a financial jam without his help, if he hadn't taken the wedding dress home for Roxy to try on, it would never have been stolen. Annie might have been able to sell it and raise the money she needed to get to Florida.

He stared at the envelope of cash. To him it wasn't a significant amount of money, but to Annie...

Maybe there was something he could do to ease his guilty conscience. After all, she wasn't supposed to leave until tomorrow.

He reached for the phone and punched in Todd's number.

"I need the names and phone numbers of any women you know who have a figure that is anywhere close in size to Annie's."

WHEN JONI GOT HOME from work, she found Annie sitting in the dark. She switched on the overhead light and gasped. "Oh—I didn't think you were here."

"Yeah. I'm here," Annie said flatly.

Joni walked quietly over to her roommate and sat down beside her. "Are you okay?"

"No." She sat with a throw pillow clutched to her chest, her eyes red from crying.

"Hey! It can't be that bad. Tomorrow you're leaving this cold, crummy climate for the sunny skies of the Caribbean and the sandy white beaches of the islands." Joni tried to sound upbeat.

Annie pointed a finger at the plastic garment bag she had left on the floor. "Look. I got the dress back."

"That's good...isn't it?"

"No. Jesse wanted his money back," she said tightly.

"Oh." Suddenly Joni understood the reason for her melancholy. Before she could offer any sympathy, however, the phone rang. She jumped up to answer it. Within a few minutes she popped her head around the corner and said, "It's someone who wants to see the dress...right now, if possible."

Annie didn't respond.

"She sounds eager," Joni said encouragingly.

Annie shrugged. "Whatever."

"There's still a chance you can sell it before tomorrow." Annie shot her a dubious glance. "I'm going to tell her to come over," Joni informed her, then went on to give the person on the phone directions to their apartment.

"She's on her way," Joni announced brightly.

Annie figured she couldn't have been very far away, for the intercom buzzed only a short while after Joni had hung up. The minute Annie saw the woman, she had a feeling the masterpiece wasn't going to fit. Although she was the same height as Annie, this prospective bride was broader through the hips.

The woman oohed and aahed over the dress, then disappeared into the bathroom to try it on. Annie and Joni exchanged knowing glances. To the surprise of both of them, however, the prospective bride emerged from the bathroom with a big grin on her face.

"It's perfect. I'll take it." She pulled a wad of hundred-dollar bills from her pocket and handed them to Annie, whose eyes widened at the sight of the money. "Thanks so much. I know I'm going to just love it."

As soon as she had gone, Joni said, "A little too much enthusiasm for me."

"Where do you suppose she got the cash?"

Joni waggled her eyebrows. "Who cares? It's yours now."

Annie dropped down on the sofa and closed her eyes. "That dress has caused me so much grief. I can't believe I finally sold it."

"Yes, and now you can take that job on the cruise ship," Joni said cheerfully. When Annie didn't comment, she asked, "You *are* going to go, aren't you?"

"I don't know," she said absently. "Maybe."

Joni sank down beside her. "Annie, are you sure you're okay?"

"Mm-hmm. I'm just tired. I'll be fine after I get a good night's rest."

ANNIE FELT TERRIBLE the next morning. Mainly because she had hardly slept the night before. When her mother called and asked her if she could take her to the doctor's office, Annie knew she had to make a decision. She either had to take the job on the cruise ship or resign herself to cooking at her mother's café until she could get another catering job.

Which was why the following Saturday she was once again behind the grill at Mom's Café flipping pancakes and frying eggs. She had just finished making a ham-and-cheese omelet when her mother called out to her.

"Annie, come take a quick peek at who came in," her mother said in a low voice from across the serving counter.

"Ma, I'm in the middle of cooking," Annie protested.

"Just take a peek. Please?"

Annie dragged her feet over to the swinging café doors and peered out over the top. Sitting in booth nine was Hank and the brunette Annie had seen coming out of Jesse's house. Annie's first thought was that Jesse had been telling the truth. It only added to her misery. She quickly returned to the grill.

"What did you think?" her mother wanted to know.

"She's too young for him," Annie retorted, knowing that was exactly what her mother wanted to hear. "Why did he bring her in here anyway?"

"He needed to drop off some insurance forms for me."

Annie thought it was more likely that he wanted to flaunt his girlfriend under her mother's nose. She mentally shrugged. Just because she was unhappy was no reason to be so jaded about men. She sighed. Now she was even thinking like her mother.

"When I waited on him, he told me Jesse's been like a bear with a sore tooth lately," her mother added, then disappeared with the plate of pancakes.

The mention of Jesse's name caused Annie's chest to tighten. For three days she had hoped that he would call her and tell her he was wrong, that he didn't want to end their relationship. He hadn't, and instead of time dulling the pain, it only seemed to increase it.

"Hank was surprised to see you were still here," her mother commented the next time she came to the serving counter. "He thought you were on the cruise ship."

"Shows you what he knows," Annie answered sarcastically.

"He told me to tell you he's sorry about the whole wedding-dress thing," her mother continued.

"Yeah, right," Annie drawled.

"He's a nice man," her mother admonished her, then disappeared once more.

In her present state of mind, Annie wasn't sure the adjective *nice* should be applied to men. It was one of those words that belonged in their gender defect. Oh, God, she really was becoming her mother.

"HANK, DID YOU DROP those papers off for Margaret Jamison like I asked you to do?" Jesse asked his uncle the following Monday morning when he showed up at the construction site.

"Yes, boss. I stopped at the diner," Hank answered, pulling out his tape measure to double-check the opening between the kitchen and the living room of the new house.

"Then Margaret's back to work?"

"Yup. She's moving a little slower, but she's up and around." He wrote some figures down on the clipboard he carried. "Annie was there, too."

Jesse had been examining the recently completed electrical work when he stopped to look at his uncle. "Annie? I thought she took the job on the cruise ship."

"Nope." Hank eyed him suspiciously. "You're not still hung up on her...." He trailed off uneasily.

"No, I'm not." He gave his uncle a look that warned him not to press the issue.

Hank ignored the warning. "Are you sure? I thought I saw that look in your eye when I mentioned her name."

"That look is because I feel responsible for the hassle with the wedding dress." He flipped a switch, and the kitchen fan whirled.

"As long as that's all it is. You don't want to get messed up with a Jamison woman."

Jesse turned the fan off. "I thought I told you I didn't need any advice in the romance department?"

He held up his hands in self-defense. "All right, all right. I won't say another word about Annie, but I think you should know that you're not the only one she jilted. She's had four fiancés."

Jesse's eyebrows lifted. "Four? How did you find that out?"

"Margie told me. Weren't the carpenters supposed to put trim around this opening?" he asked, squinting as he examined the doorway.

Jesse didn't answer. All he could think about was that Annie had had four fiancés. Three men had followed in his footsteps, yet not a one had been able to get her to the altar. Her mother had had five husbands, and she had had four fiancés. Maybe Hank was right—it was a good thing their relationship hadn't worked out.

However, the longer he thought about the two women, the clearer his relationship with Annie became. By the time he was finished work, he knew exactly what he needed to do. When he got back to the office, he called Joni Tremaine. Then he told Roxy, "Find me someone who can cater breakfast for tomorrow morning, will you?"

JONI WOKE UP AT SIX, crept quietly into the bathroom so as not to wake her roommate. She showered and put her makeup on, then tiptoed back to her room to get dressed. Only as she passed Annie's door, she noticed that it was ajar.

"Annie?" she called out tentatively. When there was no response, she repeated her name a bit louder. Still there was no answer. Gingerly she pushed the door open and gasped. She was not in her bed. "Annie?" This time she shouted the name. She hurried into the kitchen to discover a note left on the table.

> Joni,
> Got called into work unexpectedly.
> See you later,
>
>   Annie

"She's at work?" Joni screeched in dismay. She rubbed two fingers across her forehead. She hurried into the bedroom and donned her fairy gown. She slipped her feet into satin slippers, then tugged on the wig of golden curls. Just as she was reaching for her wand, the intercom buzzed.

"Oooh, he's here." She scrambled around nervously, looking for her tiara. By the time she answered the door, she was completely costumed.

"I thought I wasn't going to ring the doorbell," Jesse said in a whisper.

"It doesn't matter," Joni waved a hand. "She's not here."

Jesse's face fell. "Where is she?"

"At the diner. Working," Joni answered, then grabbed

her cape and pushed him out the door. "Come. We have to hurry or you'll miss the sunrise."

"We're going to the diner?"

"Yes. It'll work. Trust me."

ONE OF THE THINGS Annie hated most about winter was getting up in the dark and going home in the dark. There never seemed to be any daylight. And in her present state of mind, she needed all the sunlight she could get.

Seasons didn't seem to affect the customers at Mom's Café. It was busy no matter what time of year it was, especially at breakfast, when most of the patrons were regulars who stopped in on their way to work.

Normally the restaurant was quiet between six and seven, with the rush hour beginning a few minutes past seven and lasting until around nine. At six-thirty Annie glanced at the clock and couldn't believe that only half an hour had passed.

"Is it exceptionally slow or is it my imagination?" she asked her mother as she slid a bowl of oatmeal onto the serving counter.

"They'll probably all come at once," her mother warned.

Annie nodded and turned her attention back to the grill. She was busy cooking up hash browns when she heard her mother call out to her. "Come out front when you're done with that order. I want to show you something."

Annie finished frying the potatoes, which she slid onto a plate that already had two scrambled eggs and an order of toast. She set it on the counter, then walked over to the swinging café doors. As she pushed her way through, she said, "What is it, Ma?"

She gasped at the sight that greeted her. Joni stood before her wearing her fairy costume.

"It's not my birthday," she murmured as every head in the diner turned her way.

"Of course it isn't," Joni said in her sugary sweet, good-fairy voice. "It's a very special day. A day when the good fairy can make your every wish come true."

She launched into "When You Wish upon a Star," spreading sparkly fairy dust and waving her wand as she sang. Annie could only stare in disbelief. When Joni had finished singing, she pulled out her wish bag, a knapsack made out of gold lamé.

Annie's heart warmed at her roommate's attempt to cheer her up. She figured her mother must have had a hand in the scheme, and smiled affectionately at both of them.

"Now, let's see what is in my wish bag," Joni said with eyes wide. She pulled out an imaginary wish and said, "Oooh. It says here that you would like a tall, dark and handsome man." Joni giggled and said in an aside, "Wouldn't we all."

She reached again into the sack and pulled out another handful of air. "Oooh, and this one says you like break-fast picnics so you can watch the sunrise."

Annie's heart began to beat faster.

"Well, let's see if your fairy can grant your wish." Joni flitted about the room, waving her wand and spreading the glittery sprinkles until she reached the door. Then she slipped outside. When she came back in, Jesse was with her.

Annie closed her eyes, afraid she had imagined his handsome face smiling at her. But when she opened them again, he was still there, coming toward her, his dark hair hidden beneath the baseball cap, his broad shoulders covered by the brown leather jacket.

She pressed a hand to her chest, convinced that everyone in the restaurant could see it beating. Her face grew warm, not because all eyes were on her, but because Jesse was looking at her as if she were the only woman in the room.

Joni led him by the hand across the restaurant. The crowd parted as he made his way to Annie's side.

When they reached her, Joni said, "The good fairy has made two of your wishes come true." She dug into her wish bag one last time and pulled out the third imaginary wish. "This is one I'll give to you. Only you know what to do with it."

Annie opened her hand and allowed Joni to tap her magic wand on her palm.

Then Jesse reached for that hand and said, "I have bagels and cream cheese in the car. Are you ready for that picnic?"

Annie looked around. "I can't leave. There's no one to work for me."

Joni cleared her throat. "Leave it to your fairy god-mother, dear."

Then Annie's mother said, "There are extra uniforms in the storage room."

The next thing Annie knew, her jacket was being draped over her shoulders and Jesse was leading her out to his pick-up. Once inside, he kissed her long and hard, then he started up the truck, saying, "We need to hurry if we're going to make the sunrise."

They were barely out of the city when shades of pink blossomed on the horizon. Jesse pulled the pick-up into the parking lot of an abandoned service station. "We're not going to make the creek," he answered her unasked question.

"Wait here." He hopped out of the car, to return a few

moments later carrying a picnic basket. "I had it in the back," he told her with a grin.

He set two mugs of coffee and two bagels on the dash. "There's not a whole lot of room in here, but at least we'll be warm." He gave her a grin that had the power to make her heart sing out in joy.

Then his smile disappeared and his face grew sober. "I need to know something, Annie. Was Joni right about your wishes?"

She lifted her eyes to his and saw her uncertainty mirrored there. "You said it was too late for us."

"I was hurt, Annie. When you accused me of getting rid of a woman to make room for you, all I could see was that you didn't trust me. History repeating itself."

She reached across the seat to lay her hand against his cheek. "I want to trust you, Jesse."

He turned his head so that his lips met her palm. "But it's hard, isn't it?"

She nodded, swallowing back the fear.

"Annie, I know about your ex-fiancés."

"All of them?" She blushed in embarrassment.

His grin was crooked. "There have only been four, right?"

"Jesse, it's nothing to joke about." She pulled away from him. "Look at my mother."

He reached for her chin. "Annie, you're not your mother."

Again uncertainty clouded her eyes. "I don't want to make the same mistakes she made."

"Is that why you didn't marry any of them?"

"I was never in love with three of them," she confessed softly.

"And the fourth one?"

"I only discovered last week that he's the reason why

I couldn't marry the others. You see, I fell in love when I was nineteen, only I was too young and scared of what was happening to trust my instincts."

He sighed. "If you would have only told me about seeing Roxy and me."

"I couldn't. I wasn't ready to trust you yet."

"And now?"

She wrapped her arms around him and pulled him close, telling him with a kiss just how much she trusted him. "Why did you change your mind about us, Jesse?"

"Because I love you and I don't want to live without you," he answered, a warm glow in his eyes. He smiled that wonderful smile that made her heart feel as if it would jump right out of her chest.

"Annie, it's not easy for me, either. I've seen the way guys look at you and I know that there are any number of them who would just as soon step on me to get to you, but when you love someone you have to learn to trust." Once more his lips found hers and kissed her hungrily.

"I only plan on getting married once, Annie," he said close to her lips.

"Is that a marriage proposal?" she asked with a grin.

"What do you think? Can you stand to be the wife of a pick-up man?"

"I think I can." She gave him a short and sassy kiss, then reached for a bagel. "I have only one request, however."

"And that is?" he asked, reaching for the other bagel.

"We keep it simple."

"No expensive wedding dress?"

She grinned. "No. But it might interest you to know that I sold it and got exactly what I told you it was worth," she boasted proudly.

"So how come you didn't take the job on the cruise ship?"

She shrugged. "I don't know. I just couldn't leave. I would have felt as if I were running away."

"Any regrets?"

She shook her head. "I have everything I could wish for right here."

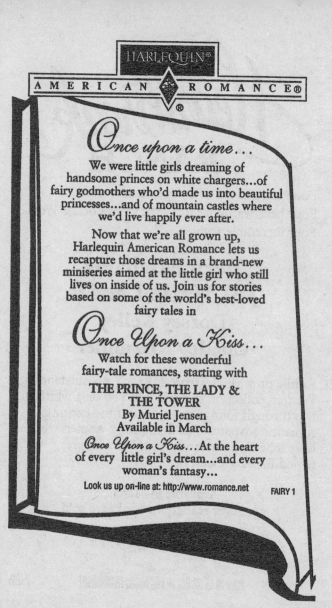

RANCH

Four generations of independent women...
Four heartwarming, romantic stories of the West...
Four incredible authors...

Fern Michaels
Jill Marie Landis
Dorsey Kelley
Chelley Kitzmiller

Saddle up with Heartbreak Ranch, an outstanding
Western collection that will take you on a whirlwind
trip through four generations and the exciting,
romantic adventures of four strong women who
have inherited the ranch from Bella Duprey,
famed Barbary Coast madam.

Available in March,
wherever Harlequin books are sold.

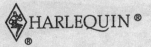

HARLEQUIN ®

HARLEQUIN®

Don't miss these Harlequin favorites by some of our most
distinguished authors!
And now, you can receive a discount by ordering two or more titles!

HT#25645	THREE GROOMS AND A WIFE by JoAnn Ross	$3.25 U.S. $3.75 CAN.	☐
HT#25647	NOT THIS GUY by Glenda Sanders	$3.25 U.S. $3.75 CAN.	☐
HP#11725	THE WRONG KIND OF WIFE by Roberta Leigh	$3.25 U.S. $3.75 CAN.	☐
HP#11755	TIGER EYES by Robyn Donald	$3.25 U.S. $3.75 CAN.	☐
HR#03416	A WIFE IN WAITING by Jessica Steele	$3.25 U.S. $3.75 CAN.	☐
HR#03419	KIT AND THE COWBOY by Rebecca Winters	$3.25 U.S. $3.75 CAN.	☐
HS#70622	KIM & THE COWBOY by Margot Dalton	$3.50 U.S. $3.99 CAN.	☐
HS#70642	MONDAY'S CHILD by Janice Kaiser	$3.75 U.S. $4.25 CAN.	☐
HI#22342	BABY VS. THE BAR by M.J. Rodgers	$3.50 U.S. $3.99 CAN.	☐
HI#22382	SEE ME IN YOUR DREAMS by Patricia Rosemoor	$3.75 U.S. $4.25 CAN.	☐
HAR#16538	KISSED BY THE SEA by Rebecca Flanders	$3.50 U.S. $3.99 CAN.	☐
HAR#16603	MOMMY ON BOARD by Muriel Jensen	$3.50 U.S. $3.99 CAN.	☐
HH#28885	DESERT ROGUE by Erine Yorke	$4.50 U.S. $4.99 CAN.	☐
HH#28911	THE NORMAN'S HEART by Margaret Moore	$4.50 U.S. $4.99 CAN.	☐

(limited quantities available on certain titles)

	AMOUNT	$
DEDUCT:	**10% DISCOUNT FOR 2+ BOOKS**	$
ADD:	**POSTAGE & HANDLING**	$
	($1.00 for one book, 50¢ for each additional)	
	APPLICABLE TAXES*	$_____
	TOTAL PAYABLE	$_____
	(check or money order—please do not send cash)	

To order, complete this form and send it, along with a check or money order for the
total above, payable to Harlequin Books, to: **In the U.S.:** 3010 Walden Avenue,
P.O. Box 9047, Buffalo, NY 14269-9047; **In Canada:** P.O. Box 613, Fort Erie, Ontario,
L2A 5X3.

Name: _____

Address: _____ City: _____

State/Prov.: _____ Zip/Postal Code: _____

*New York residents remit applicable sales taxes.
  Canadian residents remit applicable GST and provincial taxes.
  Look us up on-line at: http://www.romance.net

HBACK-JM4